Regal Academy™

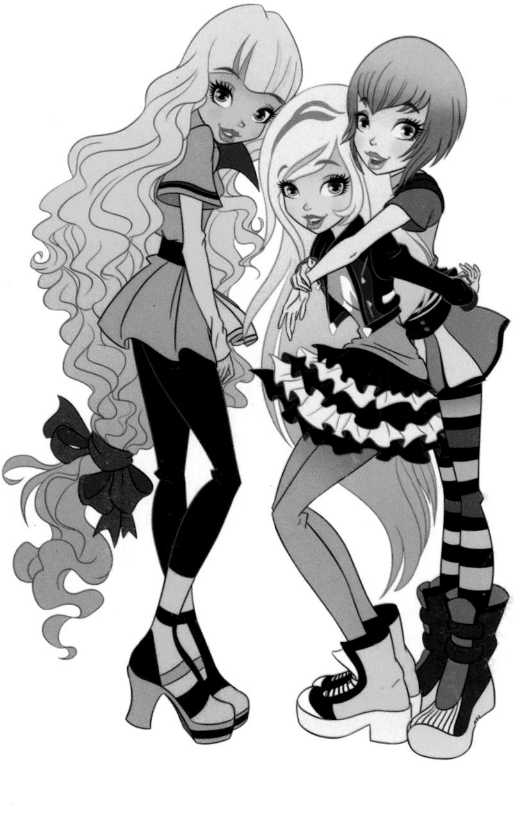

PAPERCUTZ™

Use either the QR code
or this link:

http://www.regalacademy.com/en/download/pap496

to download your exclusive digital REGAL ACADEMY booklet. Enjoy!

Magical Surprise Download Here!

#3 "A Day on Earth"
Regal Academy™© 2018 Rainbow S.p.A. All rights reserved. Regal Academy™ names,
characters and related indicia are copyright, trademark and exclusive license of Rainbow S.p.A.
Series created and directed by Iginio Straffi. www.regalacademy.com

"A Day on Earth"
Script: Rainbow S.p.A./Luana Vergari
Comics: Rainbow Srl/Red Whale

"Three Golden Apples"
Script: Rainbow S.p.A./Luana Vergari
Comics: Rainbow Srl/Red Whale

"A Great DJ"
Script: Rainbow S.p.A./Luana Vergari
Comics: Rainbow Srl/Red Whale

"The Spirit of the Mountain"
Script: Rainbow S.p.A./Luana Vergari
Comics: Rainbow Srl/Red Whale

Papercutz books may be purchased
for business or promotional use.
For information on bulk purchases please contact Macmillan
Corporate and Premium Sales Department
at (800) 221-7945 x5442

Lettering and Production – Manosaur Martin
Editorial Intern – Spenser Nellis
Editor – Jeff Whitman
Jim Salicrup
Editor-in-Chief

PB ISBN: 978-1-54580-121-5
HC ISBN: 978-1-54580-120-8

Printed in China
July 2018

Distributed by Macmillan
First Papercutz Printing

Regal Academy™

#3 "A Day on Earth"

Table of Contents

PAPERCUTZ™
New York

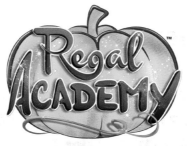

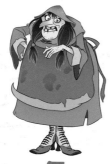

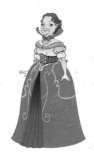

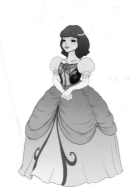

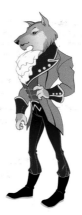

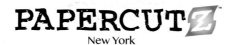

Get to know the Regal Academy students & faculty...

ROSE CINDERELLA

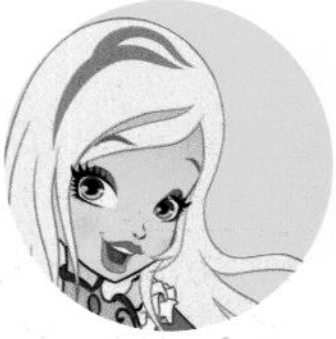

Rose is a modern teenager who never lost her love of fairy tales. Having grown up on Earth, she constantly experiences a "culture shock" between her modern, shoe-filled life on Earth and the magical Fairy Tale Land. She is a very positive girl who thinks everything is great all the time. She is happy even if she gets the worst grades in her class! She is never sad or disappointed but always full of sunshine, acting as a ray of hope for the team.

TRAVIS BEAST

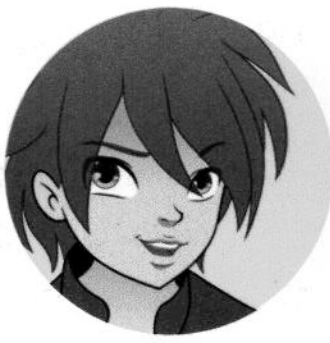

Travis is a frail, artsy sort of boy, but when he gets angry he becomes a real Beast! When it comes to getting physical though, he would much rather focus on his artistic skills. He is a true artist thanks to the talent inherited from Beauty, his grandmother, but he is totally underrated. Since he comes from Earth, Travis manages to recreate very beautiful paintings and sculptures inspired by Earthly masterpieces. He aims to control his beastly strength and become a true artist.

ASTORIA RAPUNZEL

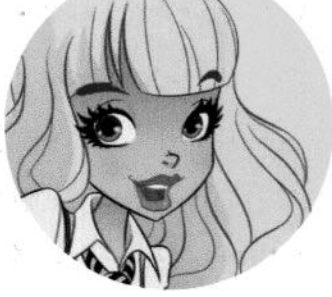

Regal Academy's resident bookworm and perfect, poised, princess... just as long as everything goes her way. Her perfectionist streak has her snapping from being absorbed in a book to up in arms, to back to studying quietly in an instant! She aims to be the best student, always the first to reply to the teacher's questions, always asking for more hours at school, more homework, or for more complicated exams.

JOY LeFROG

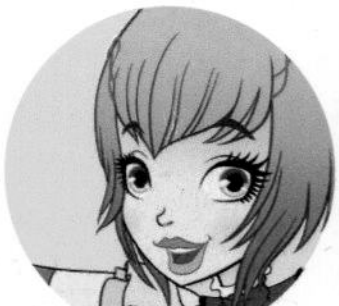

Joy loves creepy-crawlies and sometimes forgets that not everyone else does! She loves to cheer on her friends, but she's as likely to encourage their BAD ideas as well as their good ones! Because of her curse, she sometimes turns into a frog – and can't turn back unless someone is available to kiss her. Most of the times, Hawk or Travis have to save her... even if they'd rather do anything else than kiss a frog.

HAWK SNOWWHITE

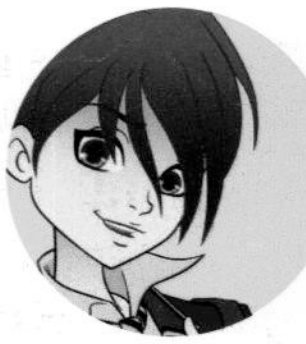

Hawk thinks he's the perfect fairy tale hero, but to his level-headed friends and the teachers, his habit of leaping head-first into trouble makes him a regal pain because he puts himself and his team in danger! His love of apples and the ladies of Regal Academy is second only to his love of proving himself. He wants to be the best fairy tale in all of history but he's got a long way to go if he's ever going to make it.

PROFESSOR SNOWWHITE

Professor SnowWhite is a stickler for the school rules and often ends up butting heads with our heroes on their adventures. This puts her at odds with her rebellious grandson Hawk, wanting him to become the most proper prince he can be. Despite her strictness, her mind is still "pure as snow" so she is very trusting. Our heroes (and the villains as well) can often get by her with a bit of cleverness.

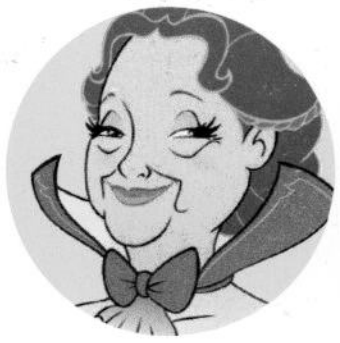

HEADMISTRESS CINDERELLA

Headmistress Cinderella was able to hold her own against her mean stepmother and stepsisters when she was a teenager, so she sure isn't afraid to speak her mind now that she's a grandmother. She often sticks up for the heroes against the strict Professor SnowWhite. She's a kindly mentor who has watched over her granddaughter Rose's entire life.

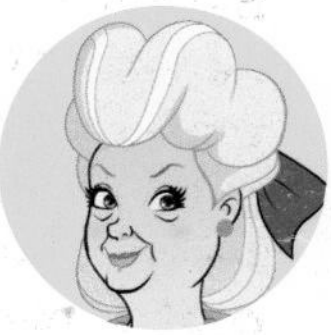

COACH BEAST

The Beast is a brash teacher, always yelling at the students to run a thousand laps or do a thousand pushups. When the Headmistress has a problem with someone breaking the rules, he scoops them up and carries them off to detention. He's always pushing his grandson Travis to give up art and become a real warrior with his beastly strength. Underneath it all, he has a heart of gold that occasionally pops up and compels him to help our heroes out of a jam.

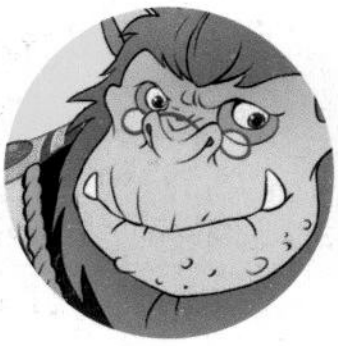

MAGISTER RAPUNZEL

Magister Rapunzel has spent way too much time locked in her tower and has a carefree attitude on life. She excitedly wants to chat or show off her books to anyone who will listen, but often accidentally forgets herself and starts talking to statues or paintings instead of real people. She tries to get her perfectionist granddaughter, Astoria, to relax and let loose at times.

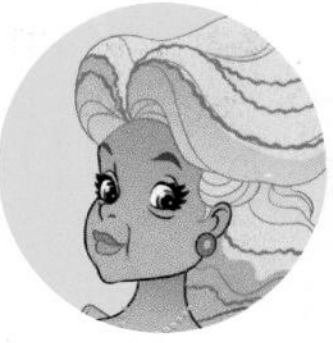

DOCTOR LeFROG

Doctor LeFrog is an old-fashioned professor at Regal Academy. He tends to be absent-minded at times, even if his classroom was exploding he would keep on teaching. He is also blind without his glasses. He always embarrasses his number-one granddaughter, Joy, by introducing frogs to her as possible dates but he really wants only the best for her.

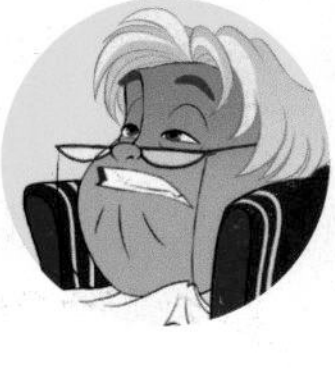

VICKY BROOMSTICK

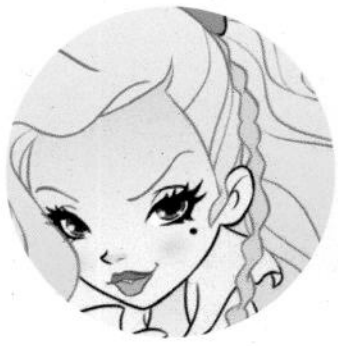

Vicky is Regal Academy's resident Mean Girl, leading her pack of villainous grandkids to accomplish her goals by any means necessary! Vicky is the intelligent and powerful granddaughter of the Broomstick Witch, but every time she tries to carry out her evil plans something goes wrong and she's thwarted by Rose and her friends. Rose and her friends are all that's preventing Vicky from opening up the Gate and releasing the old Fairytale Villains on Earth!

RUBY STEPSISTER

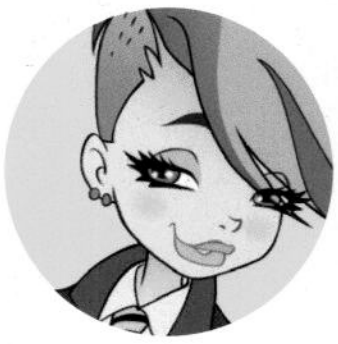

Ruby is one of Vicky's loyal henchmen in the Mean Team and not the sharpest tool in the shed. Utterly in love with Hawk SnowWhite, she helps Vicky in all of her evil plans just so she can get a chance to see her beloved. She's more than happy to do whatever dirty work Vicky couldn't be bothered with if it means being near Hawk.

CYRUS BROOMSTICK

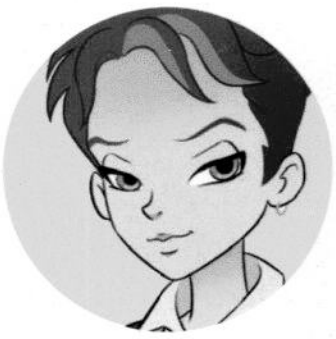

Cyrus is the lazy and cowardly grandson of the Broomstick Witch, as well as Vicky's cousin and reluctant member of the Mean Team. He is so lazy that he must be bribed by Vicky to help with her evil plans. He'd much rather be sleeping than plotting world domination.

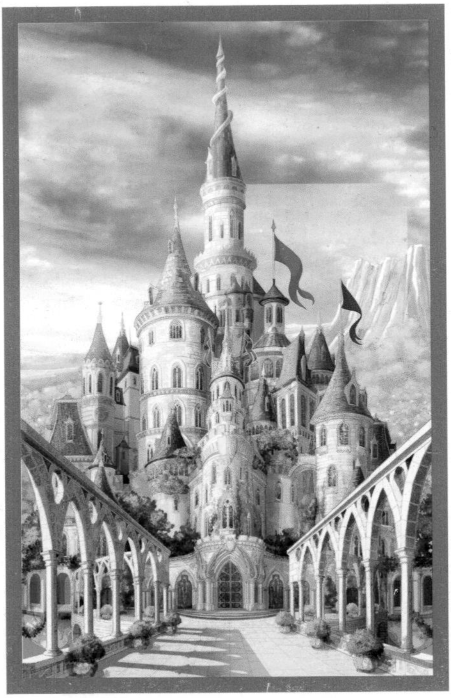

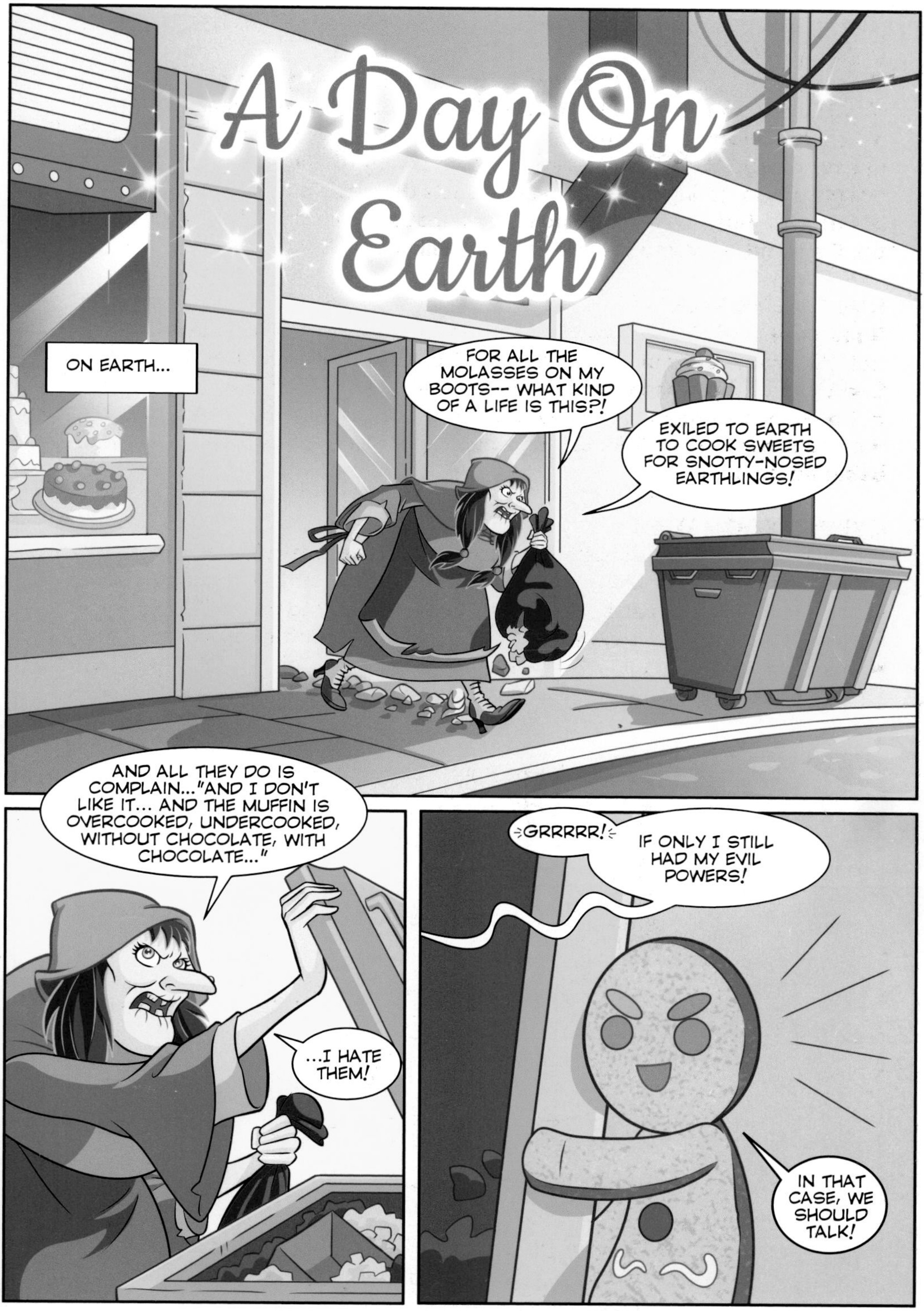
A Day On Earth
ON EARTH...
FOR ALL THE MOLASSES ON MY BOOTS-- WHAT KIND OF A LIFE IS THIS?!
EXILED TO EARTH TO COOK SWEETS FOR SNOTTY-NOSED EARTHLINGS!
AND ALL THEY DO IS COMPLAIN..."AND I DON'T LIKE IT... AND THE MUFFIN IS OVERCOOKED, UNDERCOOKED, WITHOUT CHOCOLATE, WITH CHOCOLATE..."
...I HATE THEM!
GRRRRR!
IF ONLY I STILL HAD MY EVIL POWERS!
IN THAT CASE, WE SHOULD TALK!

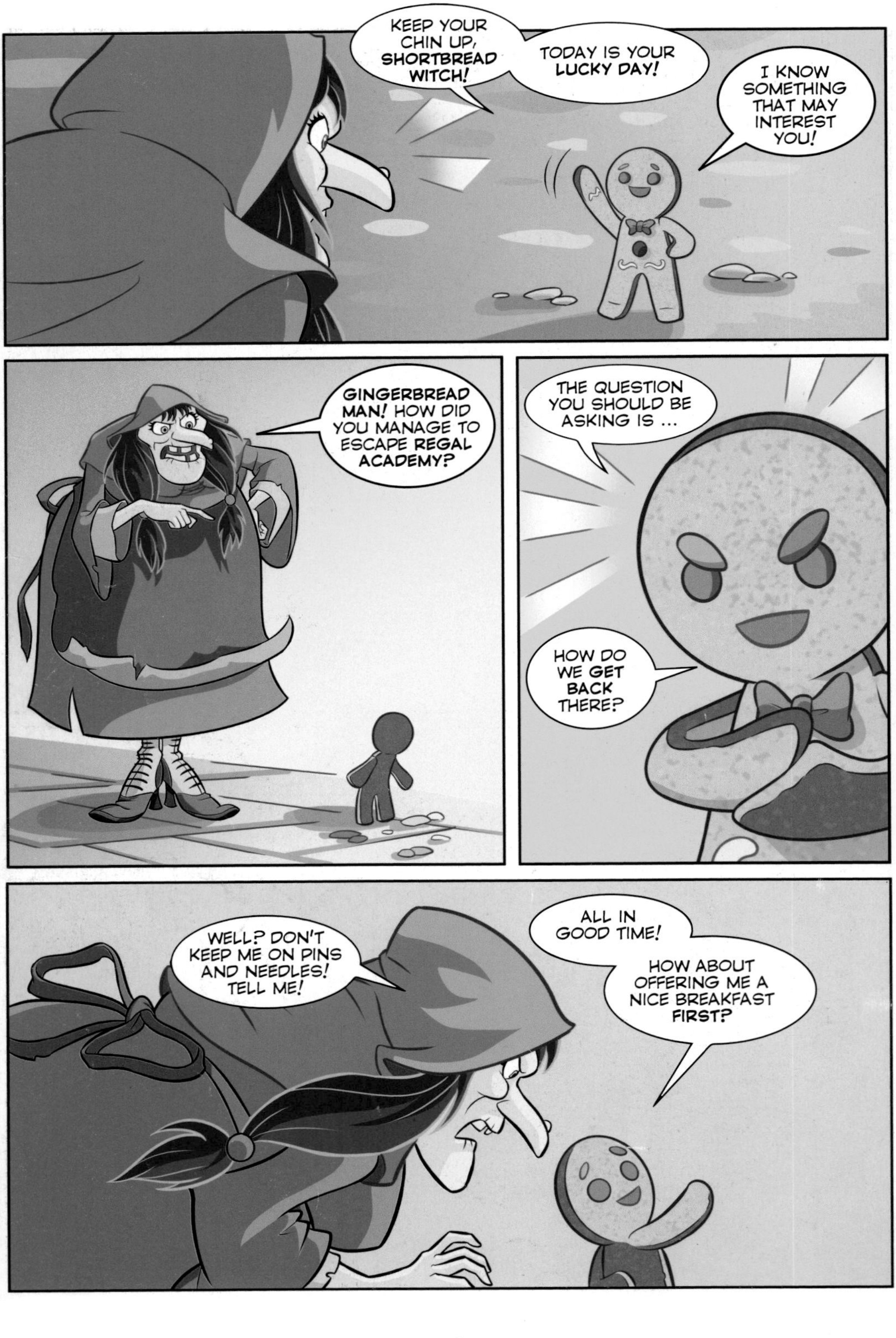
KEEP YOUR CHIN UP, SHORTBREAD WITCH!
TODAY IS YOUR LUCKY DAY!
I KNOW SOMETHING THAT MAY INTEREST YOU!
GINGERBREAD MAN! HOW DID YOU MANAGE TO ESCAPE REGAL ACADEMY?
THE QUESTION YOU SHOULD BE ASKING IS ...
HOW DO WE GET BACK THERE?
WELL? DON'T KEEP ME ON PINS AND NEEDLES! TELL ME!
ALL IN GOOD TIME!
HOW ABOUT OFFERING ME A NICE BREAKFAST FIRST?

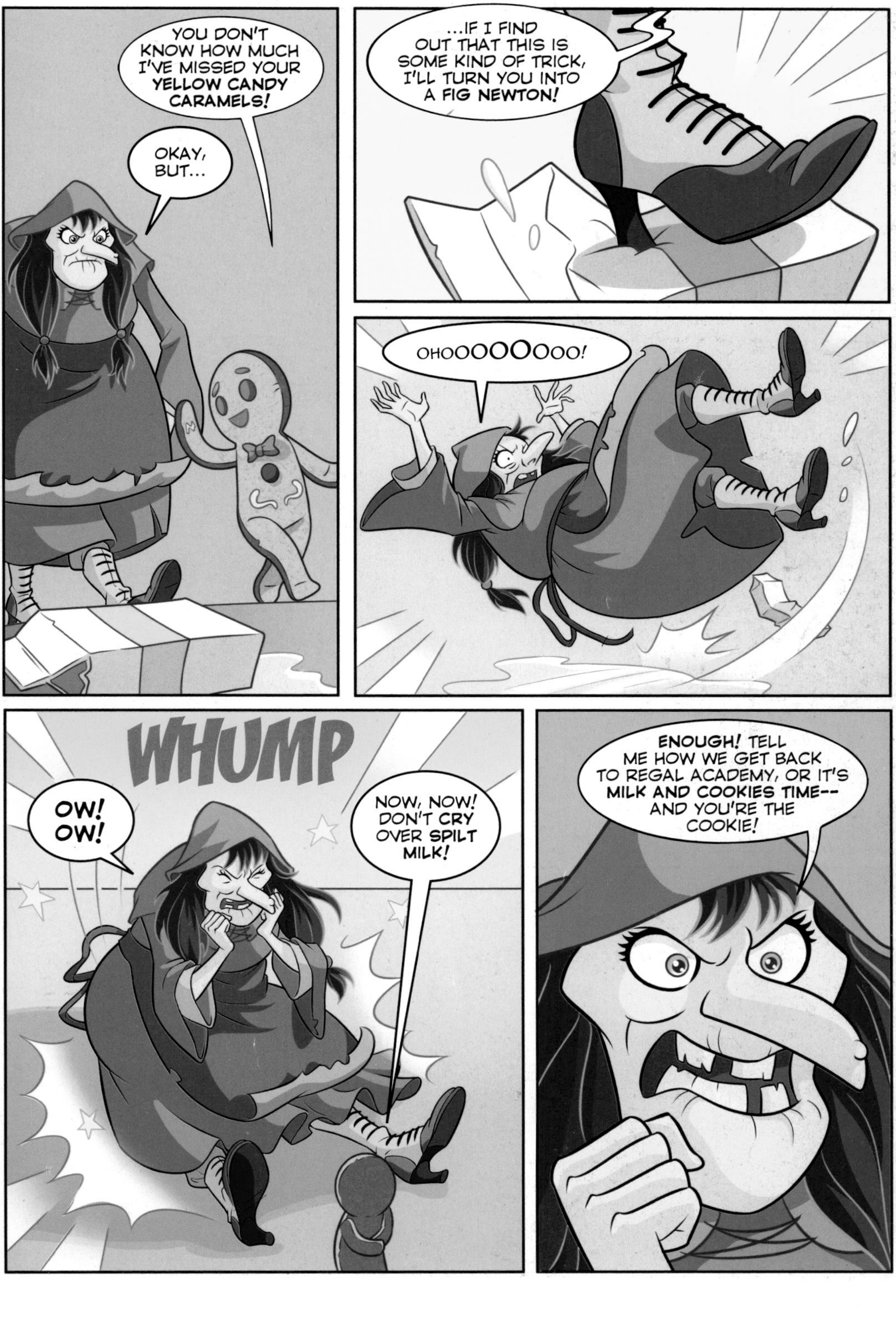
YOU DON'T KNOW HOW MUCH I'VE MISSED YOUR YELLOW CANDY CARAMELS!
OKAY, BUT...
...IF I FIND OUT THAT THIS IS SOME KIND OF TRICK, I'LL TURN YOU INTO A FIG NEWTON!
OHOOOOOOooo!
WHUMP
OW! OW!
NOW, NOW! DON'T CRY OVER SPILT MILK!
ENOUGH! TELL ME HOW WE GET BACK TO REGAL ACADEMY, OR IT'S MILK AND COOKIES TIME-- AND YOU'RE THE COOKIE!

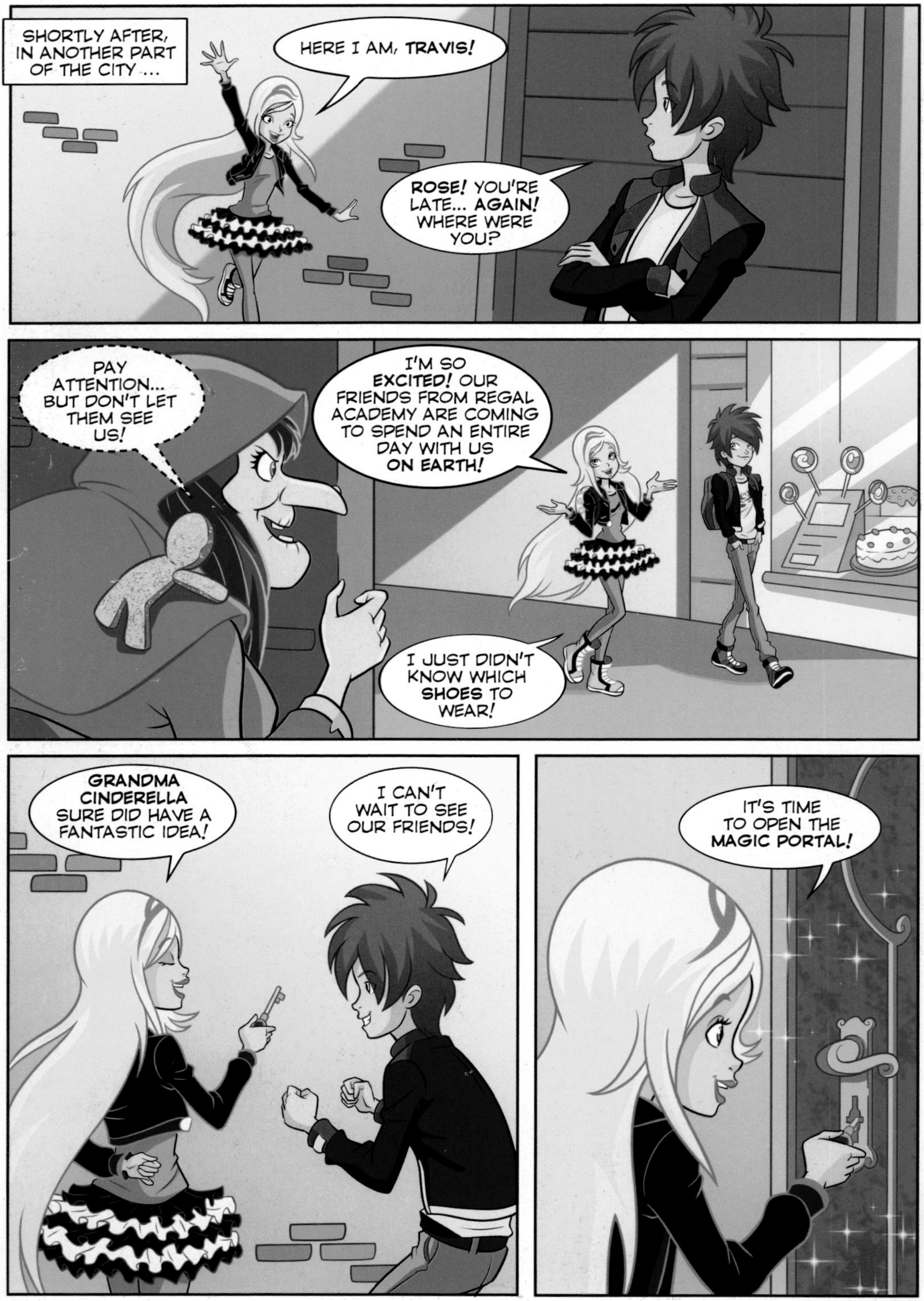
SHORTLY AFTER, IN ANOTHER PART OF THE CITY ...
HERE I AM, **TRAVIS!**
ROSE! YOU'RE LATE... **AGAIN!** WHERE WERE YOU?
PAY ATTENTION... BUT DON'T LET THEM SEE US!
I'M SO **EXCITED!** OUR FRIENDS FROM REGAL ACADEMY ARE COMING TO SPEND AN ENTIRE DAY WITH US **ON EARTH!**
I JUST DIDN'T KNOW WHICH **SHOES** TO WEAR!
GRANDMA CINDERELLA SURE DID HAVE A FANTASTIC IDEA!
I CAN'T WAIT TO SEE OUR FRIENDS!
IT'S TIME TO OPEN THE **MAGIC PORTAL!**

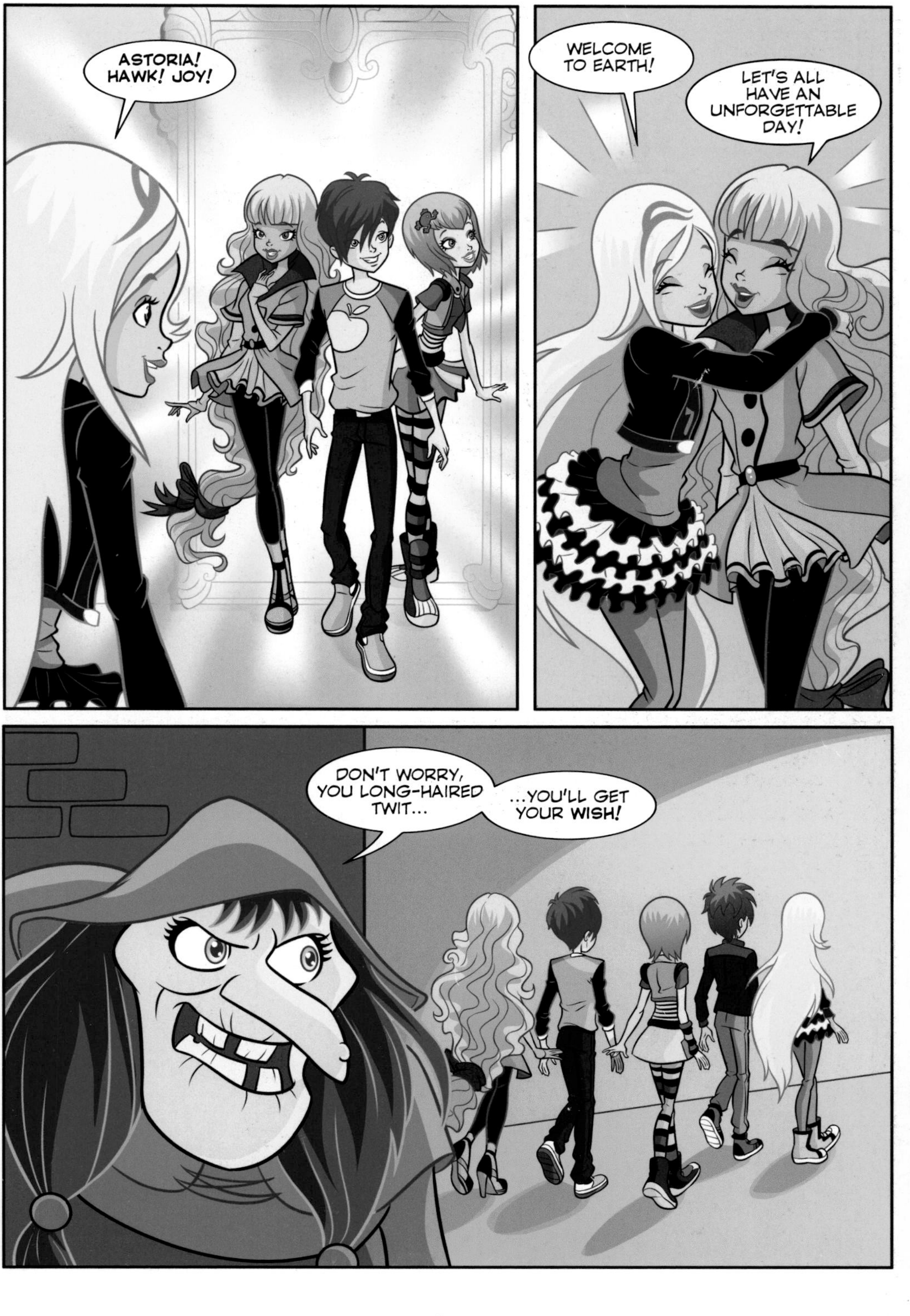
ASTORIA! HAWK! JOY!
WELCOME TO EARTH!
LET'S ALL HAVE AN UNFORGETTABLE DAY!
DON'T WORRY, YOU LONG-HAIRED TWIT...
...YOU'LL GET YOUR WISH!

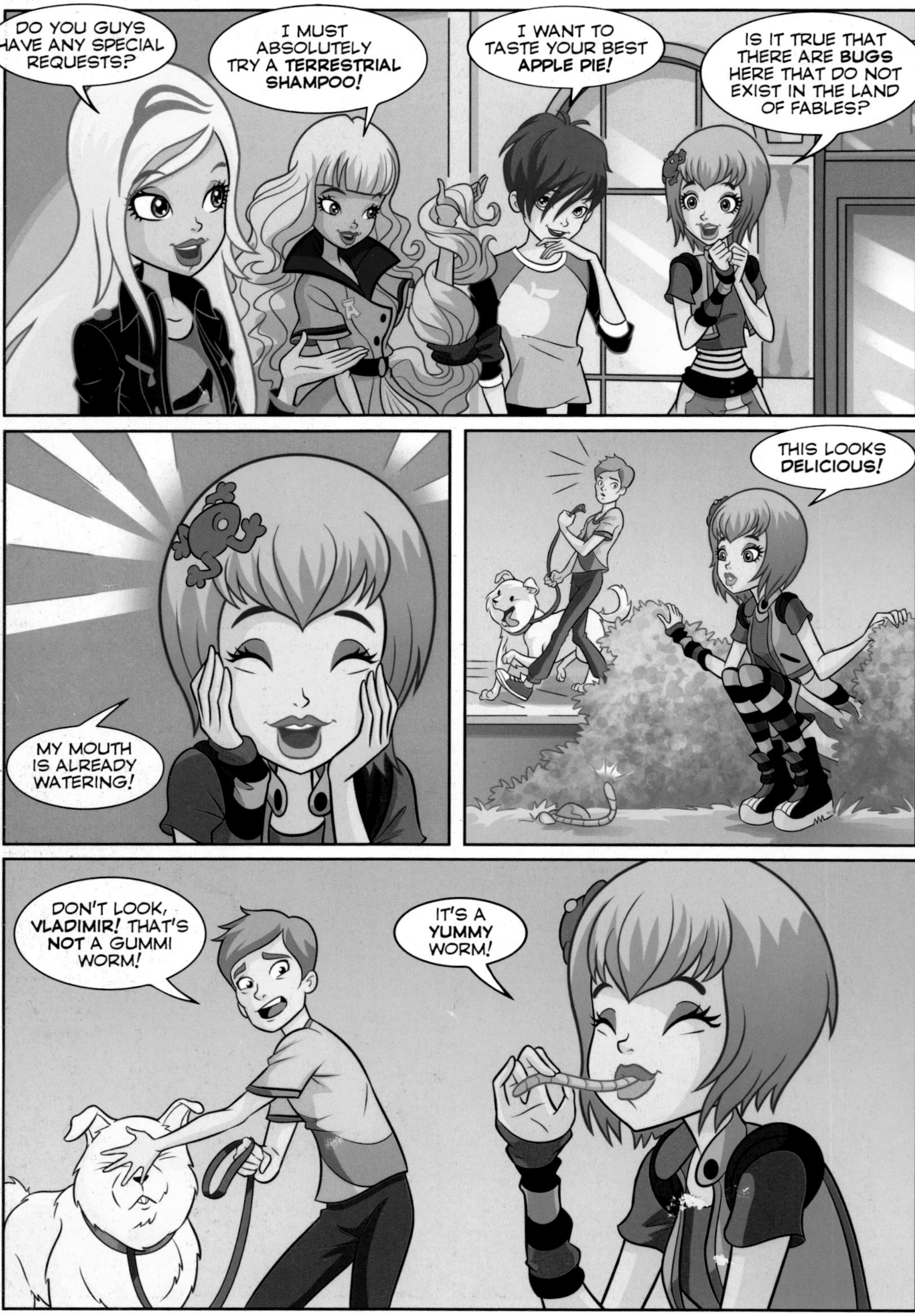
DO YOU GUYS HAVE ANY SPECIAL REQUESTS?
I MUST ABSOLUTELY TRY A TERRESTRIAL SHAMPOO!
I WANT TO TASTE YOUR BEST APPLE PIE!
IS IT TRUE THAT THERE ARE BUGS HERE THAT DO NOT EXIST IN THE LAND OF FABLES?
MY MOUTH IS ALREADY WATERING!
THIS LOOKS DELICIOUS!
DON'T LOOK, VLADIMIR! THAT'S NOT A GUMMI WORM!
IT'S A YUMMY WORM!

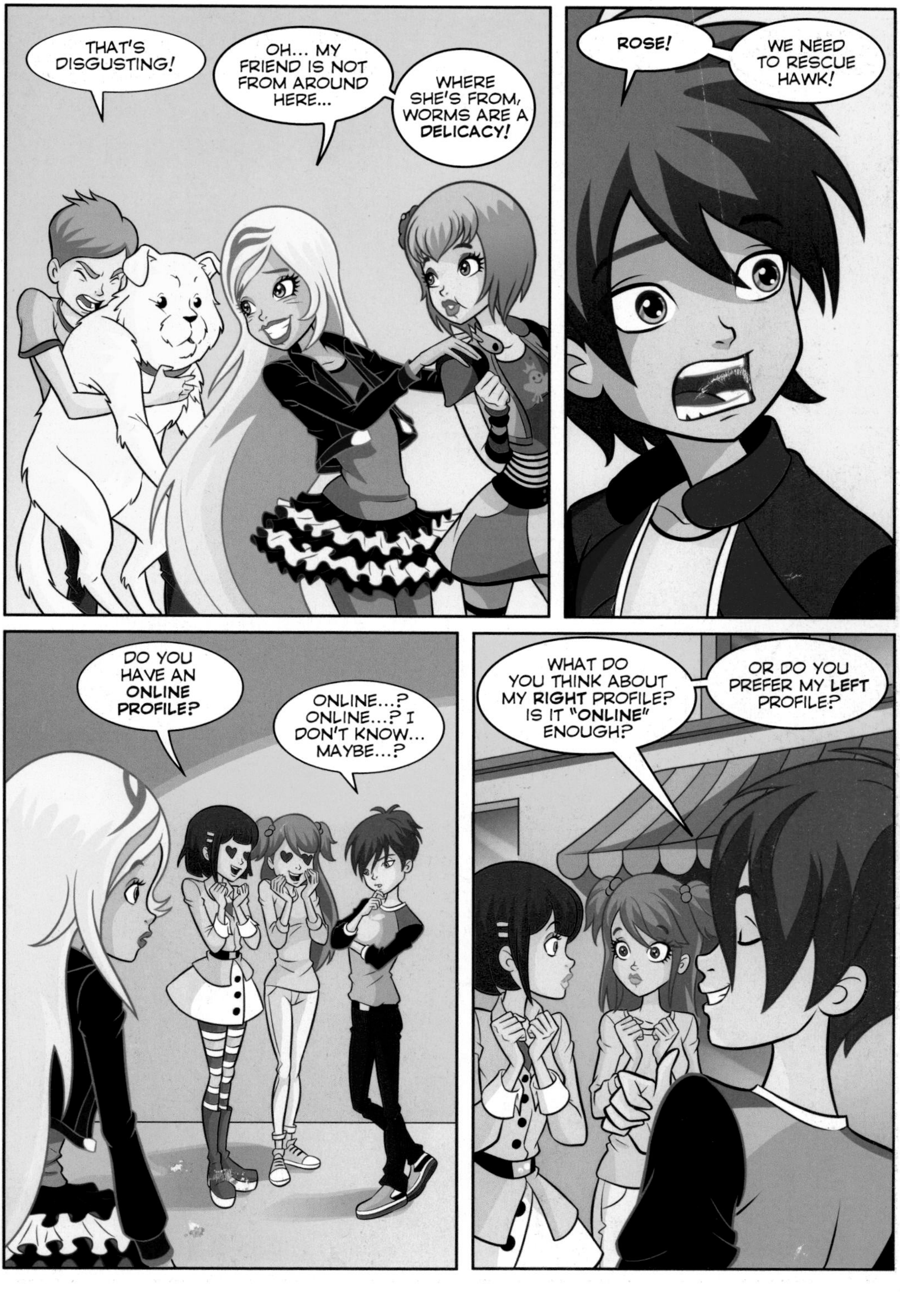
THAT'S DISGUSTING!
OH... MY FRIEND IS NOT FROM AROUND HERE...
WHERE SHE'S FROM, WORMS ARE A DELICACY!
ROSE!
WE NEED TO RESCUE HAWK!
DO YOU HAVE AN ONLINE PROFILE?
ONLINE...? ONLINE...? I DON'T KNOW... MAYBE...?
WHAT DO YOU THINK ABOUT MY RIGHT PROFILE? IS IT "ONLINE" ENOUGH?
OR DO YOU PREFER MY LEFT PROFILE?

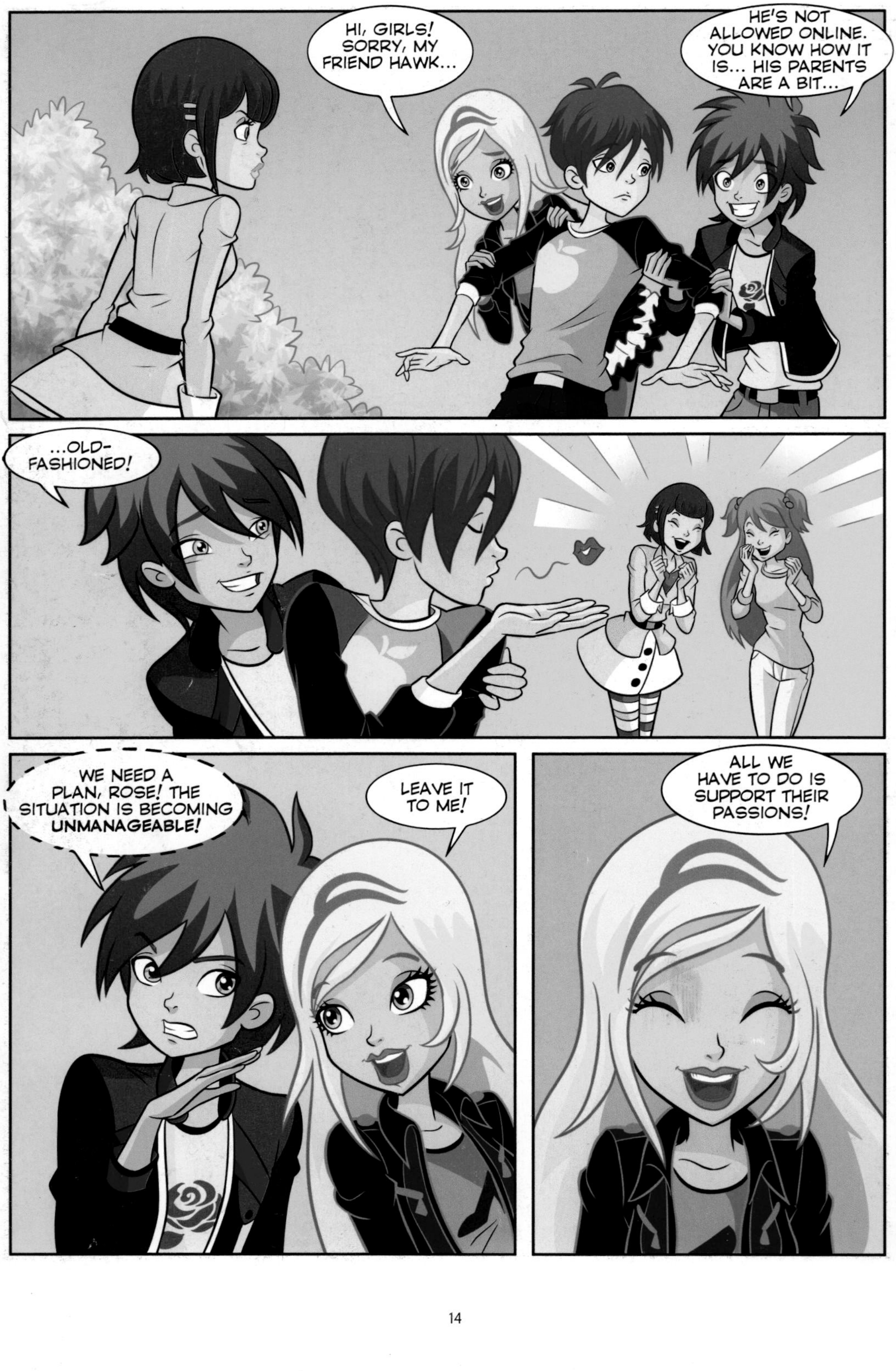
HI, GIRLS! SORRY, MY FRIEND HAWK...
HE'S NOT ALLOWED ONLINE. YOU KNOW HOW IT IS... HIS PARENTS ARE A BIT...
...OLD-FASHIONED!
WE NEED A PLAN, ROSE! THE SITUATION IS BECOMING UNMANAGEABLE!
LEAVE IT TO ME!
ALL WE HAVE TO DO IS SUPPORT THEIR PASSIONS!

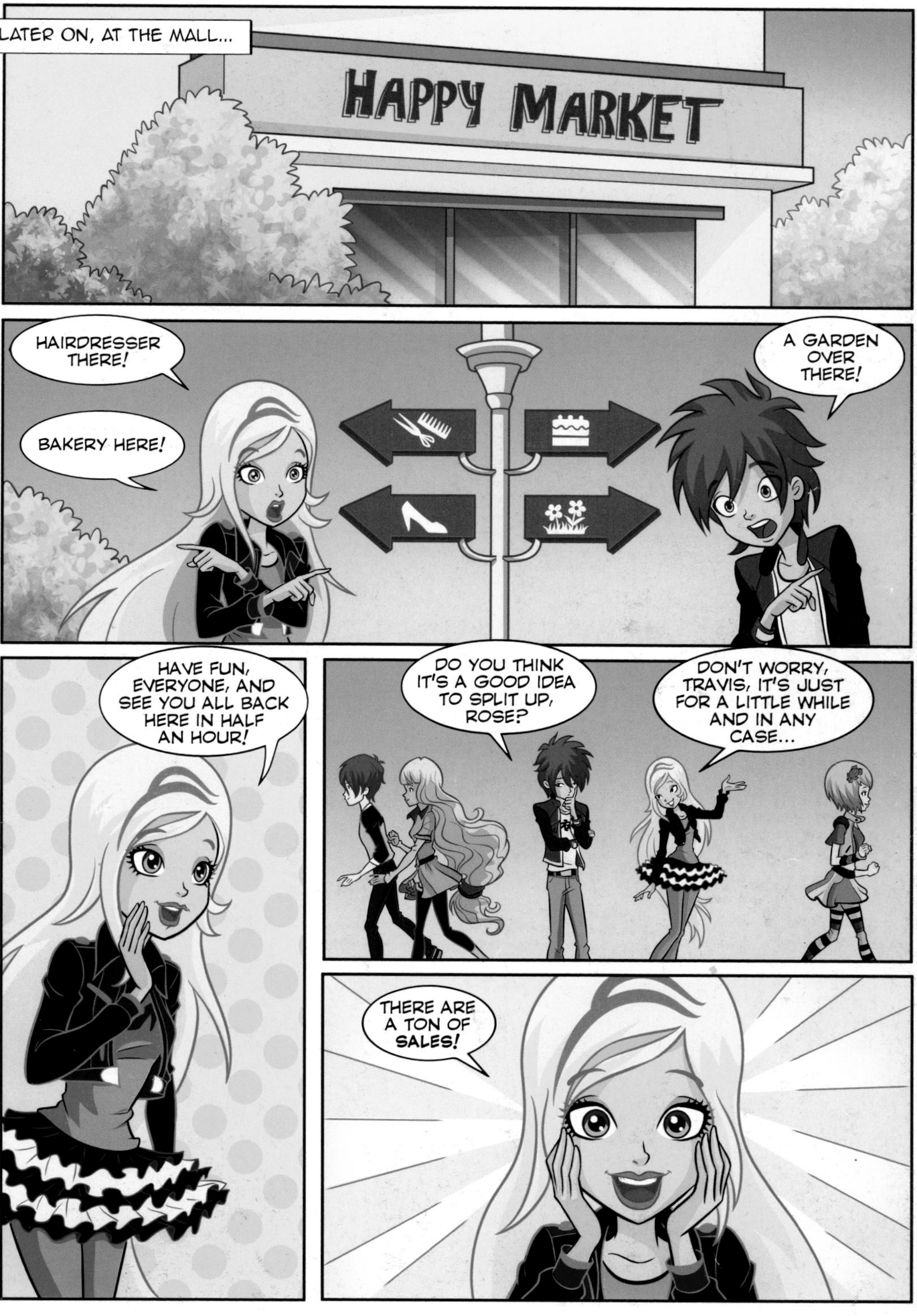
LATER ON, AT THE MALL...
HAPPY MARKET
HAIRDRESSER THERE!
BAKERY HERE!
A GARDEN OVER THERE!
HAVE FUN, EVERYONE, AND SEE YOU ALL BACK HERE IN HALF AN HOUR!
DO YOU THINK IT'S A GOOD IDEA TO SPLIT UP, ROSE?
DON'T WORRY, TRAVIS, IT'S JUST FOR A LITTLE WHILE AND IN ANY CASE...
THERE ARE A TON OF SALES!

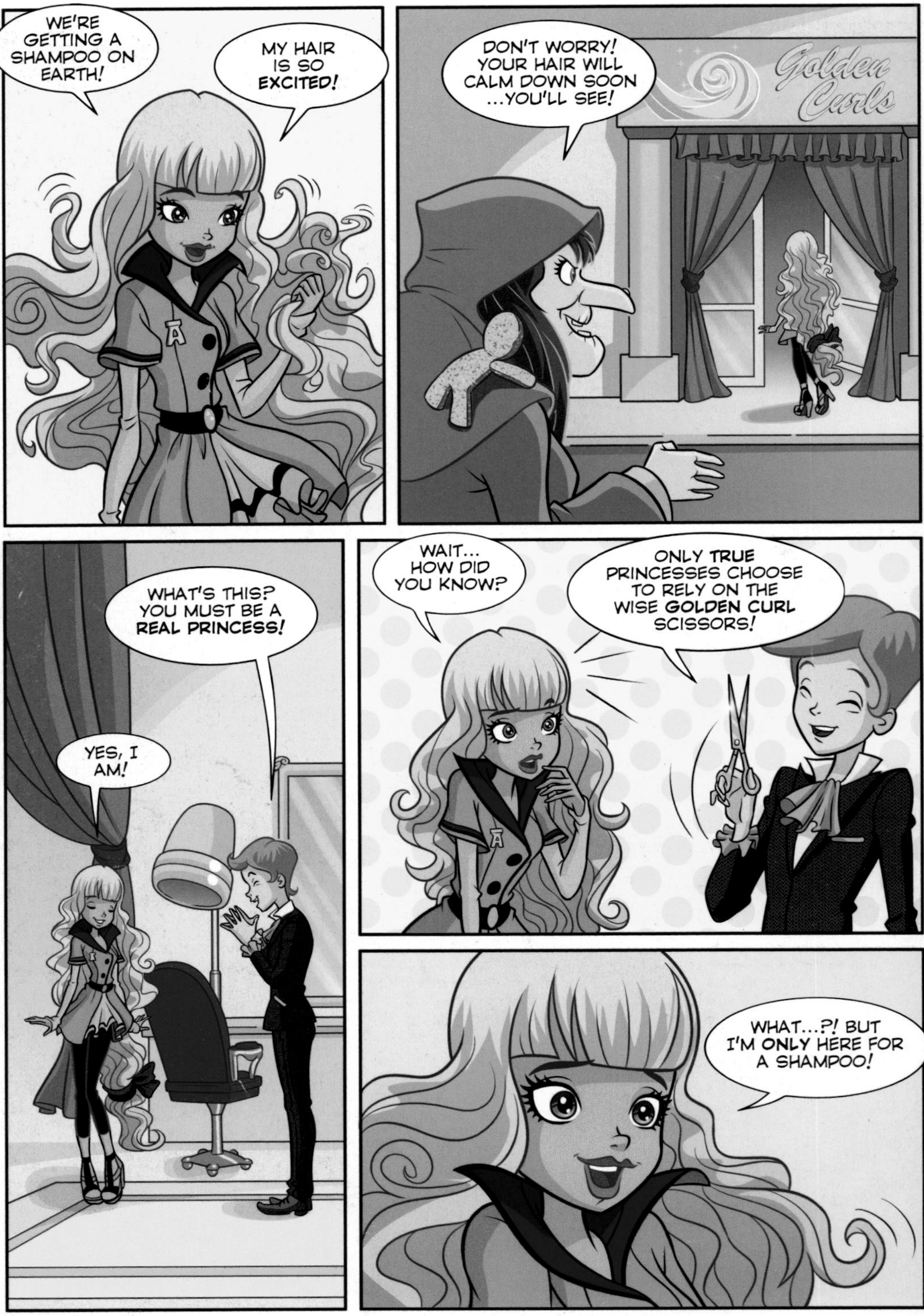

WE'RE GETTING A SHAMPOO ON EARTH!
MY HAIR IS SO **EXCITED!**
DON'T WORRY! YOUR HAIR WILL CALM DOWN SOON ...YOU'LL SEE!
Golden Curls
WHAT'S THIS? YOU MUST BE A **REAL PRINCESS!**
YES, I AM!
WAIT... HOW DID YOU KNOW?
ONLY **TRUE** PRINCESSES CHOOSE TO RELY ON THE WISE **GOLDEN CURL** SCISSORS!
WHAT...?! BUT I'M **ONLY** HERE FOR A SHAMPOO!

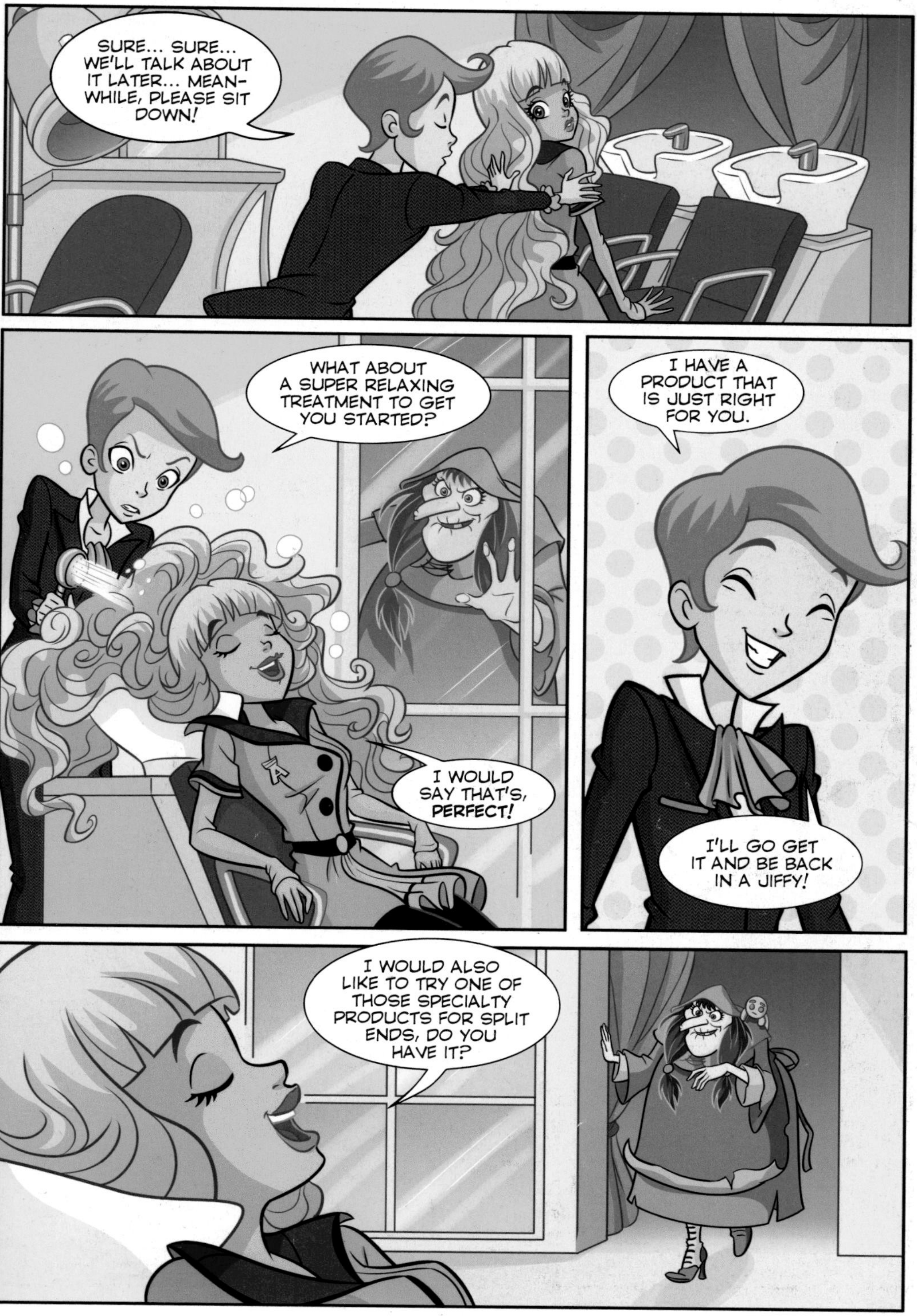
SURE... SURE... WE'LL TALK ABOUT IT LATER... MEAN-WHILE, PLEASE SIT DOWN!
WHAT ABOUT A SUPER RELAXING TREATMENT TO GET YOU STARTED?
I WOULD SAY THAT'S, PERFECT!
I HAVE A PRODUCT THAT IS JUST RIGHT FOR YOU.
I'LL GO GET IT AND BE BACK IN A JIFFY!
I WOULD ALSO LIKE TO TRY ONE OF THOSE SPECIALTY PRODUCTS FOR SPLIT ENDS, DO YOU HAVE IT?

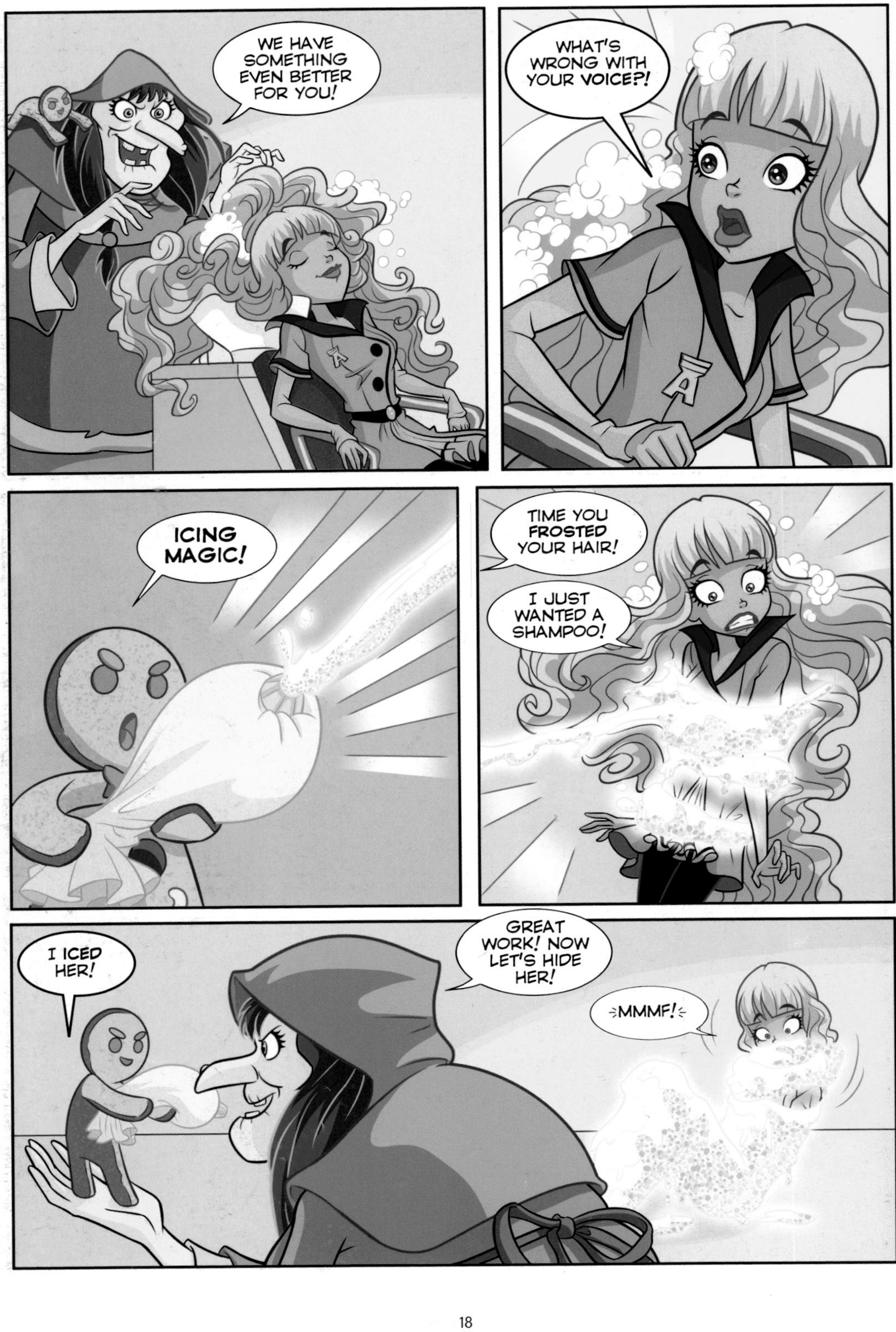
WE HAVE SOMETHING EVEN BETTER FOR YOU!
WHAT'S WRONG WITH YOUR VOICE?!
ICING MAGIC!
TIME YOU FROSTED YOUR HAIR!
I JUST WANTED A SHAMPOO!
I ICED HER!
GREAT WORK! NOW LET'S HIDE HER!
MMMF!

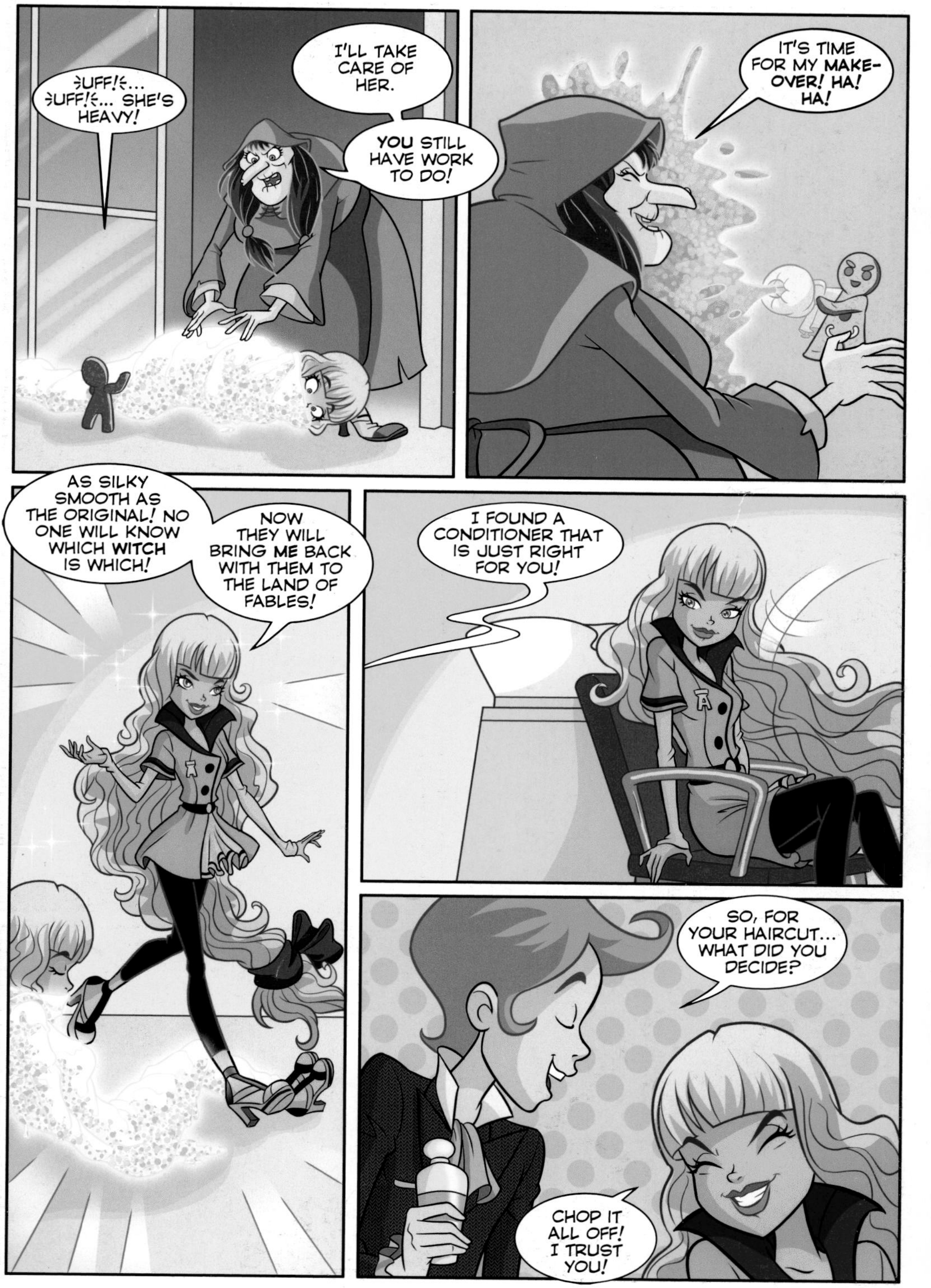

UFF!... UFF!... SHE'S HEAVY!
I'LL TAKE CARE OF HER.
YOU STILL HAVE WORK TO DO!
IT'S TIME FOR MY MAKE-OVER! HA! HA!
AS SILKY SMOOTH AS THE ORIGINAL! NO ONE WILL KNOW WHICH WITCH IS WHICH!
NOW THEY WILL BRING ME BACK WITH THEM TO THE LAND OF FABLES!
I FOUND A CONDITIONER THAT IS JUST RIGHT FOR YOU!
SO, FOR YOUR HAIRCUT... WHAT DID YOU DECIDE?
CHOP IT ALL OFF! I TRUST YOU!

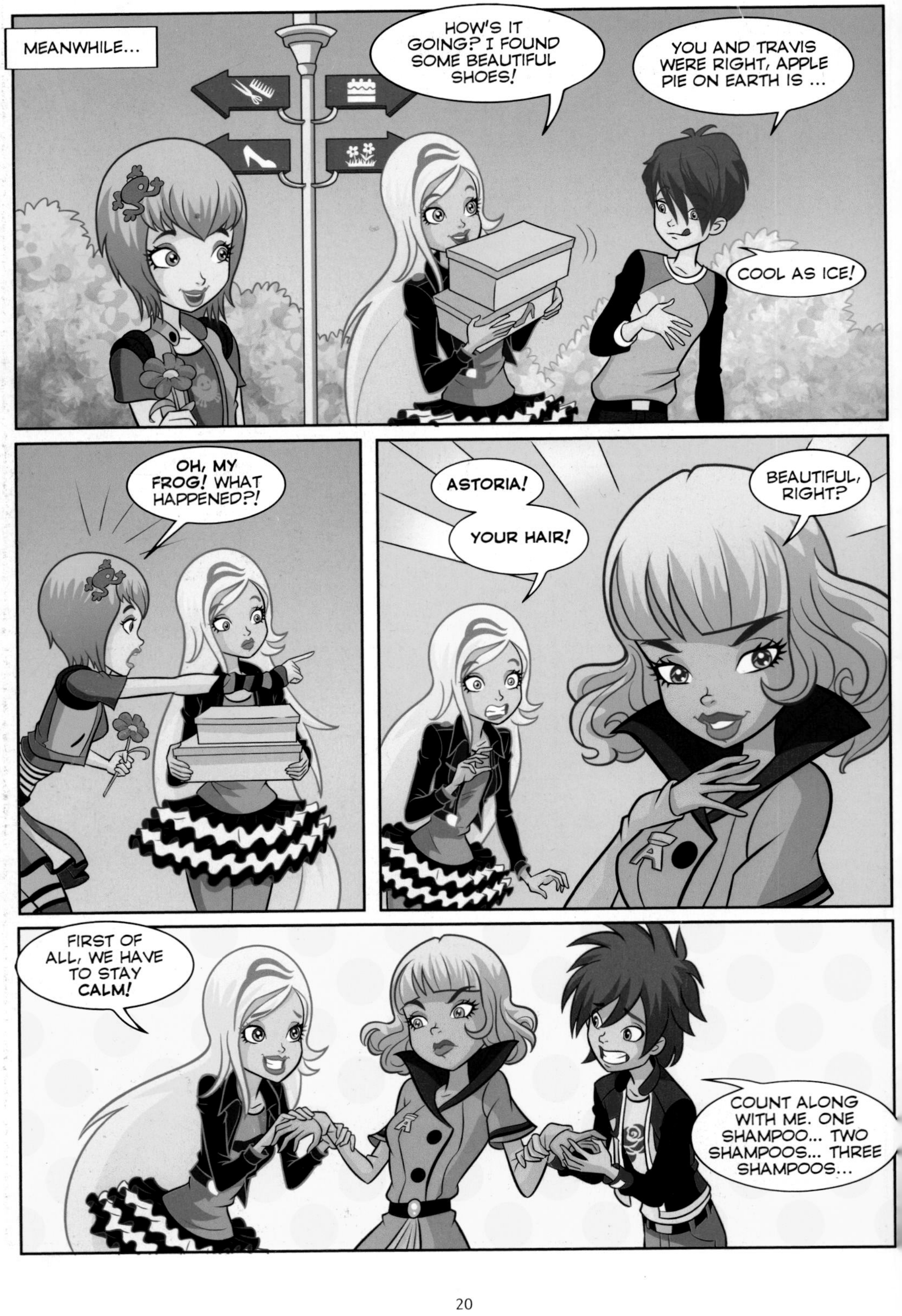
MEANWHILE...
HOW'S IT GOING? I FOUND SOME BEAUTIFUL SHOES!
YOU AND TRAVIS WERE RIGHT, APPLE PIE ON EARTH IS ...
COOL AS ICE!
OH, MY FROG! WHAT HAPPENED?!
ASTORIA!
YOUR HAIR!
BEAUTIFUL, RIGHT?
FIRST OF ALL, WE HAVE TO STAY CALM!
COUNT ALONG WITH ME. ONE SHAMPOO... TWO SHAMPOOS... THREE SHAMPOOS...

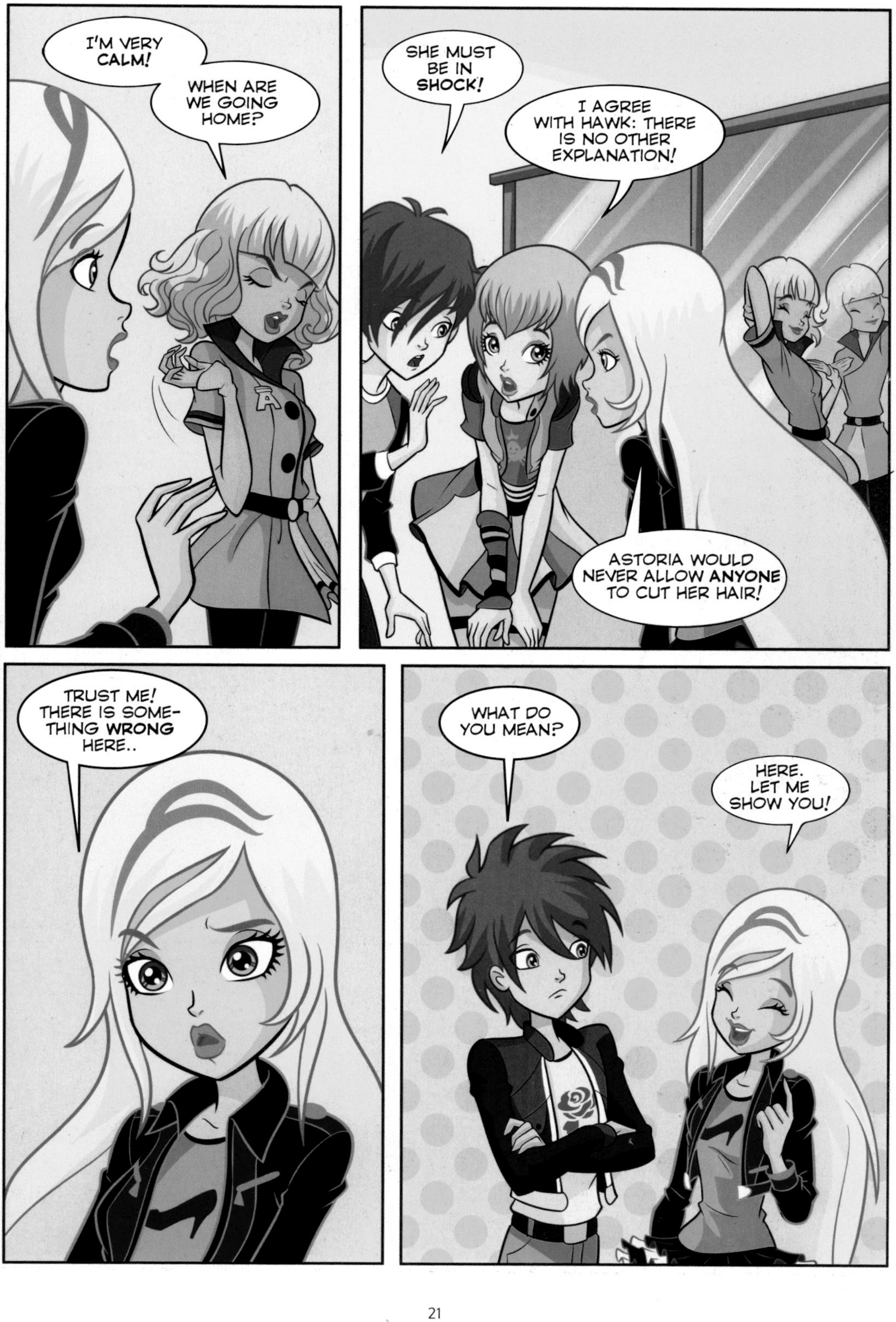
I'M VERY CALM!
WHEN ARE WE GOING HOME?
SHE MUST BE IN SHOCK!
I AGREE WITH HAWK: THERE IS NO OTHER EXPLANATION!
ASTORIA WOULD NEVER ALLOW ANYONE TO CUT HER HAIR!
TRUST ME! THERE IS SOME-THING WRONG HERE..
WHAT DO YOU MEAN?
HERE. LET ME SHOW YOU!

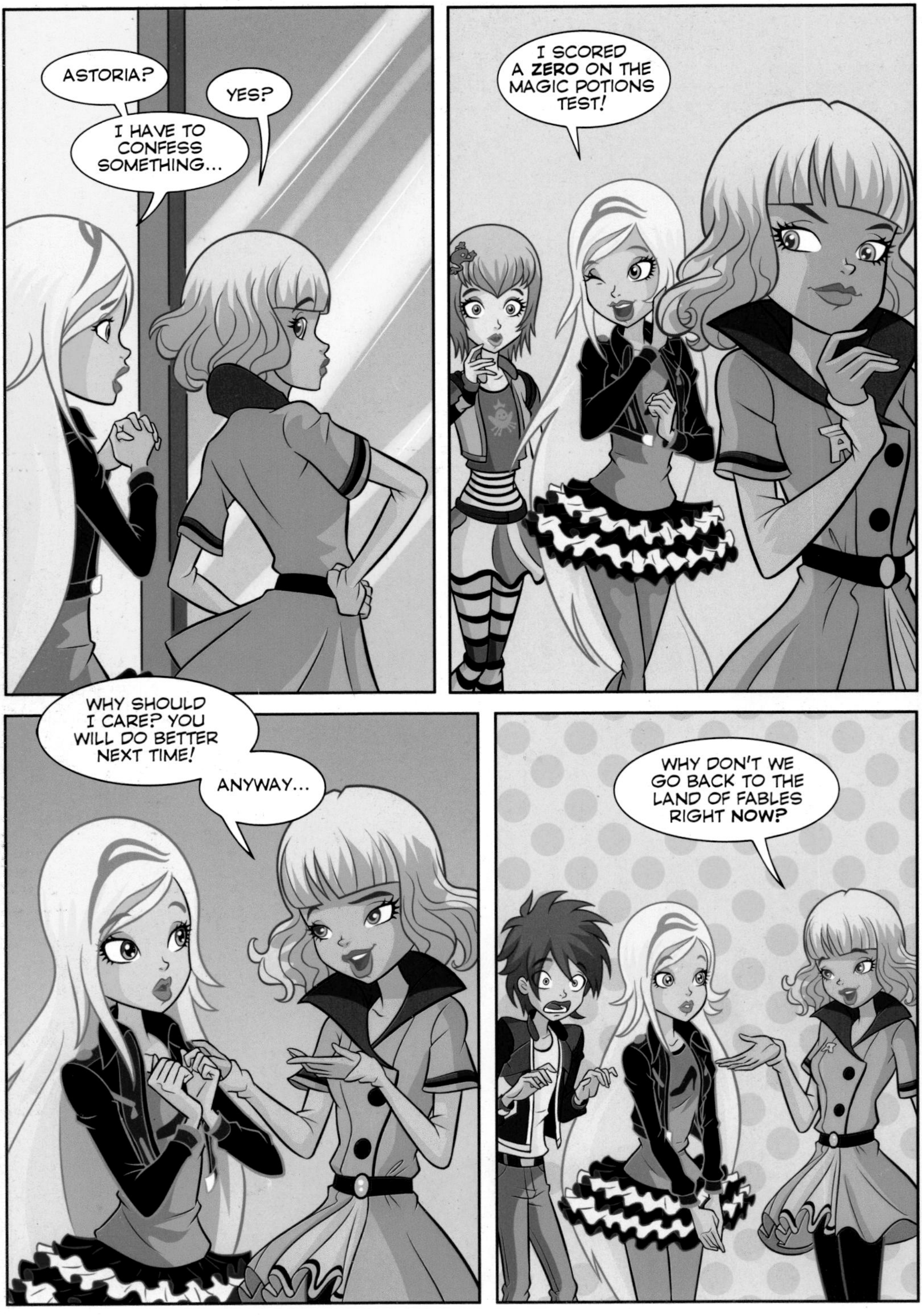
ASTORIA?
YES?
I HAVE TO CONFESS SOMETHING...
I SCORED A **ZERO** ON THE MAGIC POTIONS TEST!
WHY SHOULD I CARE? YOU WILL DO BETTER NEXT TIME!
ANYWAY...
WHY DON'T WE GO BACK TO THE LAND OF FABLES RIGHT **NOW**?

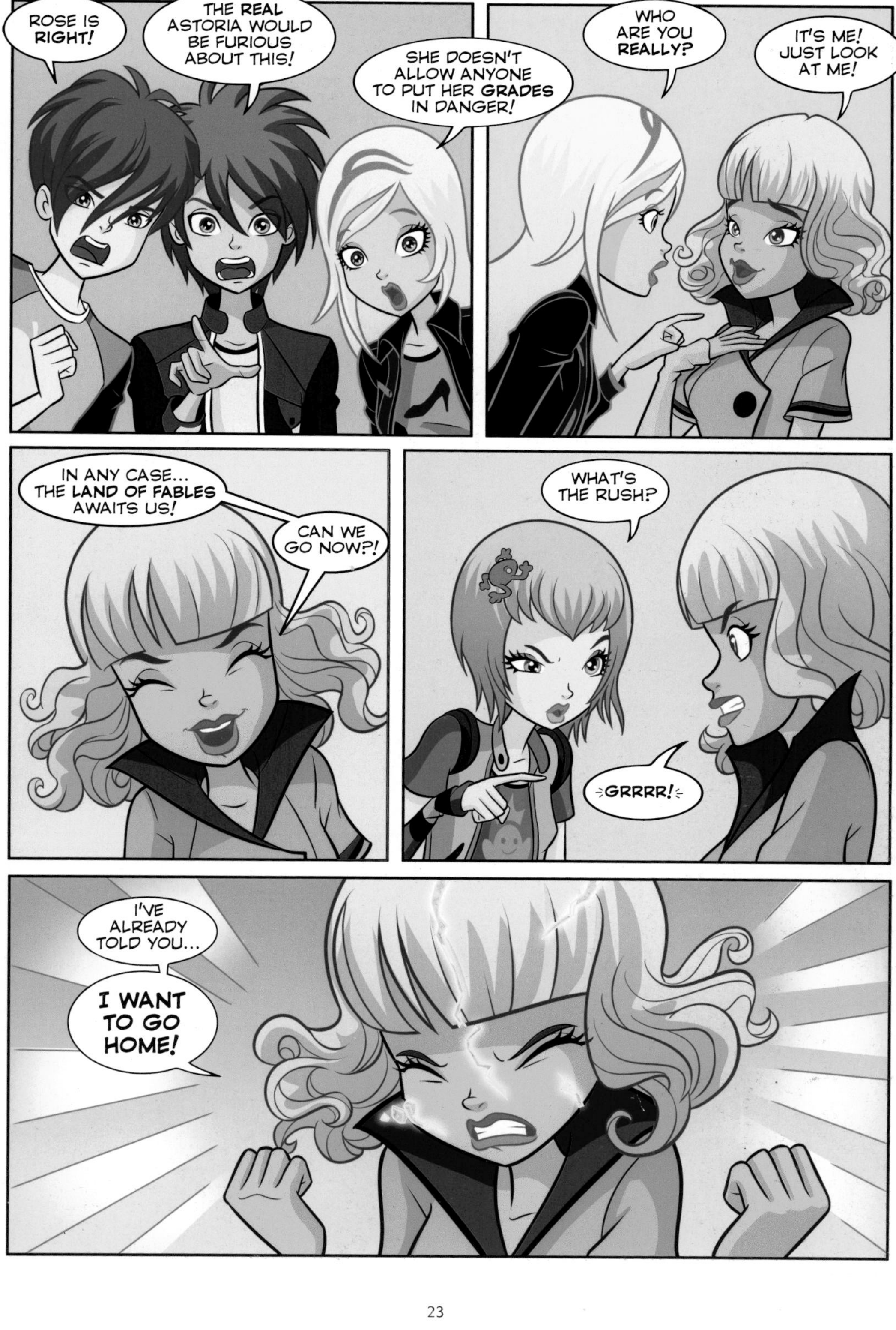
ROSE IS RIGHT!
THE REAL ASTORIA WOULD BE FURIOUS ABOUT THIS!
SHE DOESN'T ALLOW ANYONE TO PUT HER GRADES IN DANGER!
WHO ARE YOU REALLY?
IT'S ME! JUST LOOK AT ME!
IN ANY CASE... THE LAND OF FABLES AWAITS US!
CAN WE GO NOW?!
WHAT'S THE RUSH?
GRRRR!
I'VE ALREADY TOLD YOU...
I WANT TO GO HOME!

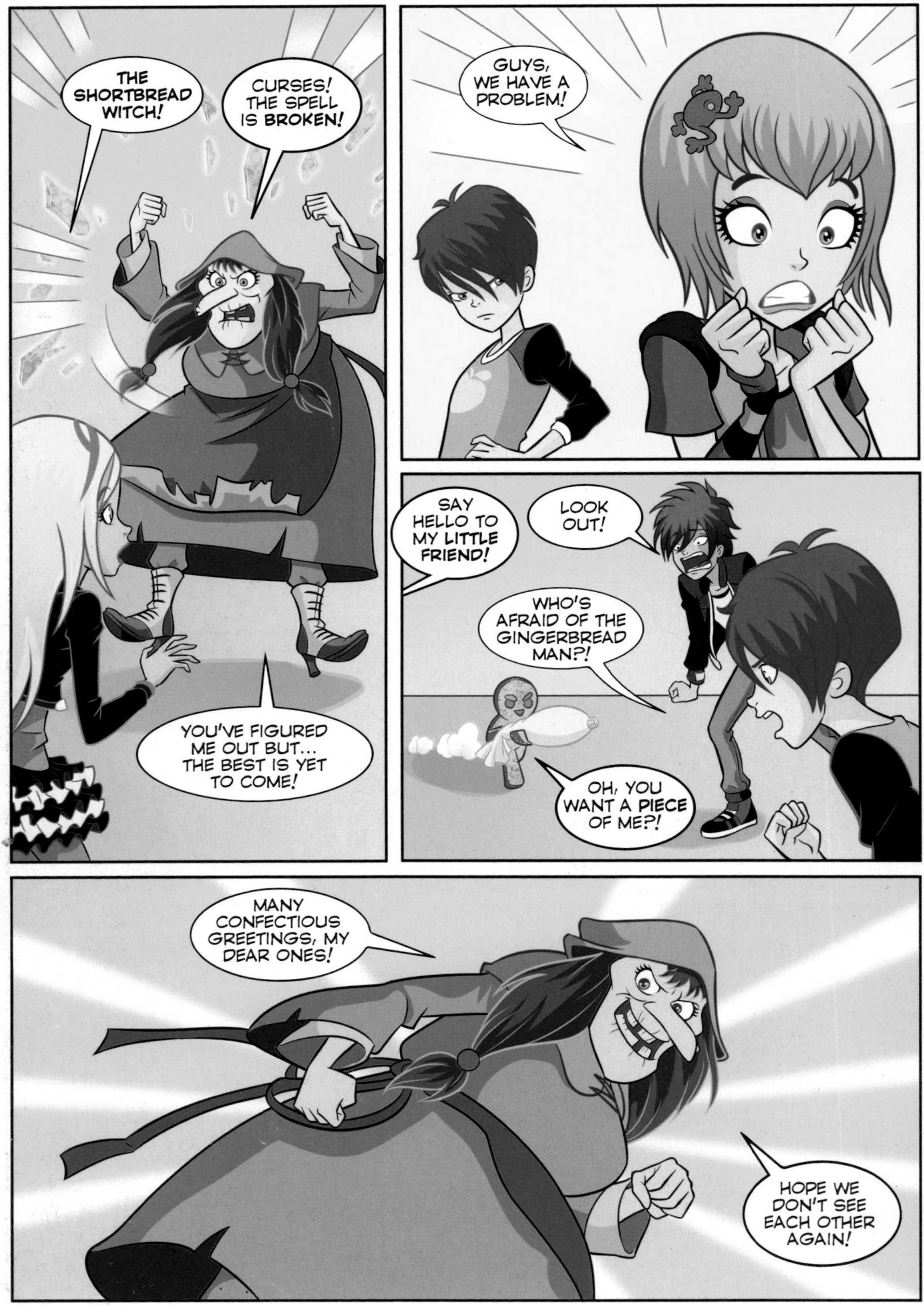
THE SHORTBREAD WITCH!
CURSES! THE SPELL IS BROKEN!
YOU'VE FIGURED ME OUT BUT... THE BEST IS YET TO COME!
GUYS, WE HAVE A PROBLEM!
SAY HELLO TO MY LITTLE FRIEND!
LOOK OUT!
WHO'S AFRAID OF THE GINGERBREAD MAN?!
OH, YOU WANT A PIECE OF ME?!
MANY CONFECTIOUS GREETINGS, MY DEAR ONES!
HOPE WE DON'T SEE EACH OTHER AGAIN!

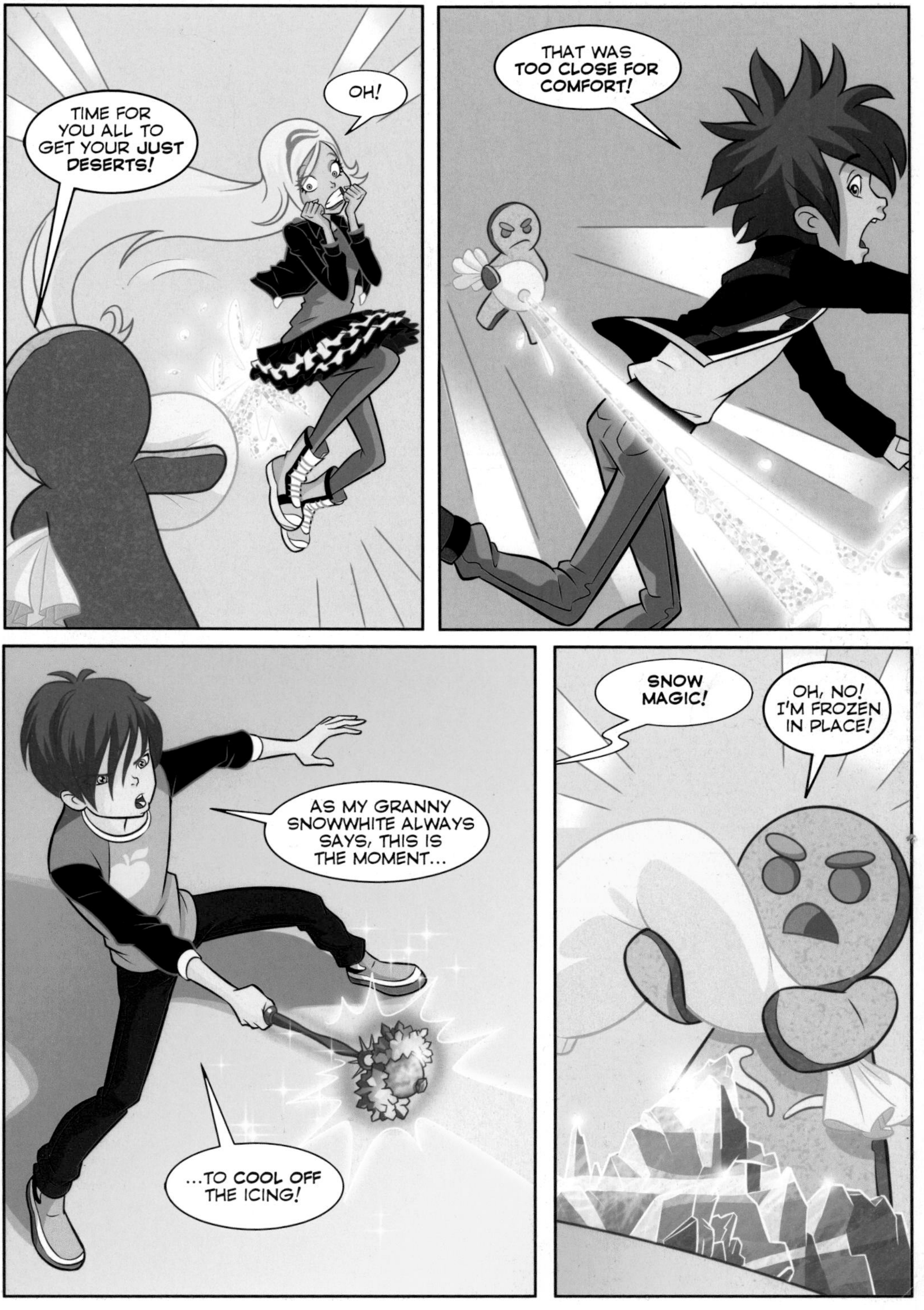
TIME FOR YOU ALL TO GET YOUR JUST DESERTS!
OH!
THAT WAS TOO CLOSE FOR COMFORT!
AS MY GRANNY SNOWWHITE ALWAYS SAYS, THIS IS THE MOMENT...
...TO COOL OFF THE ICING!
SNOW MAGIC!
OH, NO! I'M FROZEN IN PLACE!

WHAT ARE YOU DOING? YOU CAN'T LEAVE ME HERE!

YOU'RE RIGHT!

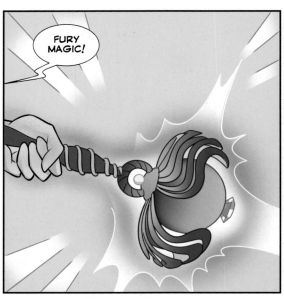

FURY MAGIC!

HE'S GONE WITH THE WIND!

NOOOOOOOOOOOOO!

THAT'S HOW THE COOKIE-MAN CRUMBLES!

BYE BYE, LITTLE GUY!

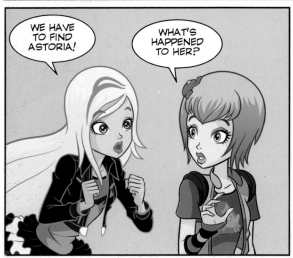

WE HAVE TO FIND ASTORIA!

WHAT'S HAPPENED TO HER?

HELP! A MUMMY!

I THINK I KNOW!

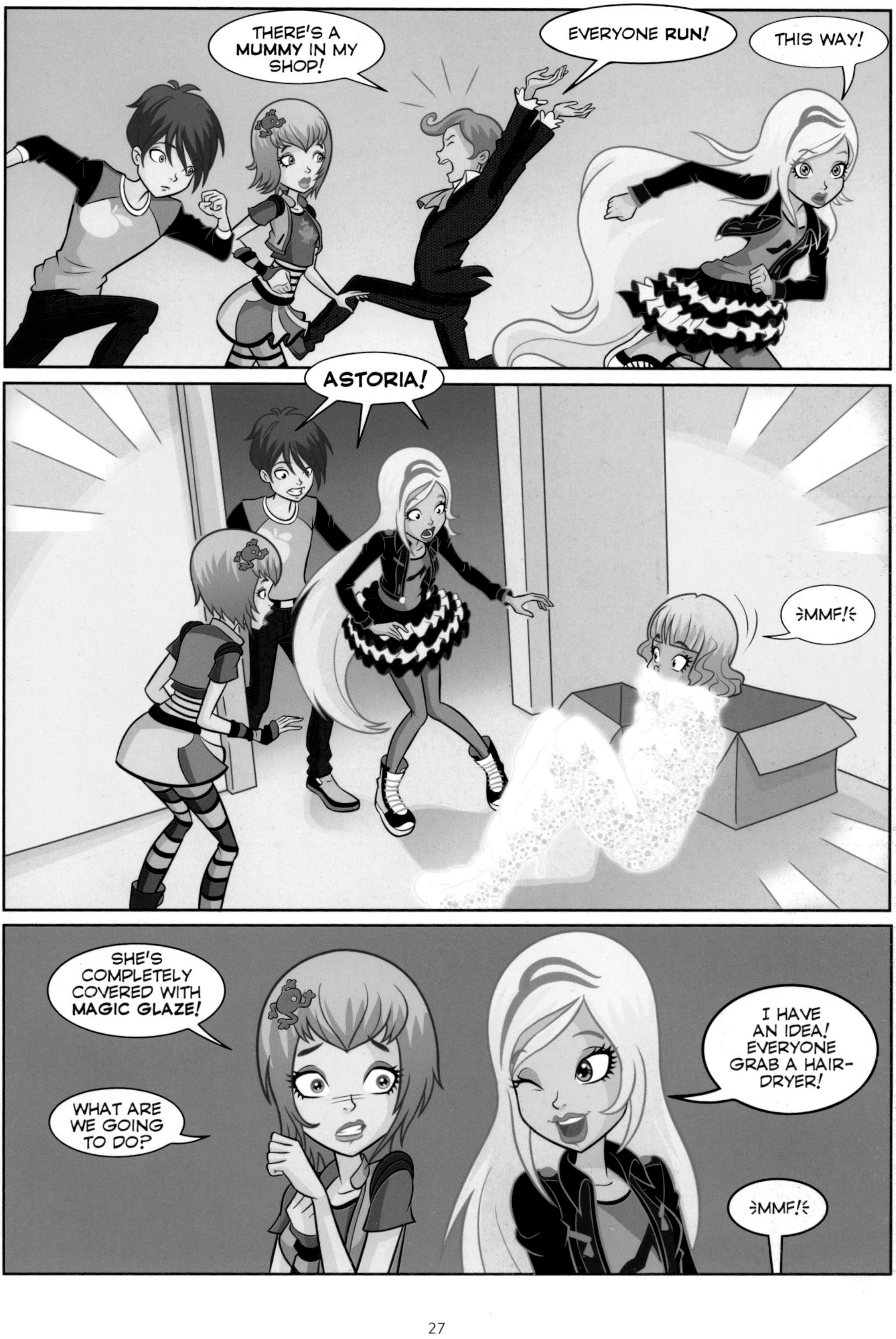
THERE'S A MUMMY IN MY SHOP!
EVERYONE RUN!
THIS WAY!
ASTORIA!
MMF!
SHE'S COMPLETELY COVERED WITH MAGIC GLAZE!
WHAT ARE WE GOING TO DO?
I HAVE AN IDEA! EVERYONE GRAB A HAIR-DRYER!
MMF!

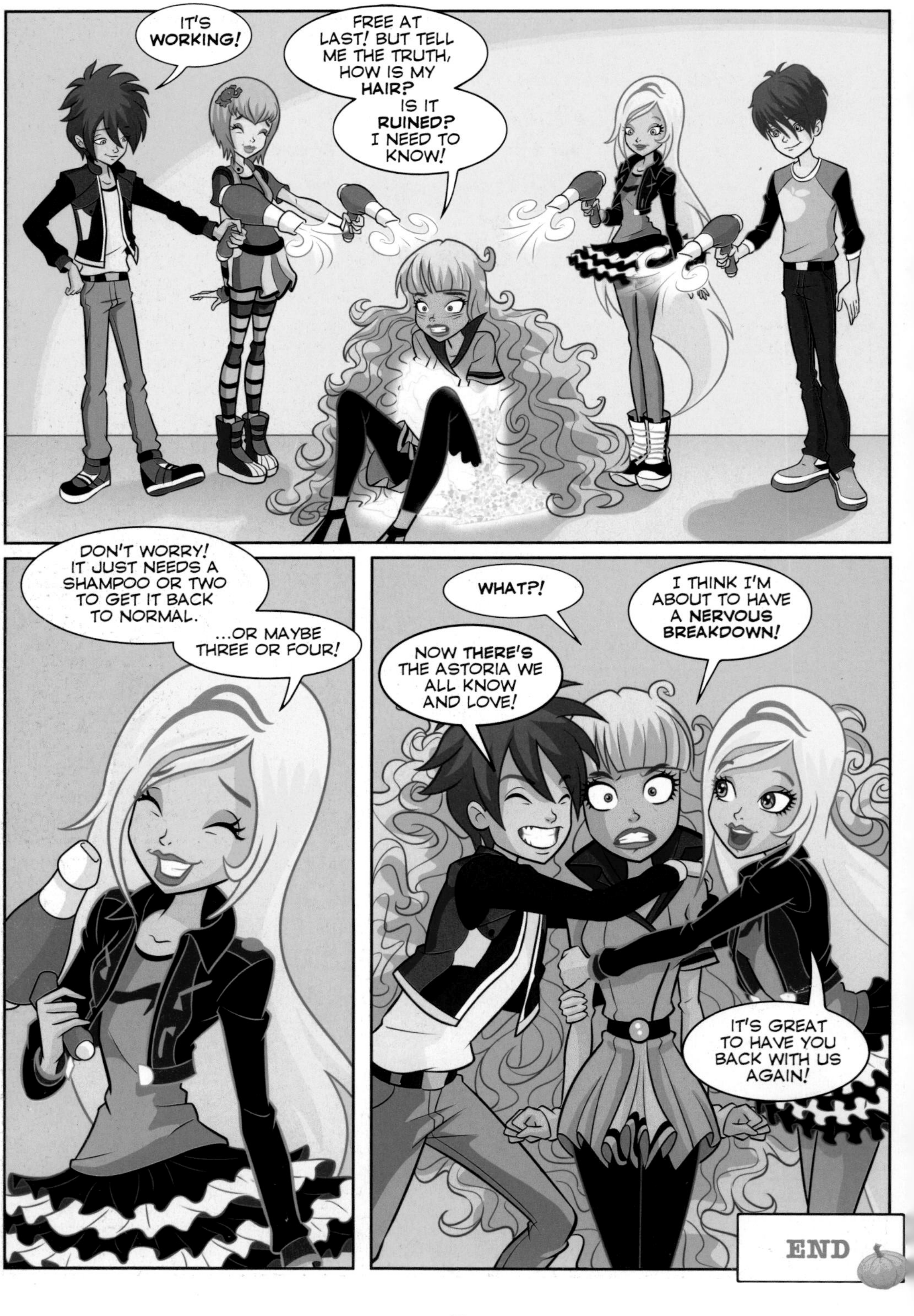
IT'S WORKING!
FREE AT LAST! BUT TELL ME THE TRUTH, HOW IS MY HAIR?
IS IT RUINED? I NEED TO KNOW!
DON'T WORRY! IT JUST NEEDS A SHAMPOO OR TWO TO GET IT BACK TO NORMAL.
...OR MAYBE THREE OR FOUR!
WHAT?!
I THINK I'M ABOUT TO HAVE A NERVOUS BREAKDOWN!
NOW THERE'S THE ASTORIA WE ALL KNOW AND LOVE!
IT'S GREAT TO HAVE YOU BACK WITH US AGAIN!
END

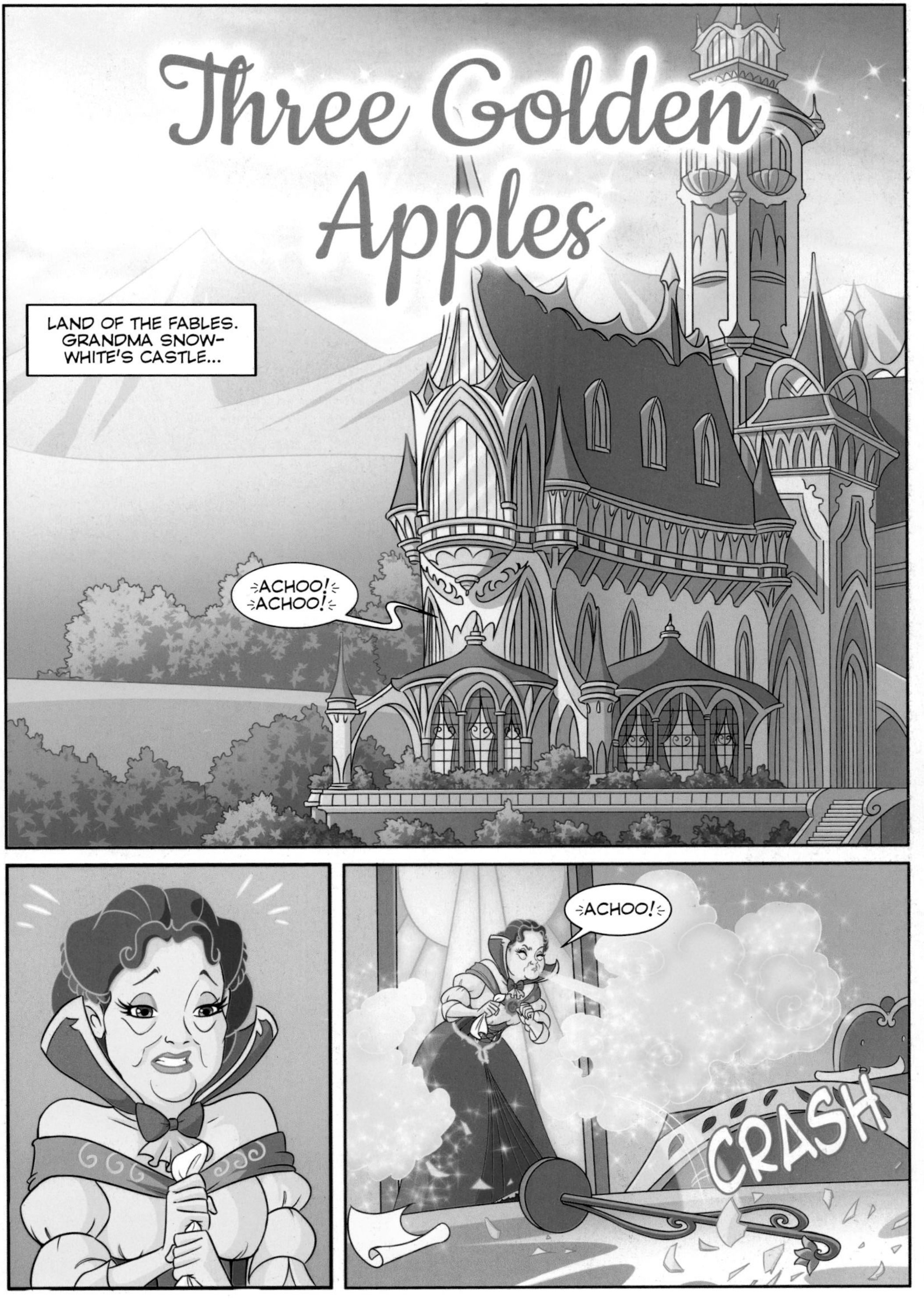
Three Golden Apples
LAND OF THE FABLES. GRANDMA SNOW-WHITE'S CASTLE...
ACHOO! ACHOO!
ACHOO!
CRASH

OH, NO! THIS ISN'T A NORMAL COLD--IT'S A **MAGIC** COLD! WHAT A MESS!

I CAN'T BLAME THAT ON THE MAN IN THE MIRROR!

THIS IS VERY IMPORTANT, ROSE, IS THAT CLEAR?

MY GRANDMA DOES NOT PERMIT ANY MISTAKES WHEN YOU'RE HER GUEST FOR TEA!

I WON'T! JUST GIVE ME HALF A CHANCE!

DON'T LET IT GET YOU DOWN, ROSE.

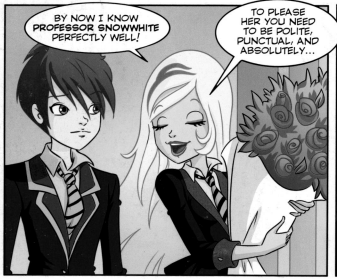

BY NOW I KNOW PROFESSOR SNOWWHITE PERFECTLY WELL!

TO PLEASE HER YOU NEED TO BE POLITE, PUNCTUAL, AND ABSOLUTELY...

...TIDY?!

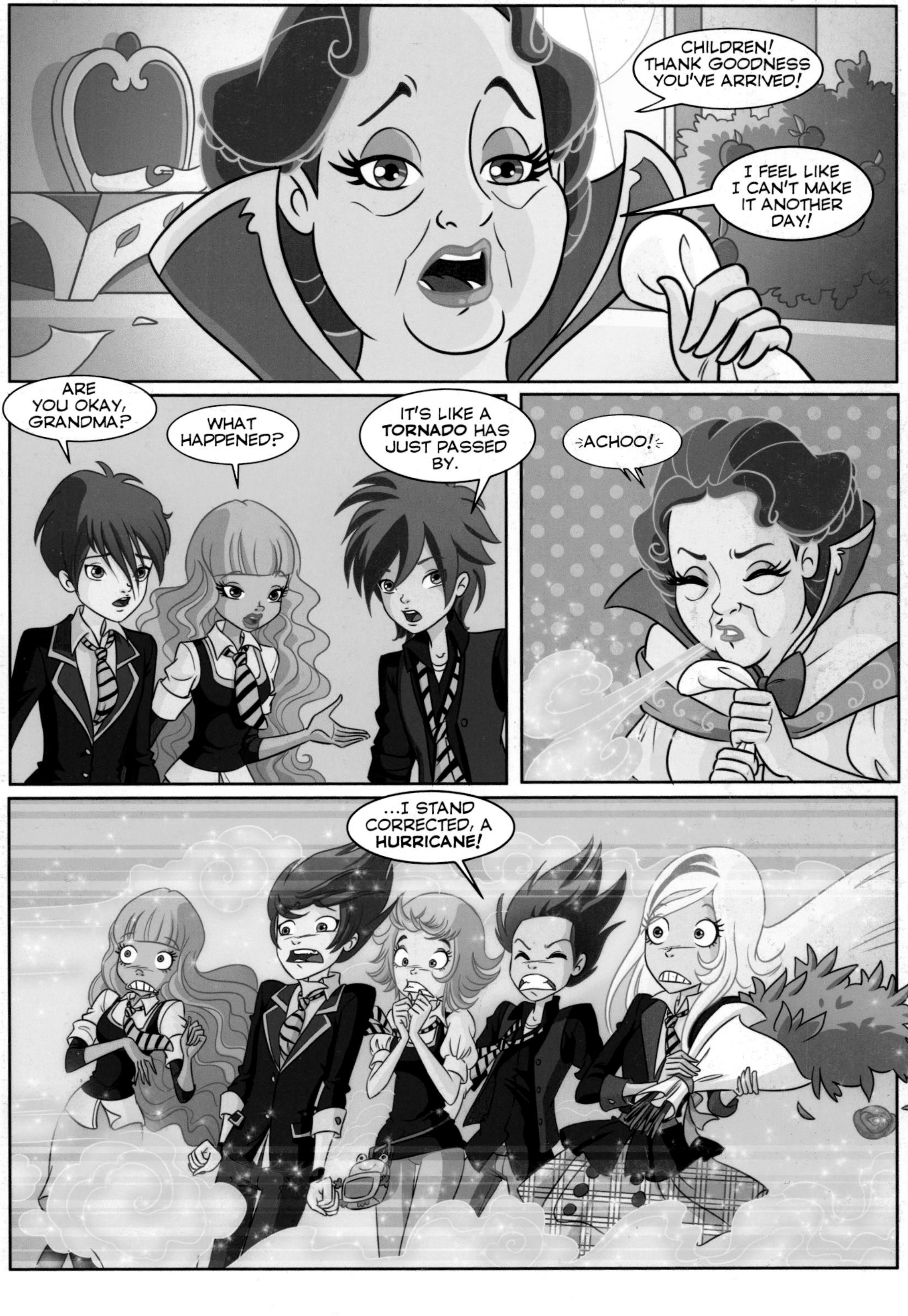
CHILDREN! THANK GOODNESS YOU'VE ARRIVED!
I FEEL LIKE I CAN'T MAKE IT ANOTHER DAY!
ARE YOU OKAY, GRANDMA?
WHAT HAPPENED?
IT'S LIKE A TORNADO HAS JUST PASSED BY.
ACHOO!
...I STAND CORRECTED, A HURRICANE!

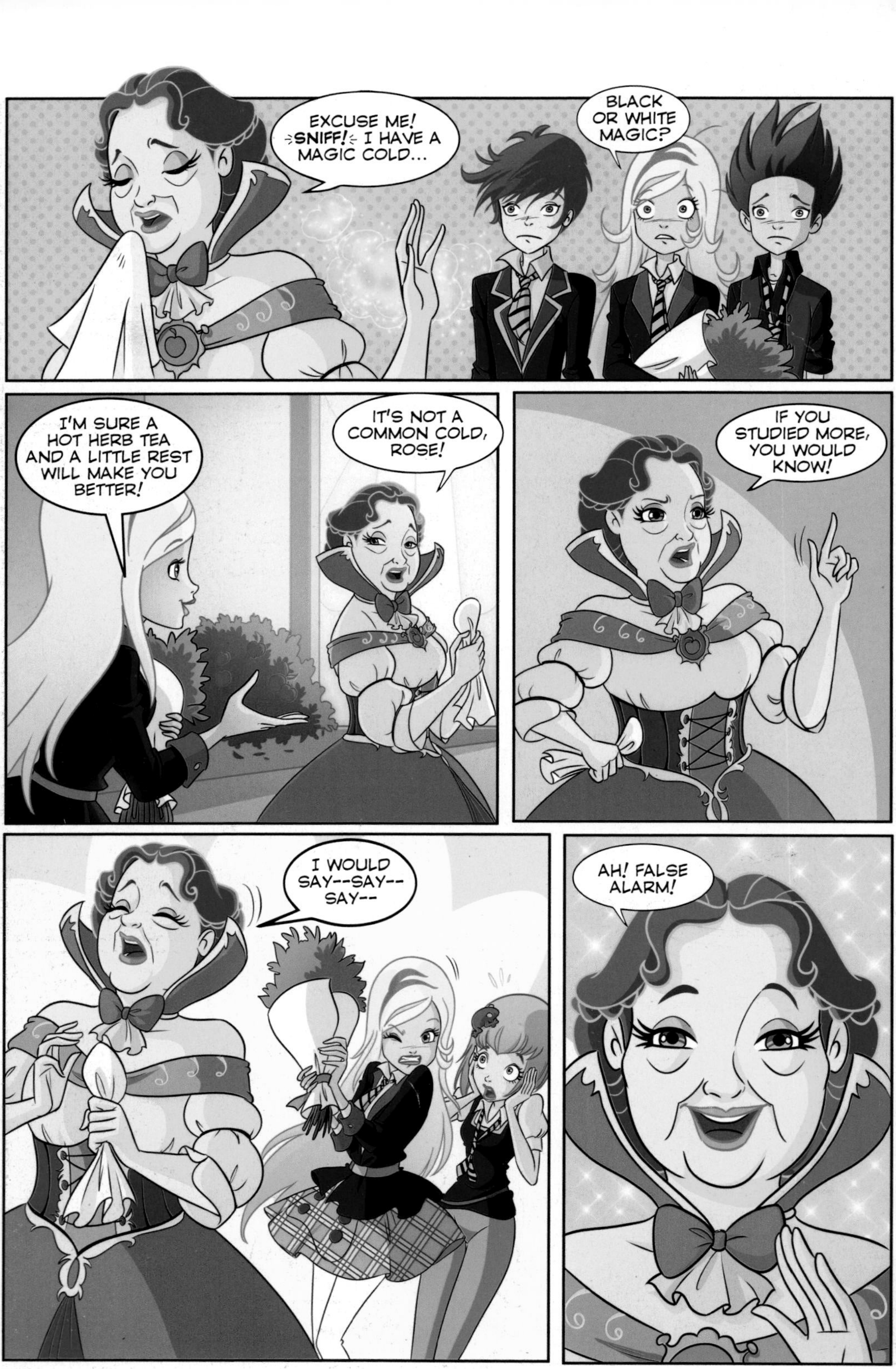

EXCUSE ME! SNIFF! I HAVE A MAGIC COLD...
BLACK OR WHITE MAGIC?
I'M SURE A HOT HERB TEA AND A LITTLE REST WILL MAKE YOU BETTER!
IT'S NOT A COMMON COLD, ROSE!
IF YOU STUDIED MORE, YOU WOULD KNOW!
I WOULD SAY--SAY--SAY--
AH! FALSE ALARM!

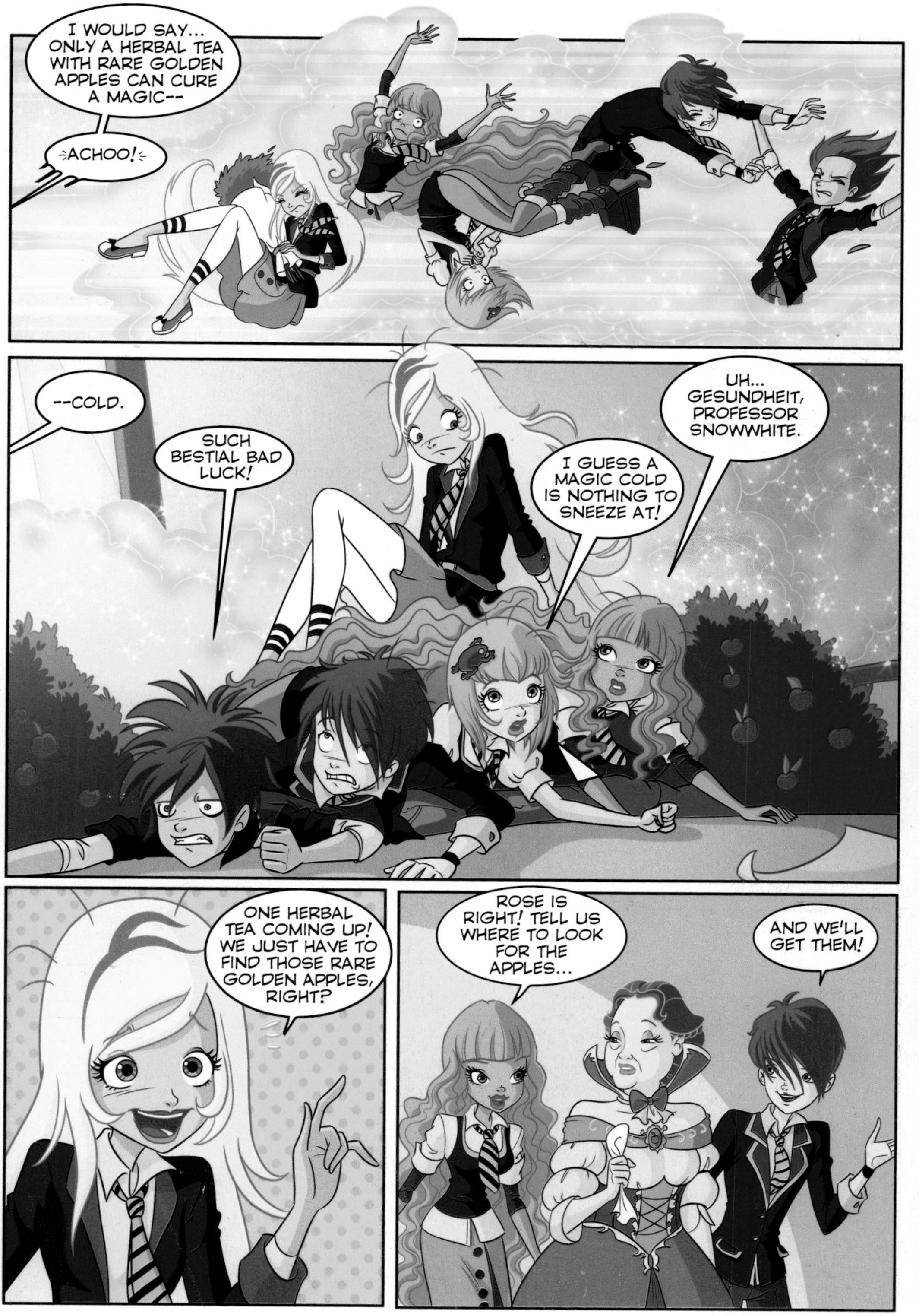
I WOULD SAY... ONLY A HERBAL TEA WITH RARE GOLDEN APPLES CAN CURE A MAGIC--
ACHOO!
--COLD.
SUCH BESTIAL BAD LUCK!
I GUESS A MAGIC COLD IS NOTHING TO SNEEZE AT!
UH... GESUNDHEIT, PROFESSOR SNOWWHITE.
ONE HERBAL TEA COMING UP! WE JUST HAVE TO FIND THOSE RARE GOLDEN APPLES, RIGHT?
ROSE IS RIGHT! TELL US WHERE TO LOOK FOR THE APPLES...
AND WE'LL GET THEM!

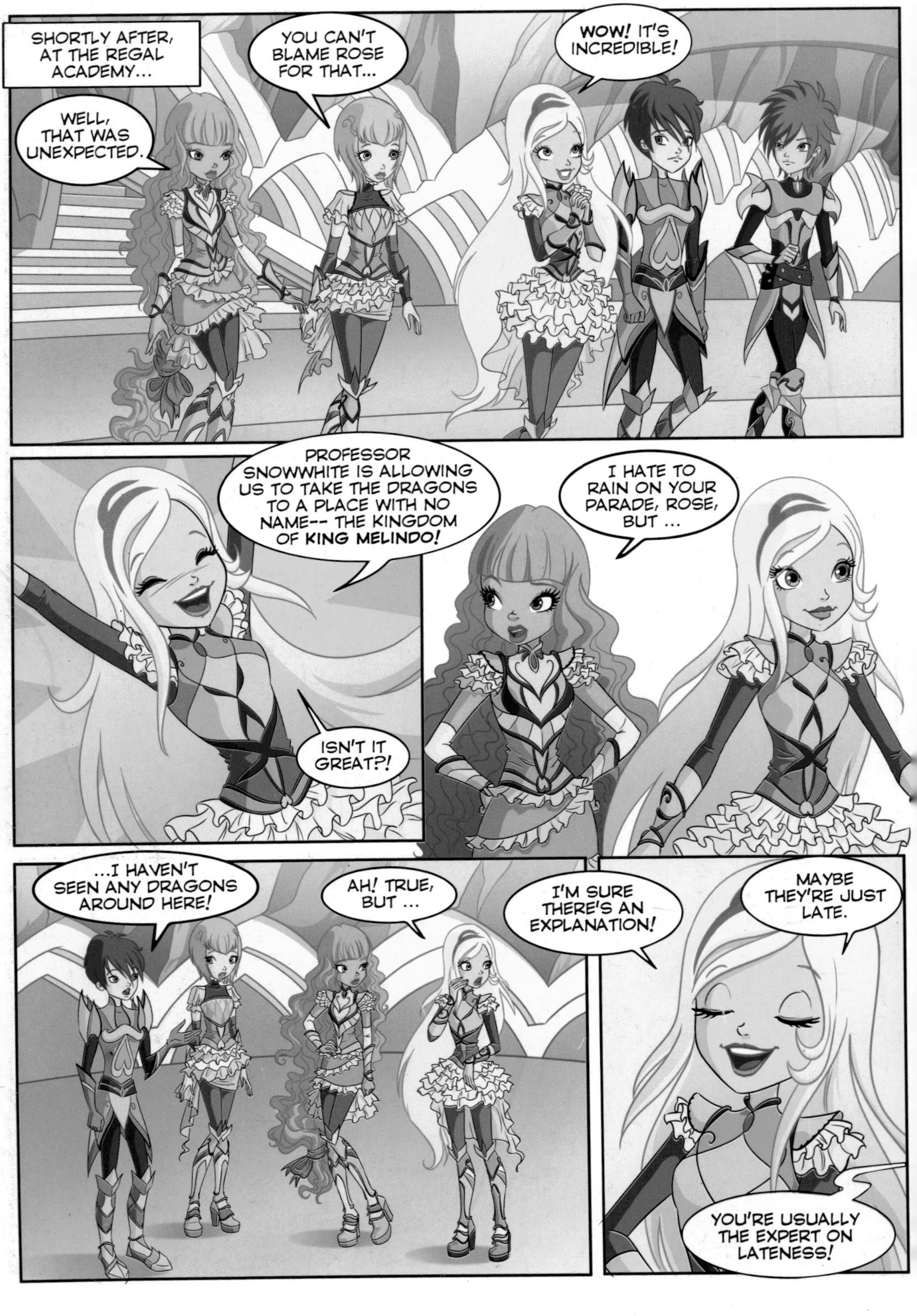
SHORTLY AFTER, AT THE REGAL ACADEMY...
WELL, THAT WAS UNEXPECTED.
YOU CAN'T BLAME ROSE FOR THAT...
WOW! IT'S INCREDIBLE!
PROFESSOR SNOWWHITE IS ALLOWING US TO TAKE THE DRAGONS TO A PLACE WITH NO NAME-- THE KINGDOM OF KING MELINDO!
ISN'T IT GREAT?!
I HATE TO RAIN ON YOUR PARADE, ROSE, BUT ...
...I HAVEN'T SEEN ANY DRAGONS AROUND HERE!
AH! TRUE, BUT ...
I'M SURE THERE'S AN EXPLANATION!
MAYBE THEY'RE JUST LATE.
YOU'RE USUALLY THE EXPERT ON LATENESS!

ISN'T THAT RIGHT, ROSE?

EHM...

I WAS ONLY LATE TWICE THIS WEEK!

WHERE ARE THE OTHER DRAGONS?

THEY'RE ALL AT THE DRAGON-RALLY, DIDN'T THEY WARN YOU?

I LEFT BEFORE EVERYONE ELSE. CROWDS IRRITATE MY SCALES ...

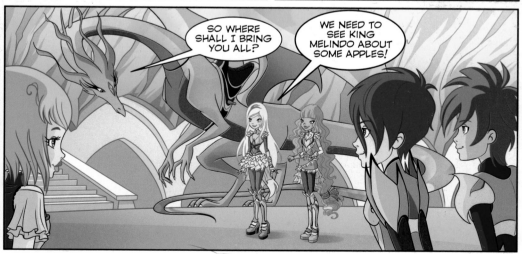

SO WHERE SHALL I BRING YOU ALL?

WE NEED TO SEE KING MELINDO ABOUT SOME APPLES!

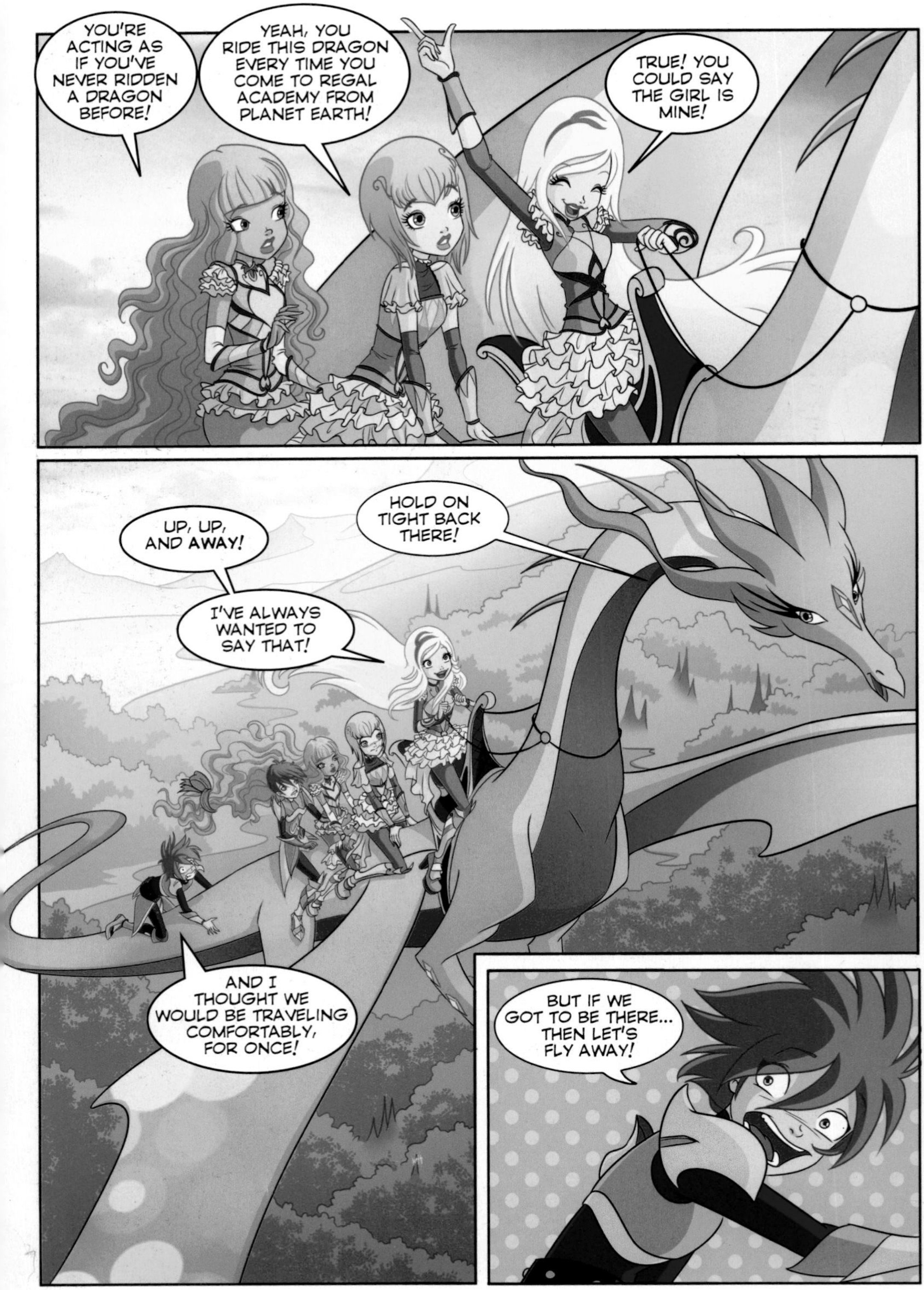
YOU'RE ACTING AS IF YOU'VE NEVER RIDDEN A DRAGON BEFORE!
YEAH, YOU RIDE THIS DRAGON EVERY TIME YOU COME TO REGAL ACADEMY FROM PLANET EARTH!
TRUE! YOU COULD SAY THE GIRL IS MINE!
UP, UP, AND AWAY!
I'VE ALWAYS WANTED TO SAY THAT!
HOLD ON TIGHT BACK THERE!
AND I THOUGHT WE WOULD BE TRAVELING COMFORTABLY, FOR ONCE!
BUT IF WE GOT TO BE THERE... THEN LET'S FLY AWAY!

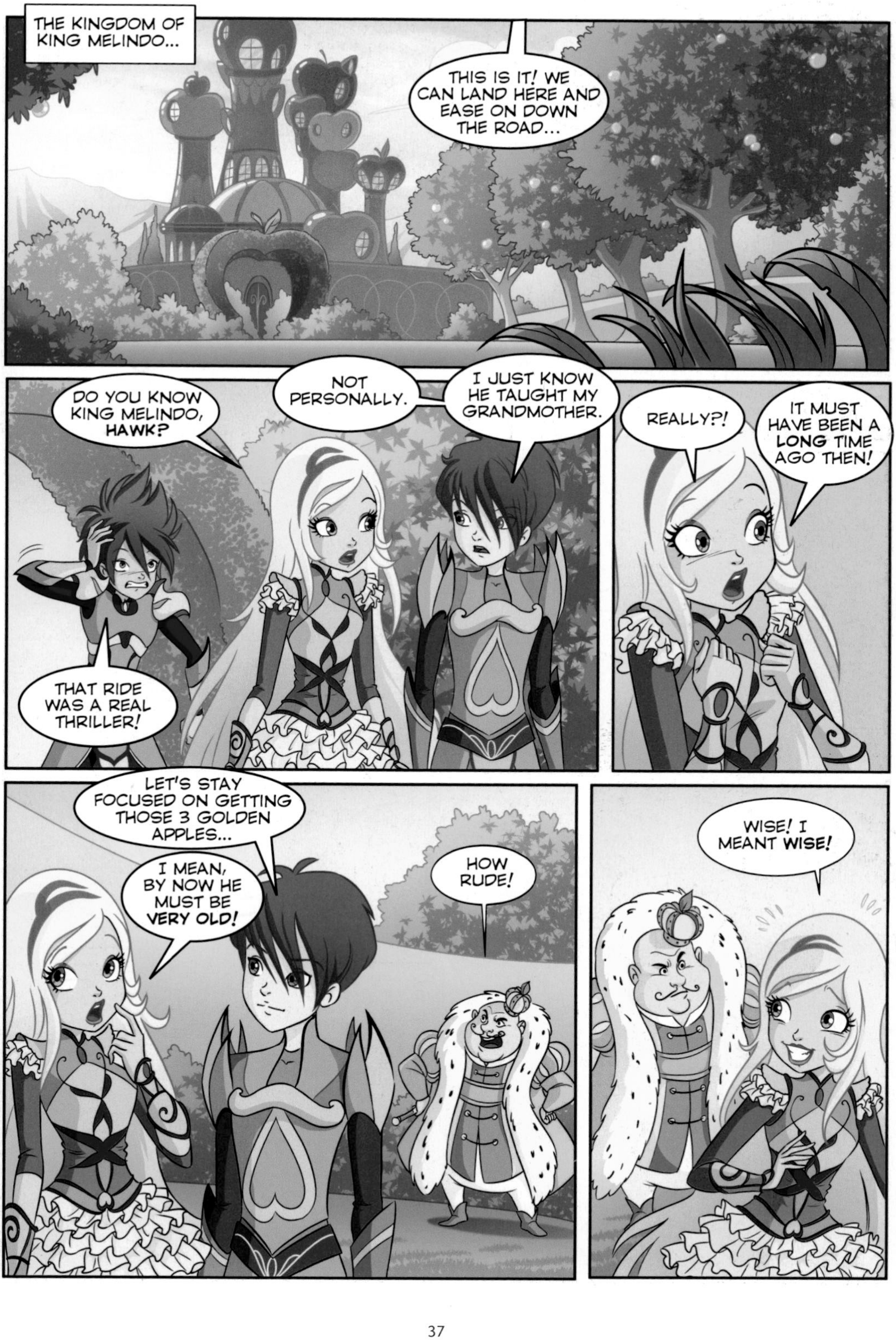
THE KINGDOM OF KING MELINDO...
THIS IS IT! WE CAN LAND HERE AND EASE ON DOWN THE ROAD...
DO YOU KNOW KING MELINDO, HAWK?
NOT PERSONALLY.
I JUST KNOW HE TAUGHT MY GRANDMOTHER.
THAT RIDE WAS A REAL THRILLER!
REALLY?!
IT MUST HAVE BEEN A LONG TIME AGO THEN!
LET'S STAY FOCUSED ON GETTING THOSE 3 GOLDEN APPLES...
I MEAN, BY NOW HE MUST BE VERY OLD!
HOW RUDE!
WISE! I MEANT WISE!

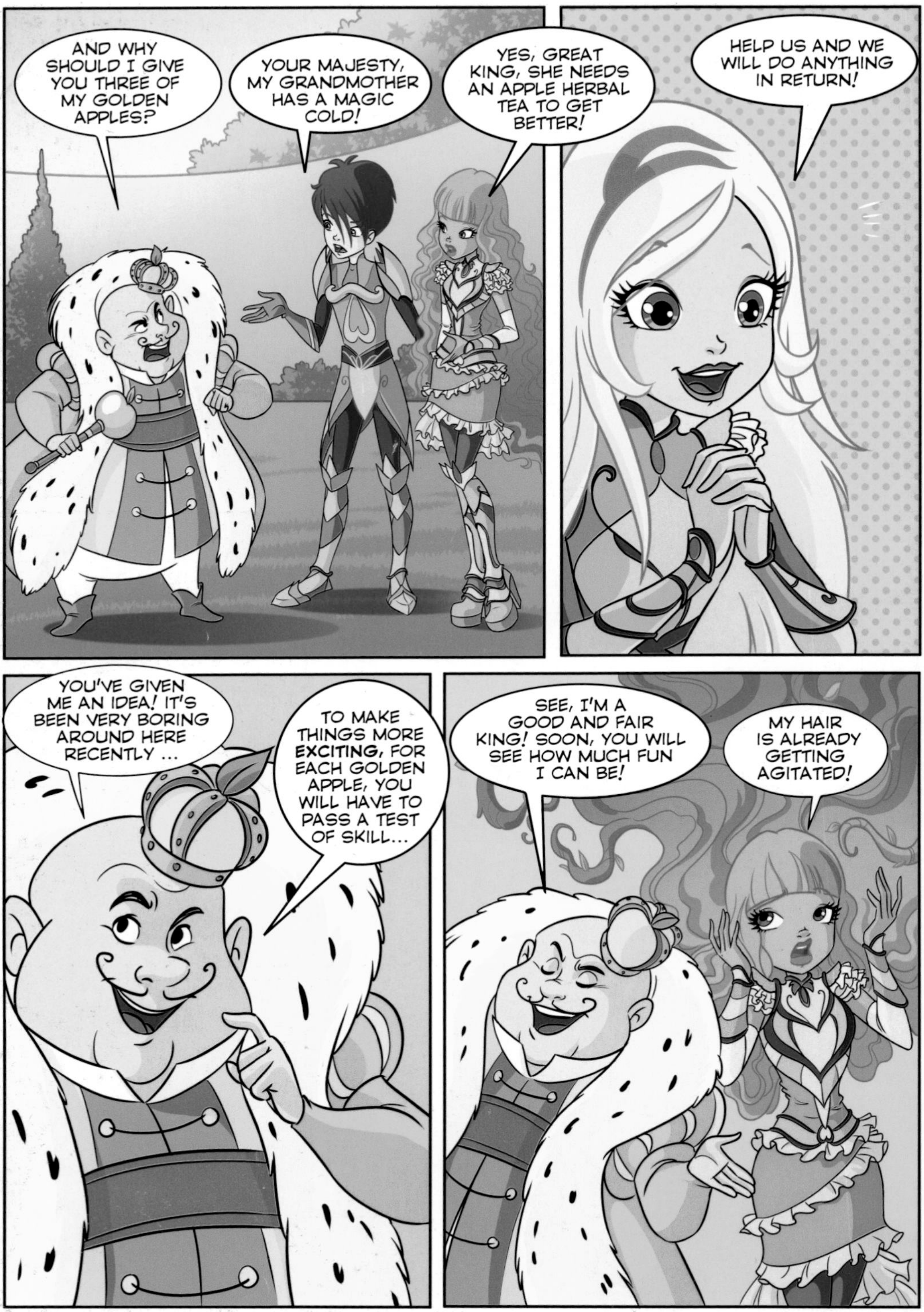
AND WHY SHOULD I GIVE YOU THREE OF MY GOLDEN APPLES?
YOUR MAJESTY, MY GRANDMOTHER HAS A MAGIC COLD!
YES, GREAT KING, SHE NEEDS AN APPLE HERBAL TEA TO GET BETTER!
HELP US AND WE WILL DO ANYTHING IN RETURN!
YOU'VE GIVEN ME AN IDEA! IT'S BEEN VERY BORING AROUND HERE RECENTLY ...
TO MAKE THINGS MORE **EXCITING,** FOR EACH GOLDEN APPLE, YOU WILL HAVE TO PASS A TEST OF SKILL...
SEE, I'M A GOOD AND FAIR KING! SOON, YOU WILL SEE HOW MUCH FUN I CAN BE!
MY HAIR IS ALREADY GETTING AGITATED!

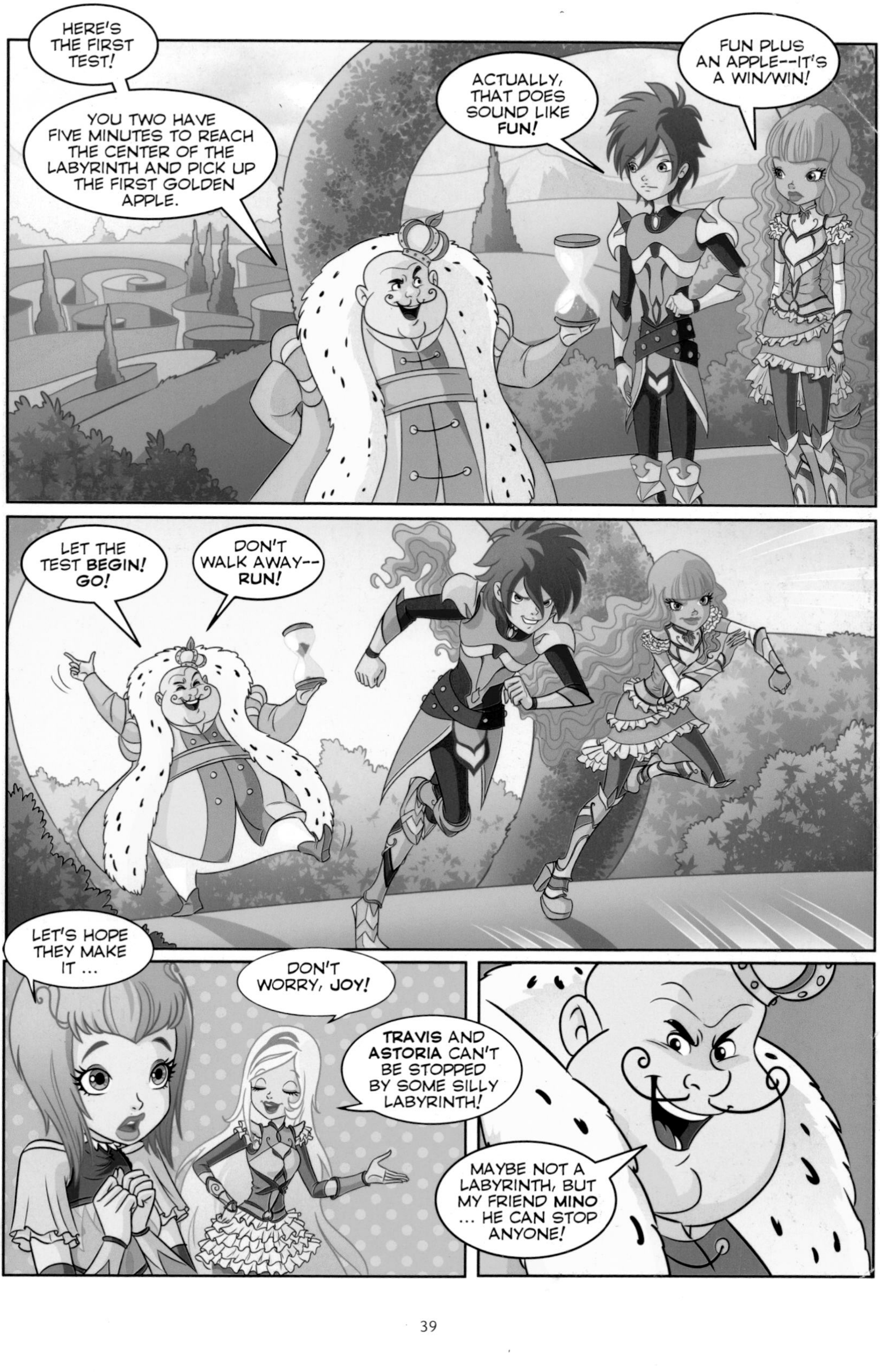
HERE'S THE FIRST TEST!
YOU TWO HAVE FIVE MINUTES TO REACH THE CENTER OF THE LABYRINTH AND PICK UP THE FIRST GOLDEN APPLE.
ACTUALLY, THAT DOES SOUND LIKE FUN!
FUN PLUS AN APPLE--IT'S A WIN/WIN!
LET THE TEST BEGIN! GO!
DON'T WALK AWAY--RUN!
LET'S HOPE THEY MAKE IT ...
DON'T WORRY, JOY!
TRAVIS AND ASTORIA CAN'T BE STOPPED BY SOME SILLY LABYRINTH!
MAYBE NOT A LABYRINTH, BUT MY FRIEND MINO ... HE CAN STOP ANYONE!

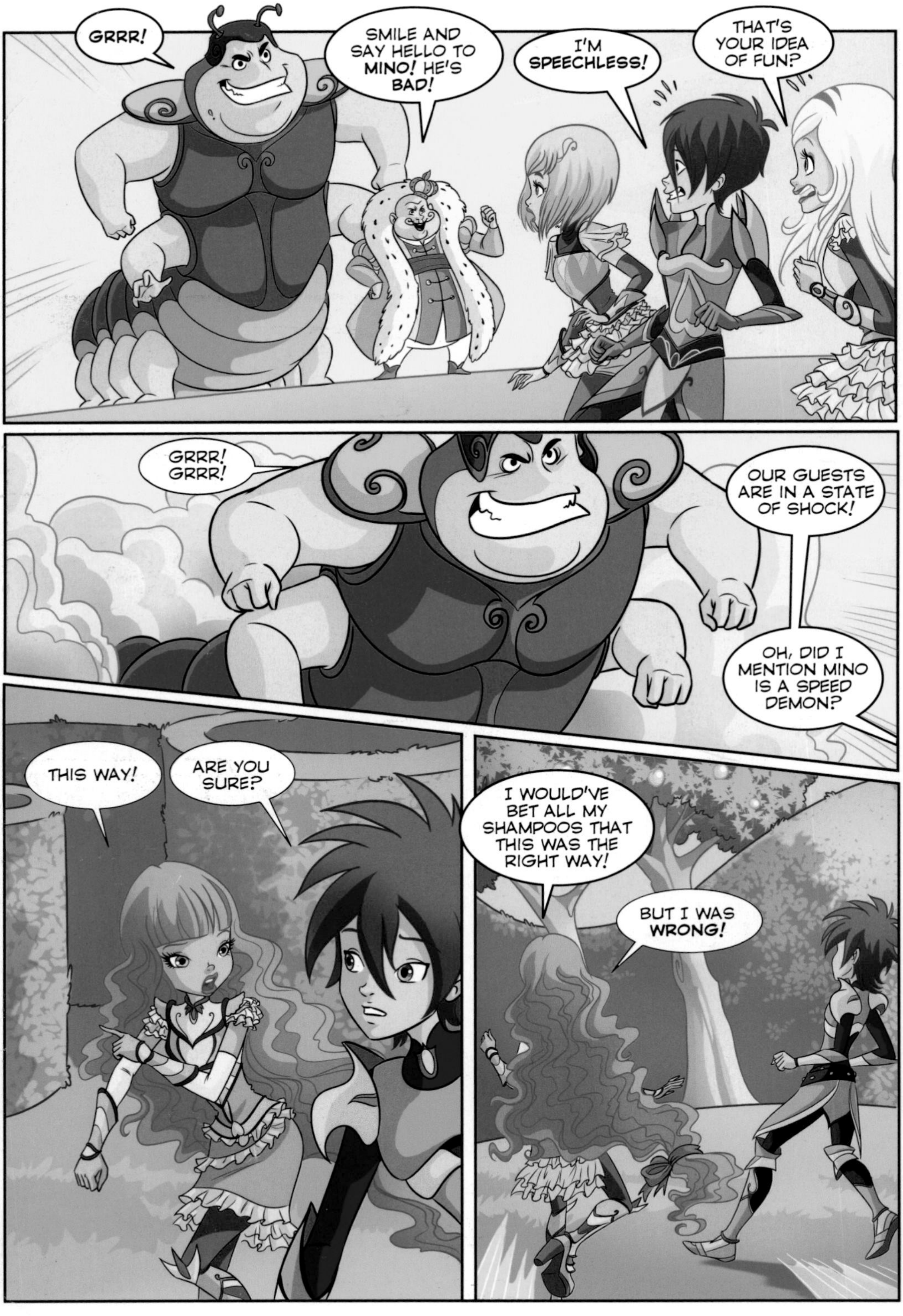
GRRR!
SMILE AND SAY HELLO TO MINO! HE'S BAD!
I'M SPEECHLESS!
THAT'S YOUR IDEA OF FUN?
GRRR! GRRR!
OUR GUESTS ARE IN A STATE OF SHOCK!
OH, DID I MENTION MINO IS A SPEED DEMON?
THIS WAY!
ARE YOU SURE?
I WOULD'VE BET ALL MY SHAMPOOS THAT THIS WAS THE RIGHT WAY!
BUT I WAS WRONG!

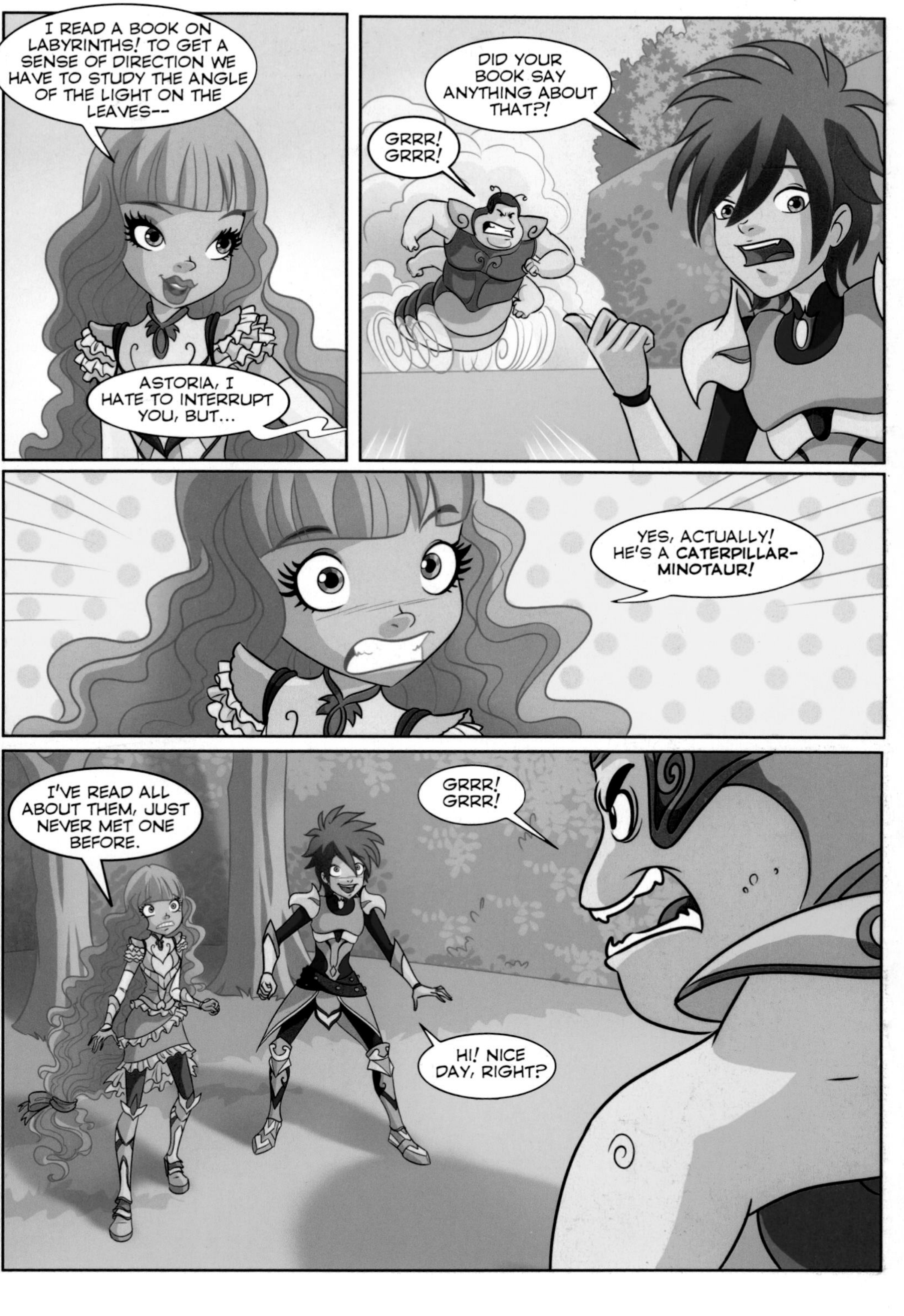
I READ A BOOK ON LABYRINTHS! TO GET A SENSE OF DIRECTION WE HAVE TO STUDY THE ANGLE OF THE LIGHT ON THE LEAVES--
ASTORIA, I HATE TO INTERRUPT YOU, BUT...
DID YOUR BOOK SAY ANYTHING ABOUT THAT?!
GRRR! GRRR!
YES, ACTUALLY! HE'S A CATERPILLAR-MINOTAUR!
I'VE READ ALL ABOUT THEM, JUST NEVER MET ONE BEFORE.
GRRR! GRRR!
HI! NICE DAY, RIGHT?

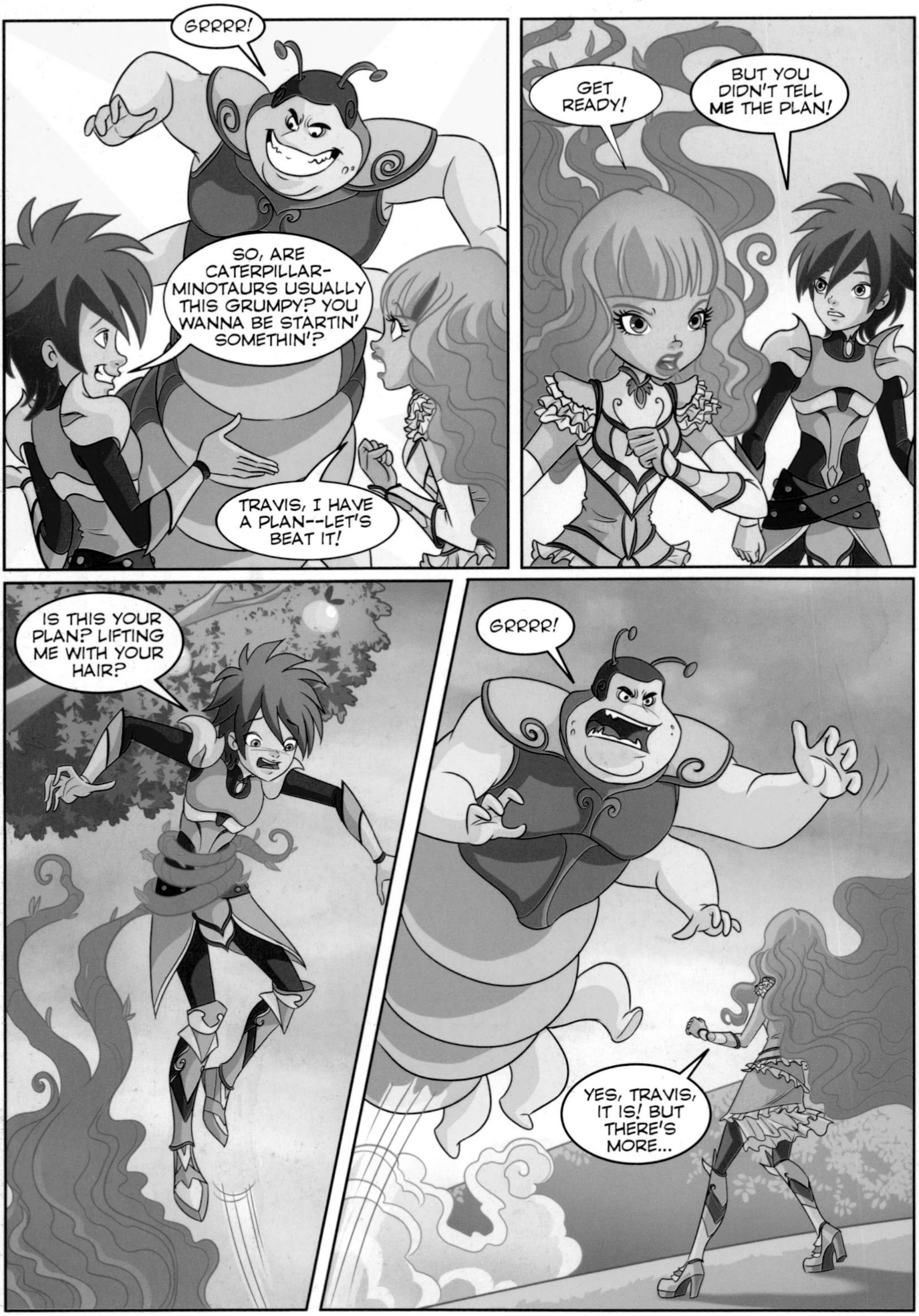
GRRRR!
SO, ARE CATERPILLAR-MINOTAURS USUALLY THIS GRUMPY? YOU WANNA BE STARTIN' SOMETHIN'?
TRAVIS, I HAVE A PLAN--LET'S BEAT IT!
GET READY!
BUT YOU DIDN'T TELL ME THE PLAN!
IS THIS YOUR PLAN? LIFTING ME WITH YOUR HAIR?
GRRRR!
YES, TRAVIS, IT IS! BUT THERE'S MORE...

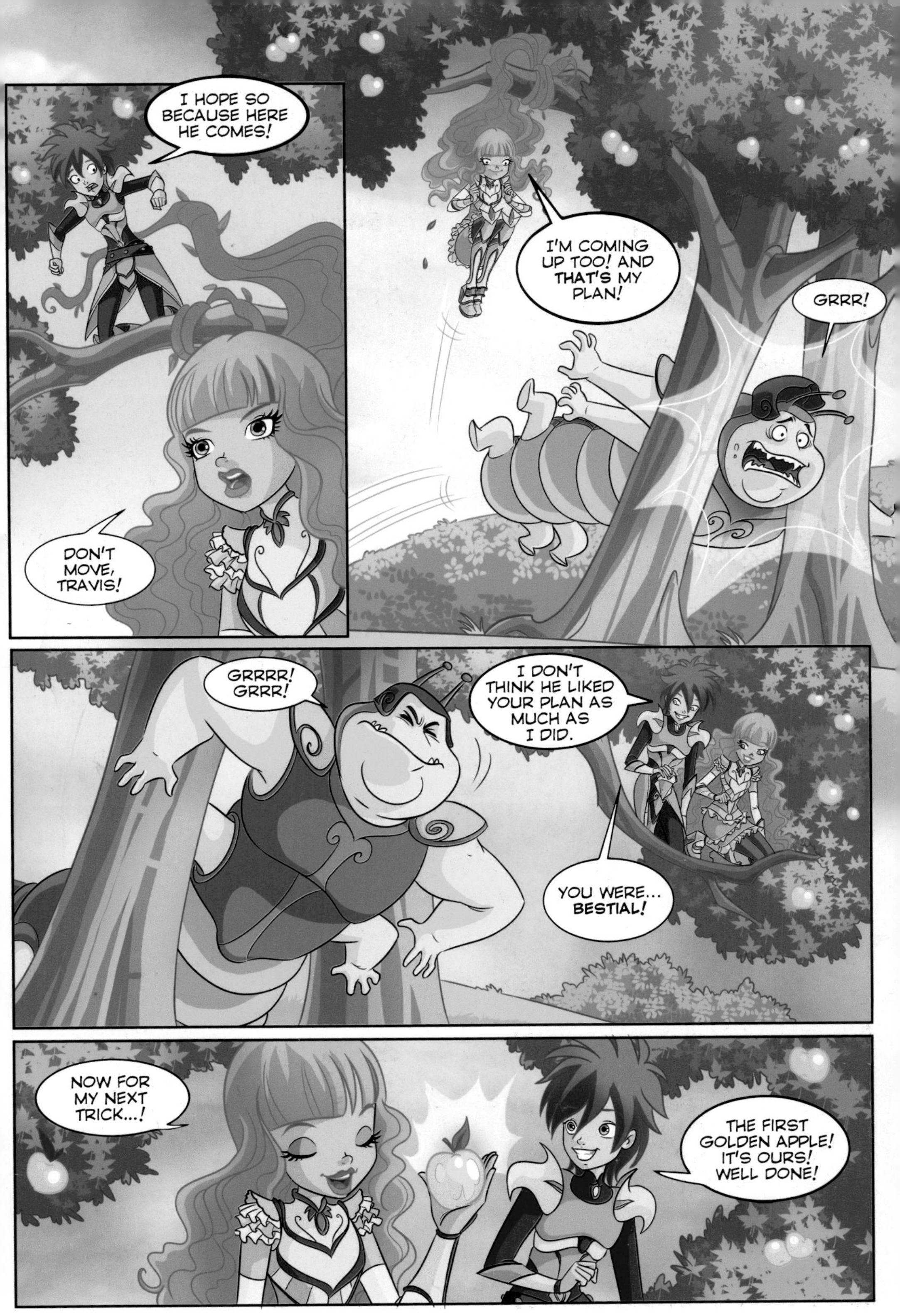
I HOPE SO BECAUSE HERE HE COMES!
DON'T MOVE, TRAVIS!
I'M COMING UP TOO! AND THAT'S MY PLAN!
GRRR!
GRRRR! GRRR!
I DON'T THINK HE LIKED YOUR PLAN AS MUCH AS I DID.
YOU WERE... BESTIAL!
NOW FOR MY NEXT TRICK...!
THE FIRST GOLDEN APPLE! IT'S OURS! WELL DONE!

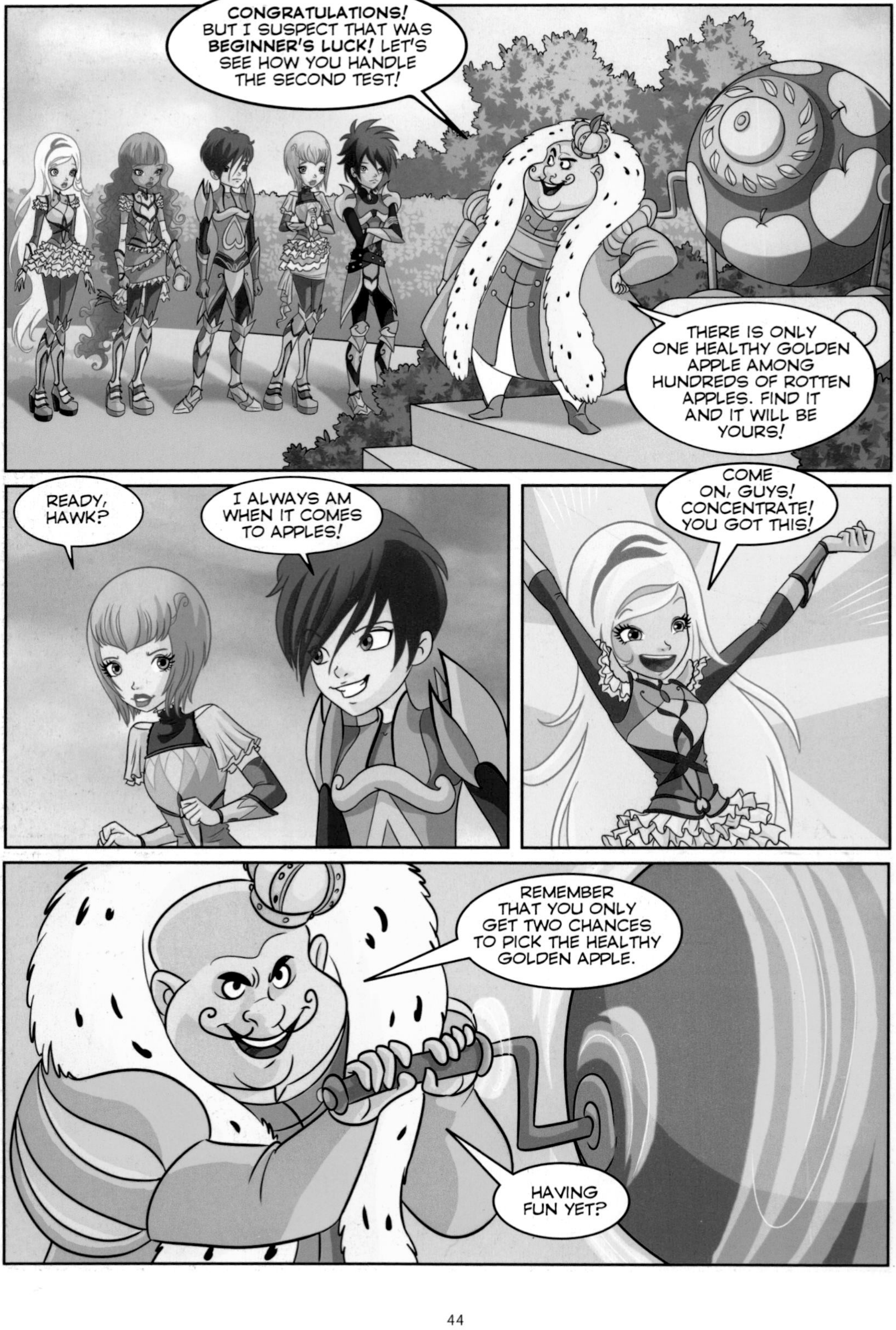
CONGRATULATIONS! BUT I SUSPECT THAT WAS BEGINNER'S LUCK! LET'S SEE HOW YOU HANDLE THE SECOND TEST!
THERE IS ONLY ONE HEALTHY GOLDEN APPLE AMONG HUNDREDS OF ROTTEN APPLES. FIND IT AND IT WILL BE YOURS!
READY, HAWK?
I ALWAYS AM WHEN IT COMES TO APPLES!
COME ON, GUYS! CONCENTRATE! YOU GOT THIS!
REMEMBER THAT YOU ONLY GET TWO CHANCES TO PICK THE HEALTHY GOLDEN APPLE.
HAVING FUN YET?

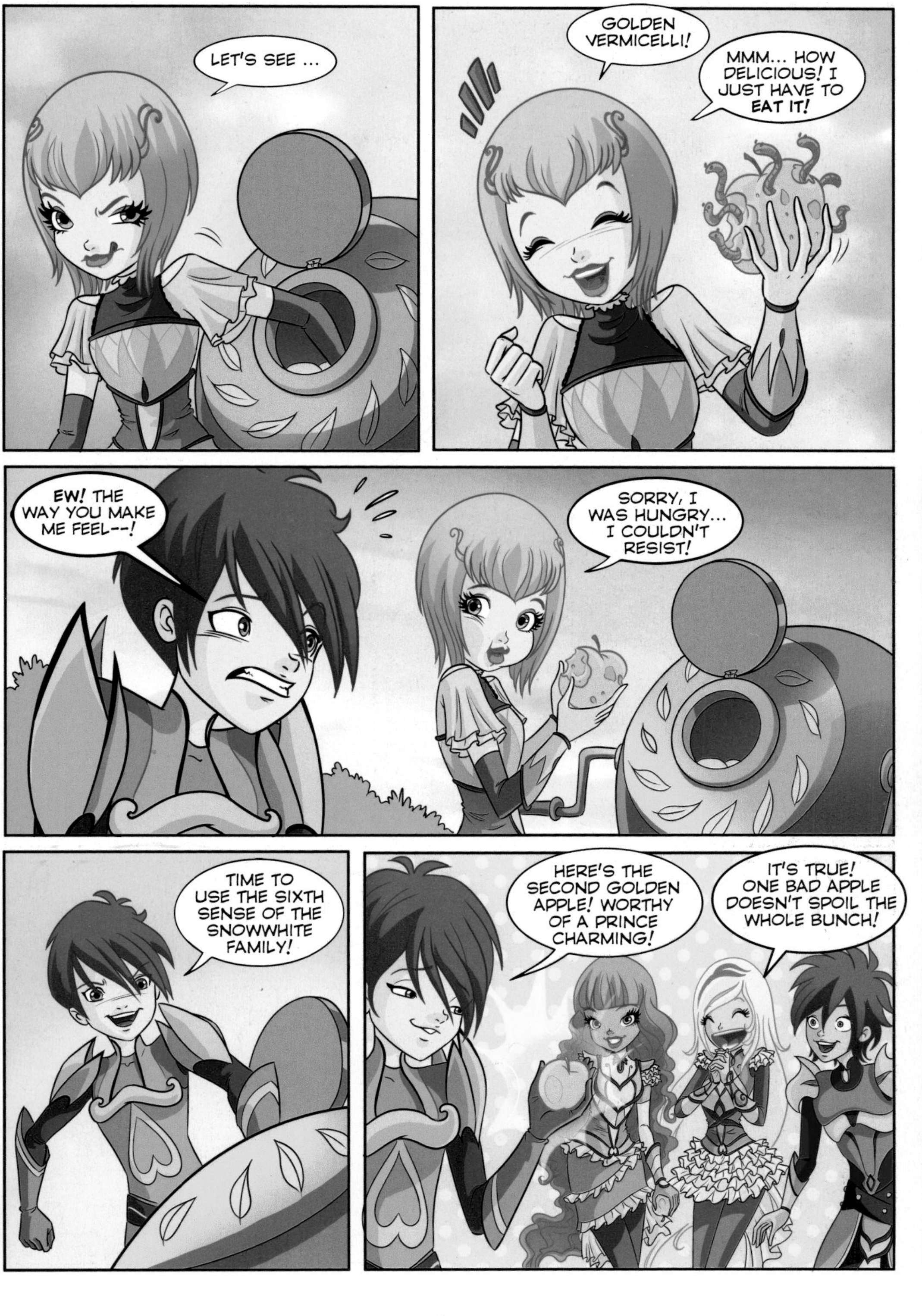
LET'S SEE ...
GOLDEN VERMICELLI!
MMM... HOW DELICIOUS! I JUST HAVE TO EAT IT!
EW! THE WAY YOU MAKE ME FEEL--!
SORRY, I WAS HUNGRY... I COULDN'T RESIST!
TIME TO USE THE SIXTH SENSE OF THE SNOWWHITE FAMILY!
HERE'S THE SECOND GOLDEN APPLE! WORTHY OF A PRINCE CHARMING!
IT'S TRUE! ONE BAD APPLE DOESN'T SPOIL THE WHOLE BUNCH!

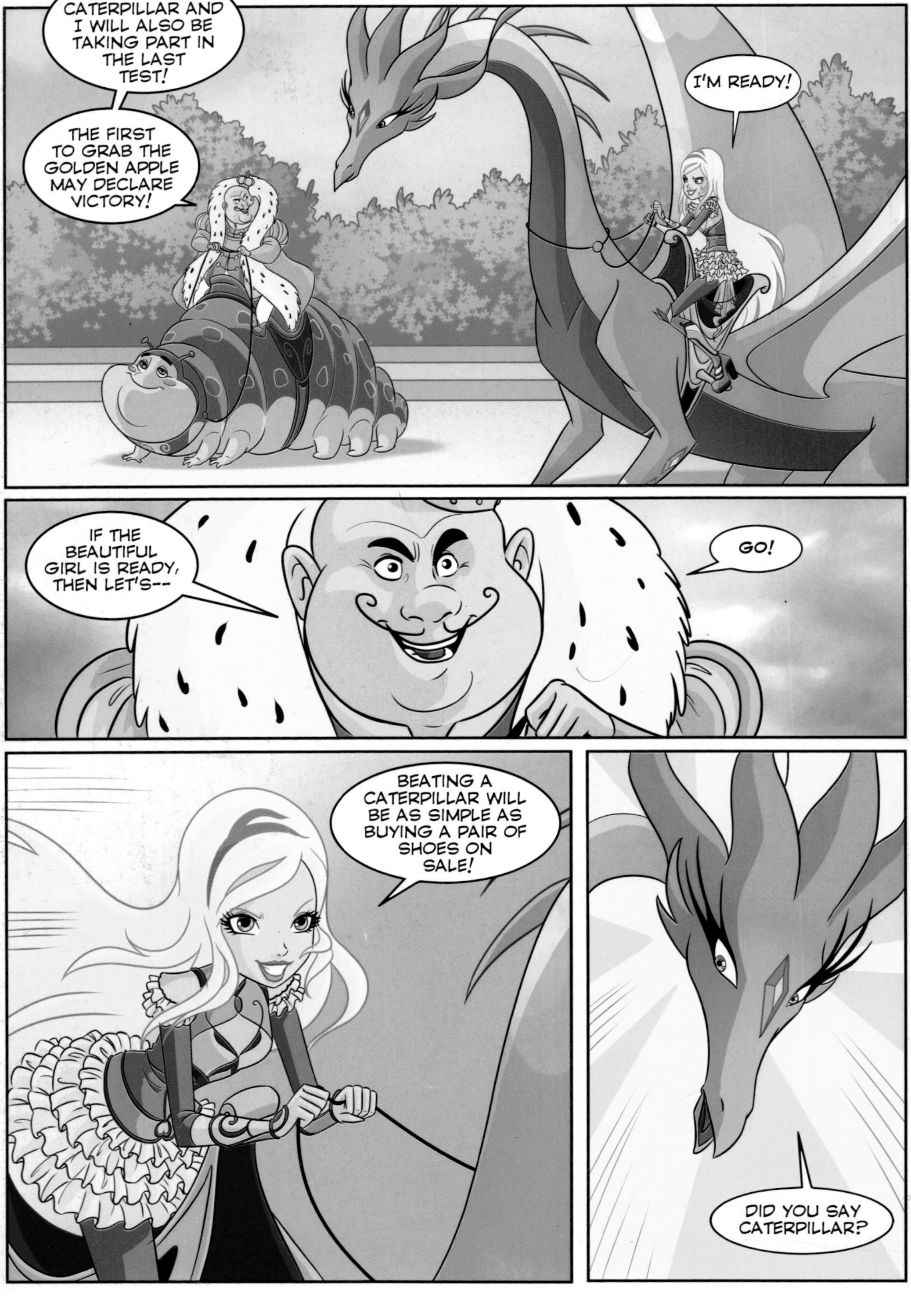
MY RACING CATERPILLAR AND I WILL ALSO BE TAKING PART IN THE LAST TEST!
THE FIRST TO GRAB THE GOLDEN APPLE MAY DECLARE VICTORY!
I'M READY!
IF THE BEAUTIFUL GIRL IS READY, THEN LET'S--
GO!
BEATING A CATERPILLAR WILL BE AS SIMPLE AS BUYING A PAIR OF SHOES ON SALE!
DID YOU SAY CATERPILLAR?

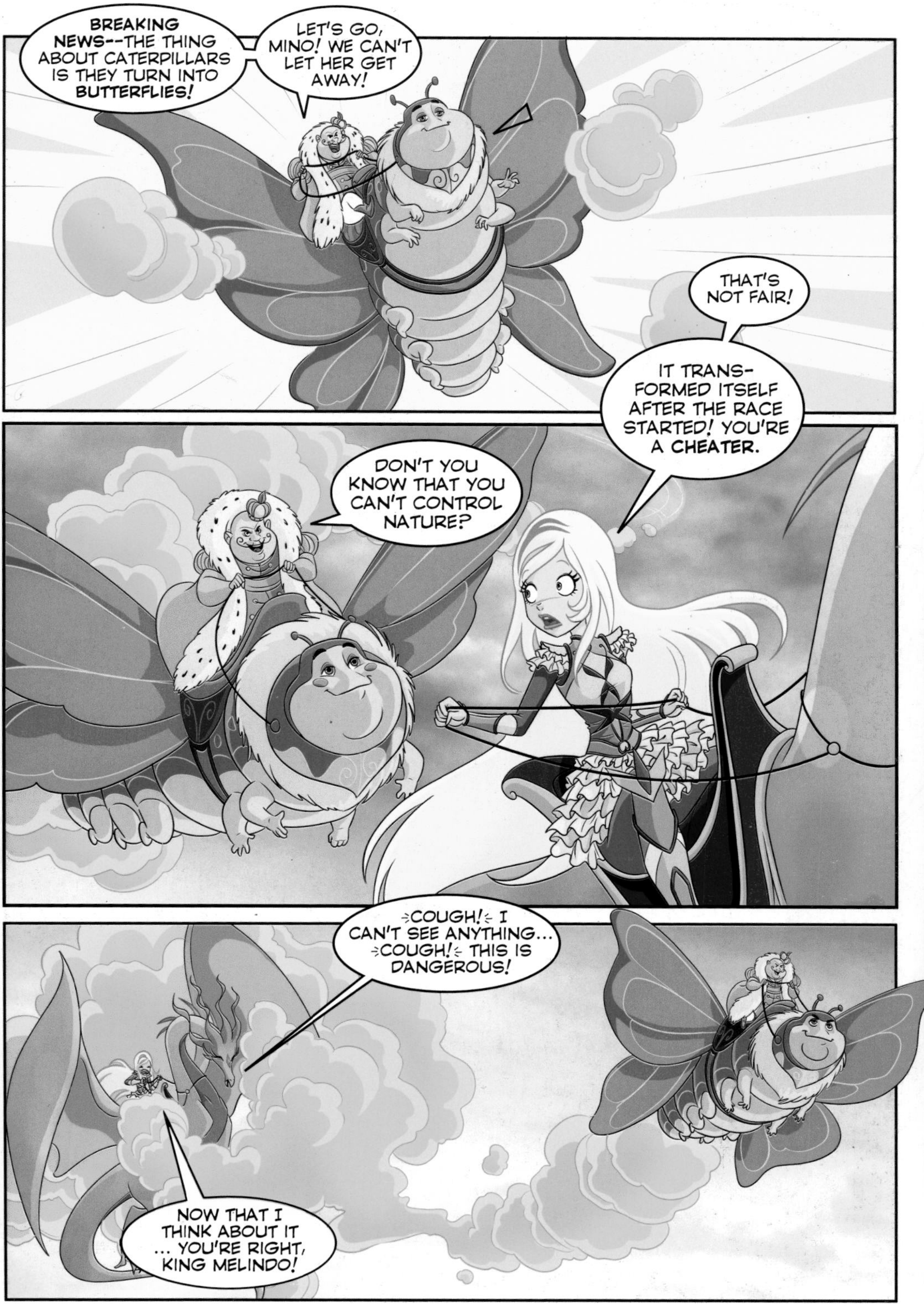
BREAKING NEWS--THE THING ABOUT CATERPILLARS IS THEY TURN INTO BUTTERFLIES!
LET'S GO, MINO! WE CAN'T LET HER GET AWAY!
THAT'S NOT FAIR!
IT TRANS-FORMED ITSELF AFTER THE RACE STARTED! YOU'RE A CHEATER.
DON'T YOU KNOW THAT YOU CAN'T CONTROL NATURE?
COUGH! I CAN'T SEE ANYTHING... COUGH! THIS IS DANGEROUS!
NOW THAT I THINK ABOUT IT ... YOU'RE RIGHT, KING MELINDO!

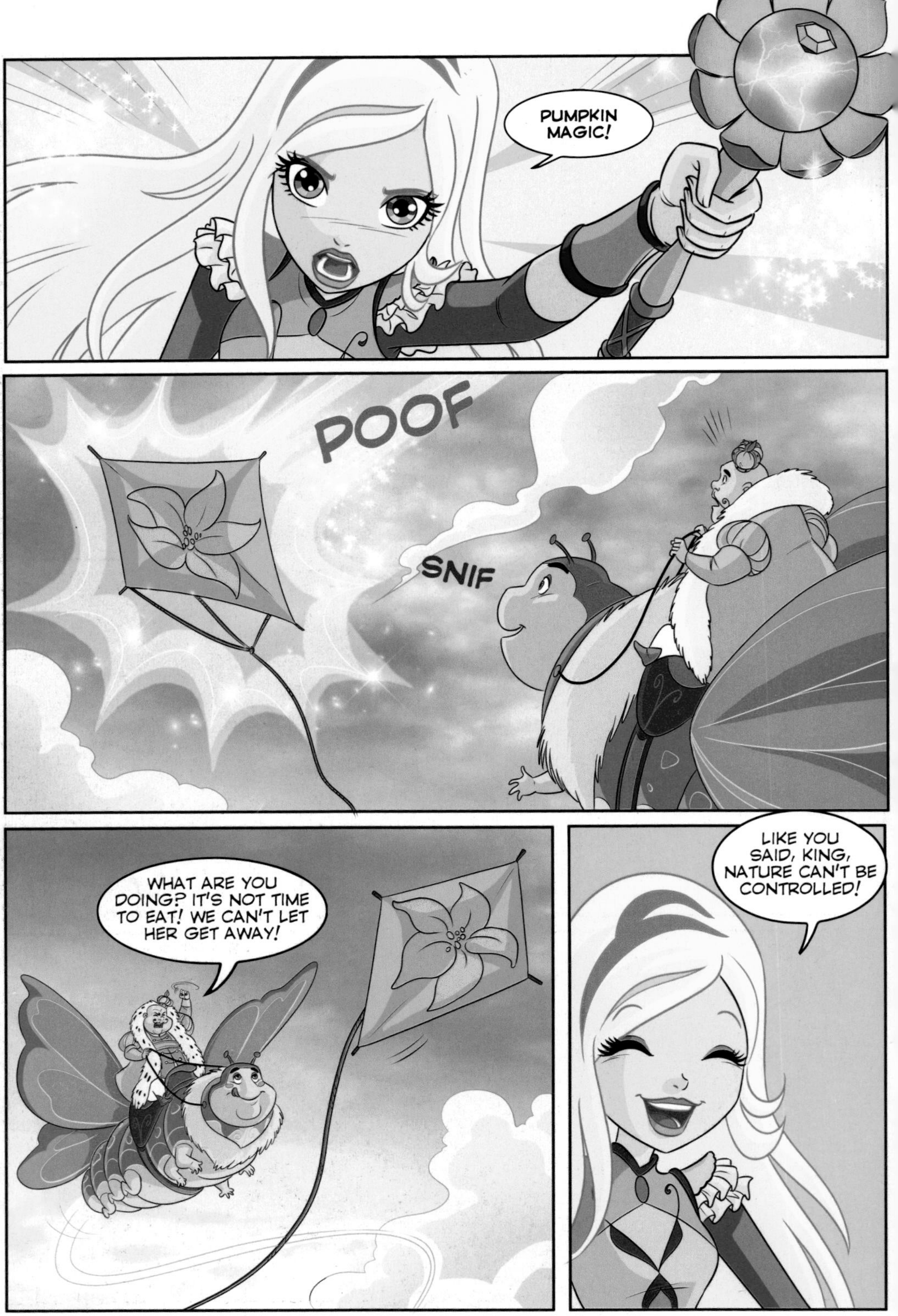
PUMPKIN MAGIC!
POOF
SNIF
WHAT ARE YOU DOING? IT'S NOT TIME TO EAT! WE CAN'T LET HER GET AWAY!
LIKE YOU SAID, KING, NATURE CAN'T BE CONTROLLED!

YOU CAN'T WIN! WHERE ARE YOU GOING? STOP!

DON'T BE SILLY, KING! IF YOU NEED THREE APPLES, YOU DON'T STOP 'TIL YOU GET ENOUGH!

YES! NOW WE HAVE ENOUGH!

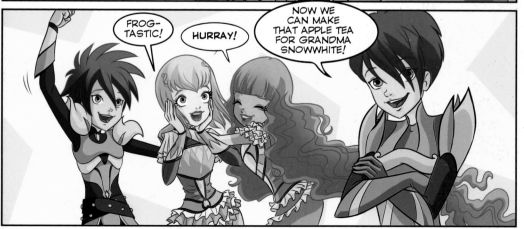

FROG-TASTIC!

HURRAY!

NOW WE CAN MAKE THAT APPLE TEA FOR GRANDMA SNOWWHITE!

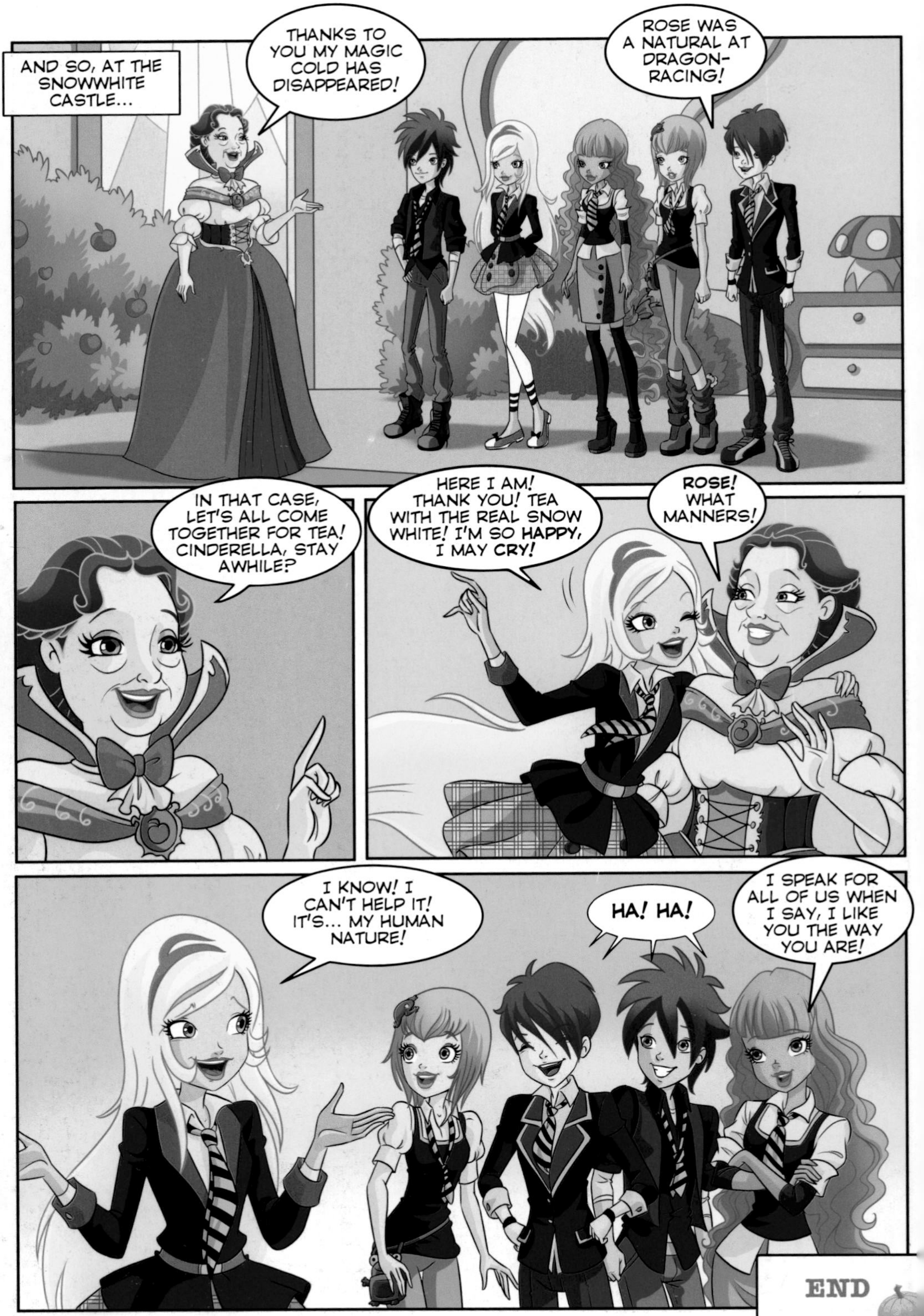
AND SO, AT THE SNOWWHITE CASTLE...
THANKS TO YOU MY MAGIC COLD HAS DISAPPEARED!
ROSE WAS A NATURAL AT DRAGON-RACING!
IN THAT CASE, LET'S ALL COME TOGETHER FOR TEA! CINDERELLA, STAY AWHILE?
HERE I AM! THANK YOU! TEA WITH THE REAL SNOW WHITE! I'M SO **HAPPY**, I MAY **CRY**!
ROSE! WHAT MANNERS!
I KNOW! I CAN'T HELP IT! IT'S... MY HUMAN NATURE!
HA! HA!
I SPEAK FOR ALL OF US WHEN I SAY, I LIKE YOU THE WAY YOU ARE!
END

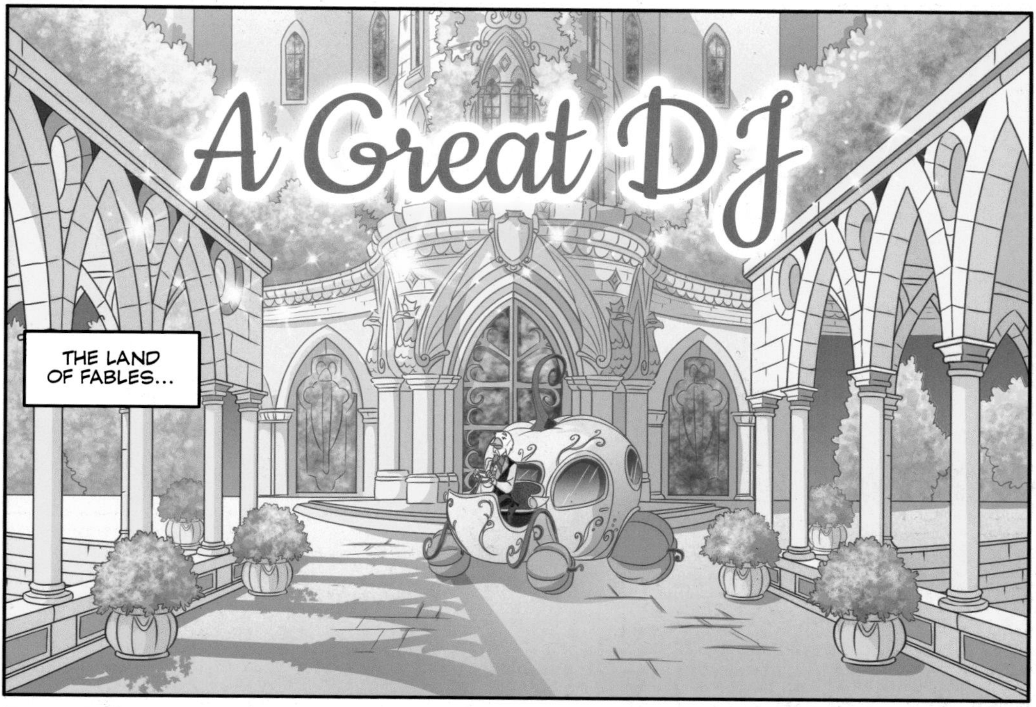
A Great DJ
THE LAND OF FABLES...

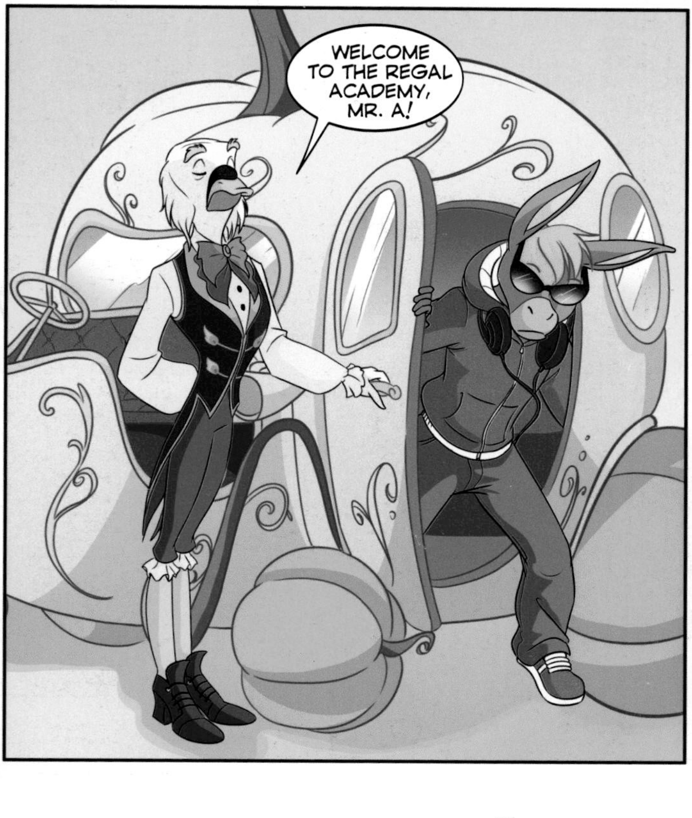
WELCOME TO THE REGAL ACADEMY, MR. A!

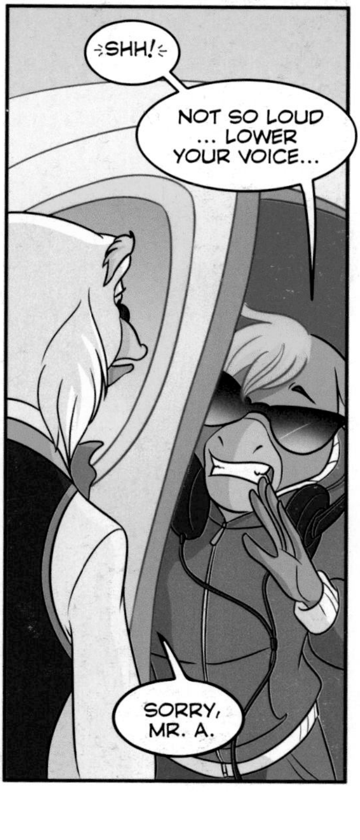
SHH!
NOT SO LOUD ... LOWER YOUR VOICE...
SORRY, MR. A.

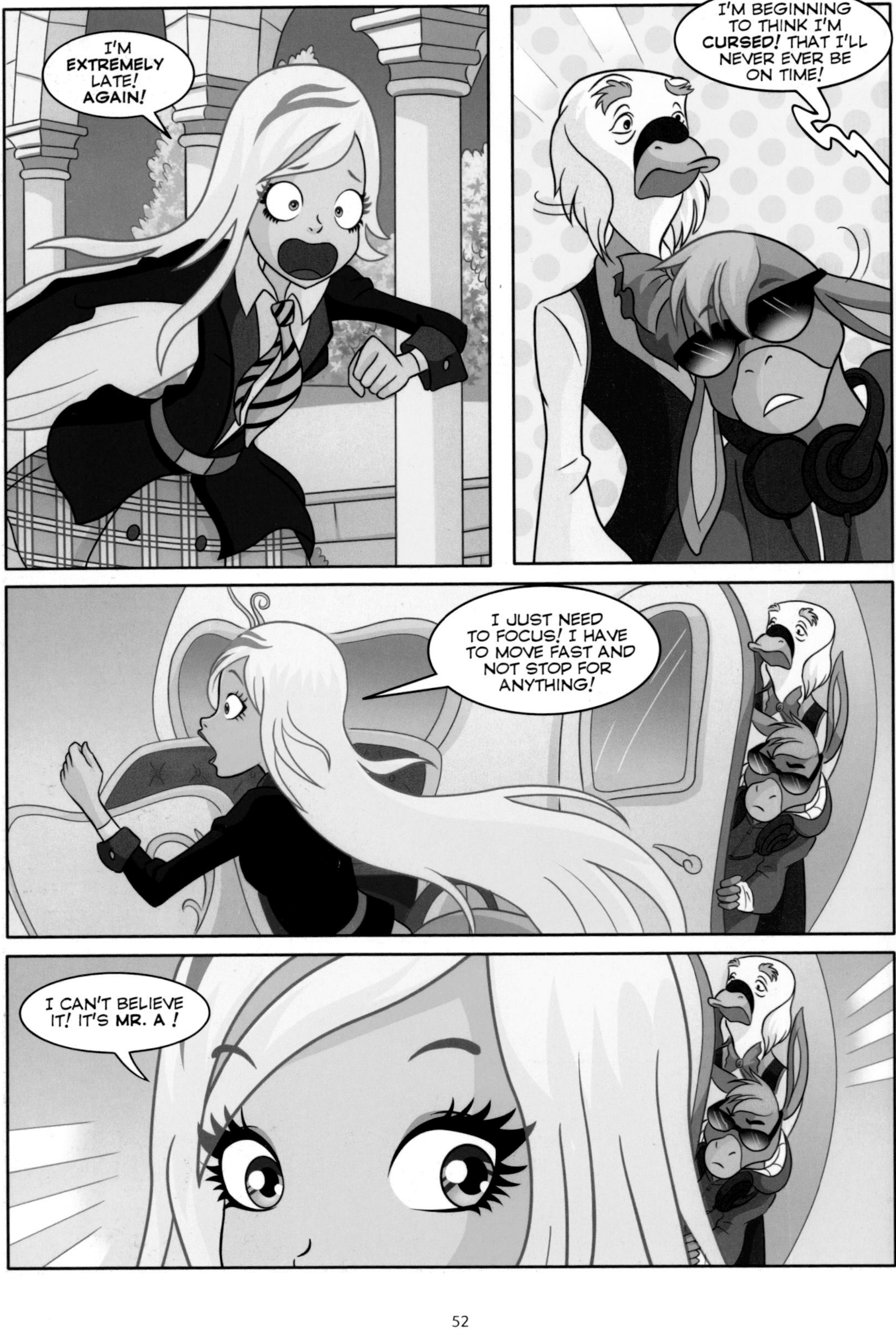
I'M EXTREMELY LATE! AGAIN!
I'M BEGINNING TO THINK I'M CURSED! THAT I'LL NEVER EVER BE ON TIME!
I JUST NEED TO FOCUS! I HAVE TO MOVE FAST AND NOT STOP FOR ANYTHING!
I CAN'T BELIEVE IT! IT'S MR. A !

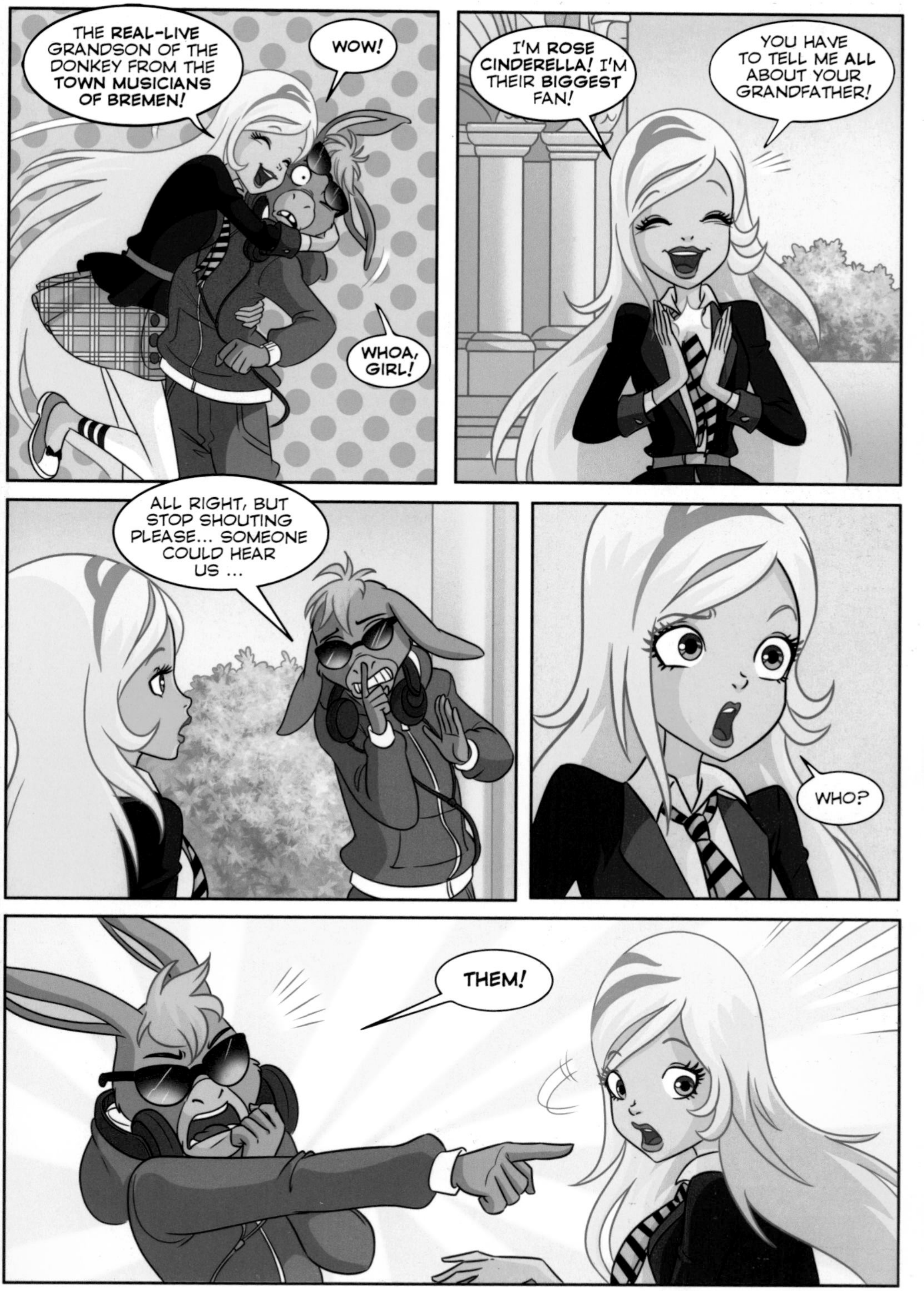
THE REAL-LIVE GRANDSON OF THE DONKEY FROM THE TOWN MUSICIANS OF BREMEN!
WOW!
WHOA, GIRL!
I'M ROSE CINDERELLA! I'M THEIR BIGGEST FAN!
YOU HAVE TO TELL ME ALL ABOUT YOUR GRANDFATHER!
ALL RIGHT, BUT STOP SHOUTING PLEASE... SOMEONE COULD HEAR US ...
WHO?
THEM!

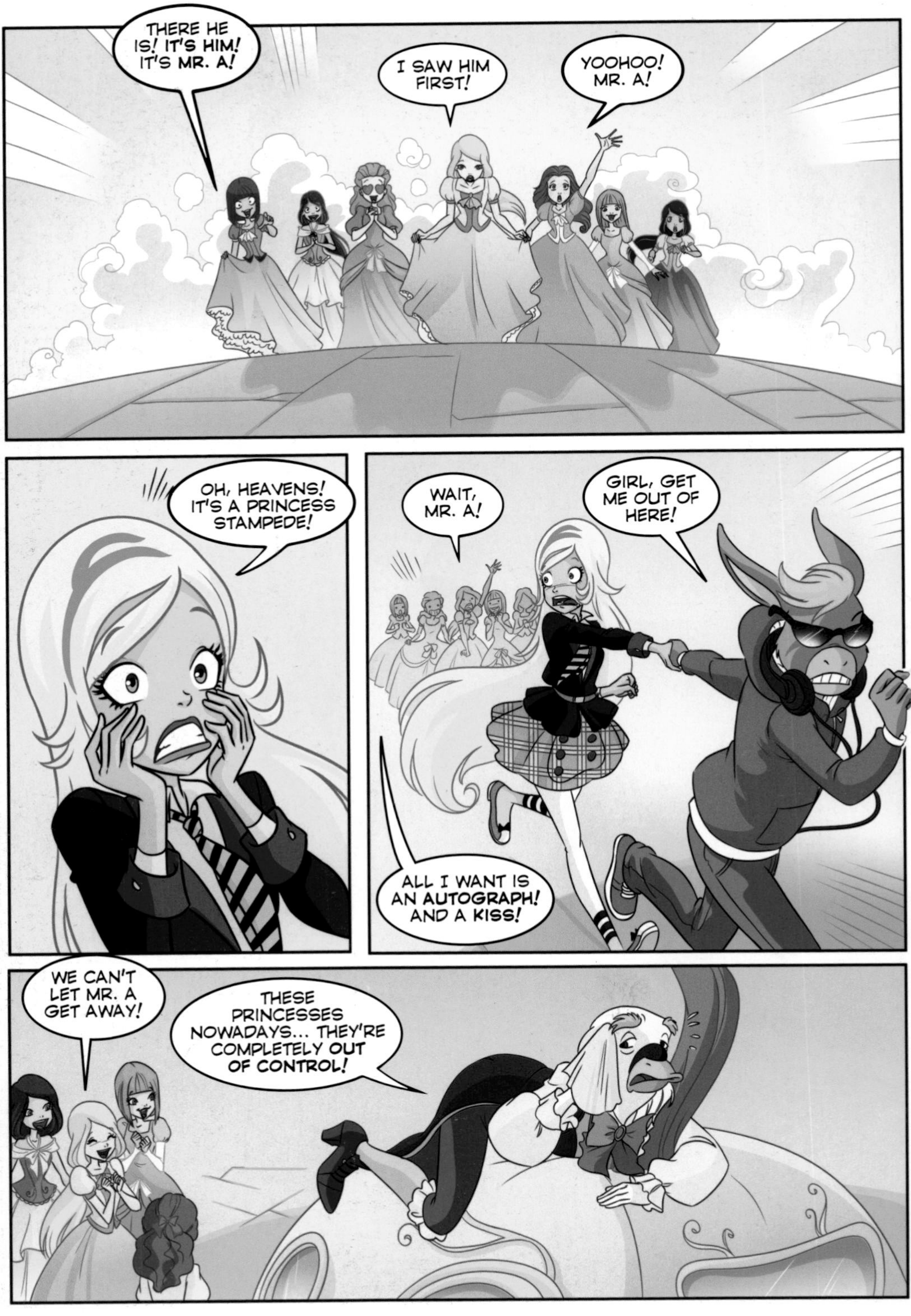
THERE HE IS! IT'S HIM! IT'S MR. A!
I SAW HIM FIRST!
YOOHOO! MR. A!
OH, HEAVENS! IT'S A PRINCESS STAMPEDE!
WAIT, MR. A!
GIRL, GET ME OUT OF HERE!
ALL I WANT IS AN AUTOGRAPH! AND A KISS!
WE CAN'T LET MR. A GET AWAY!
THESE PRINCESSES NOWADAYS... THEY'RE COMPLETELY OUT OF CONTROL!

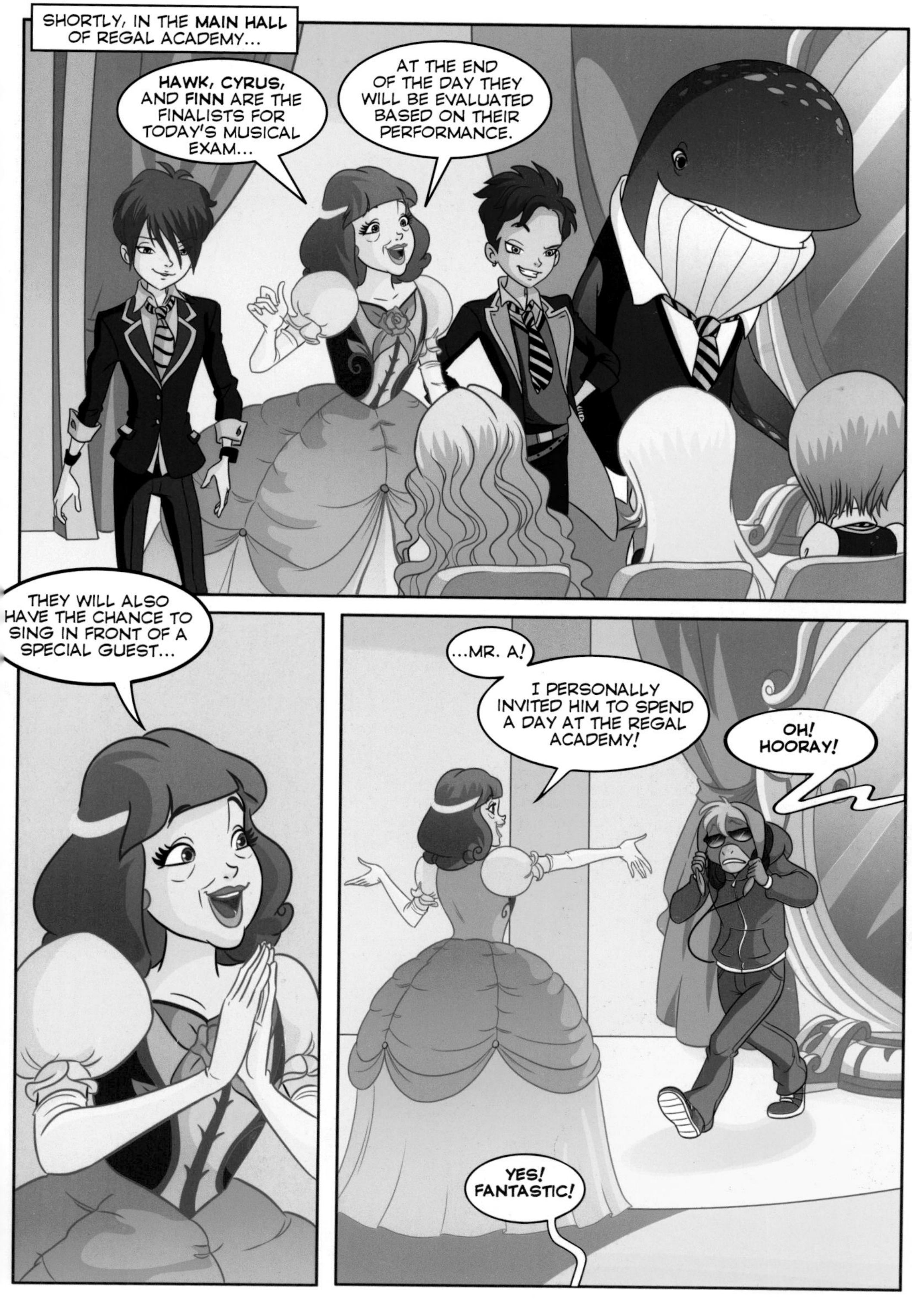
SHORTLY, IN THE MAIN HALL OF REGAL ACADEMY...
HAWK, CYRUS, AND FINN ARE THE FINALISTS FOR TODAY'S MUSICAL EXAM...
AT THE END OF THE DAY THEY WILL BE EVALUATED BASED ON THEIR PERFORMANCE.
THEY WILL ALSO HAVE THE CHANCE TO SING IN FRONT OF A SPECIAL GUEST...
...MR. A!
I PERSONALLY INVITED HIM TO SPEND A DAY AT THE REGAL ACADEMY!
OH! HOORAY!
YES! FANTASTIC!

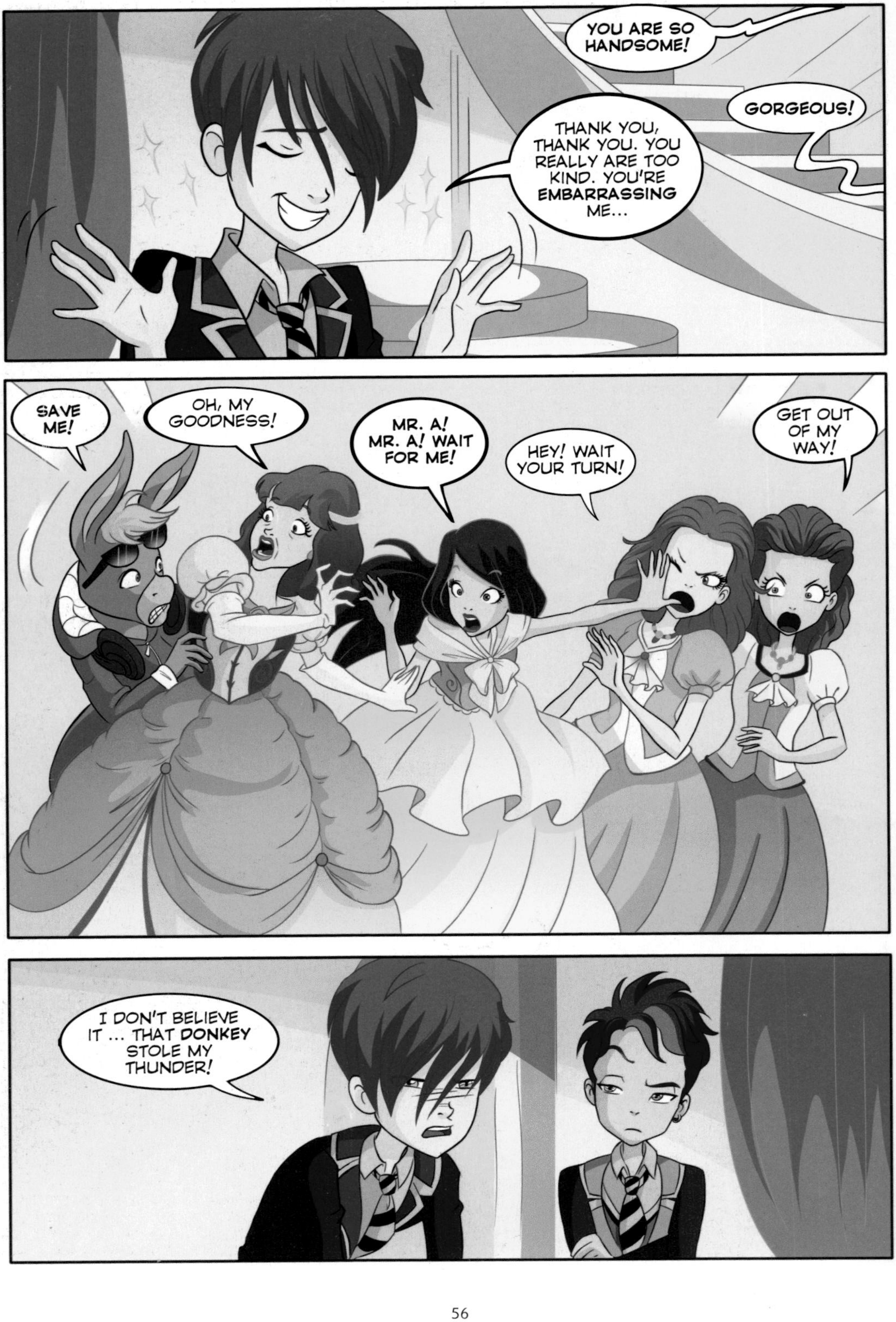
YOU ARE SO HANDSOME!
GORGEOUS!
THANK YOU, THANK YOU. YOU REALLY ARE TOO KIND. YOU'RE EMBARRASSING ME...
SAVE ME!
OH, MY GOODNESS!
MR. A! MR. A! WAIT FOR ME!
HEY! WAIT YOUR TURN!
GET OUT OF MY WAY!
I DON'T BELIEVE IT ... THAT DONKEY STOLE MY THUNDER!

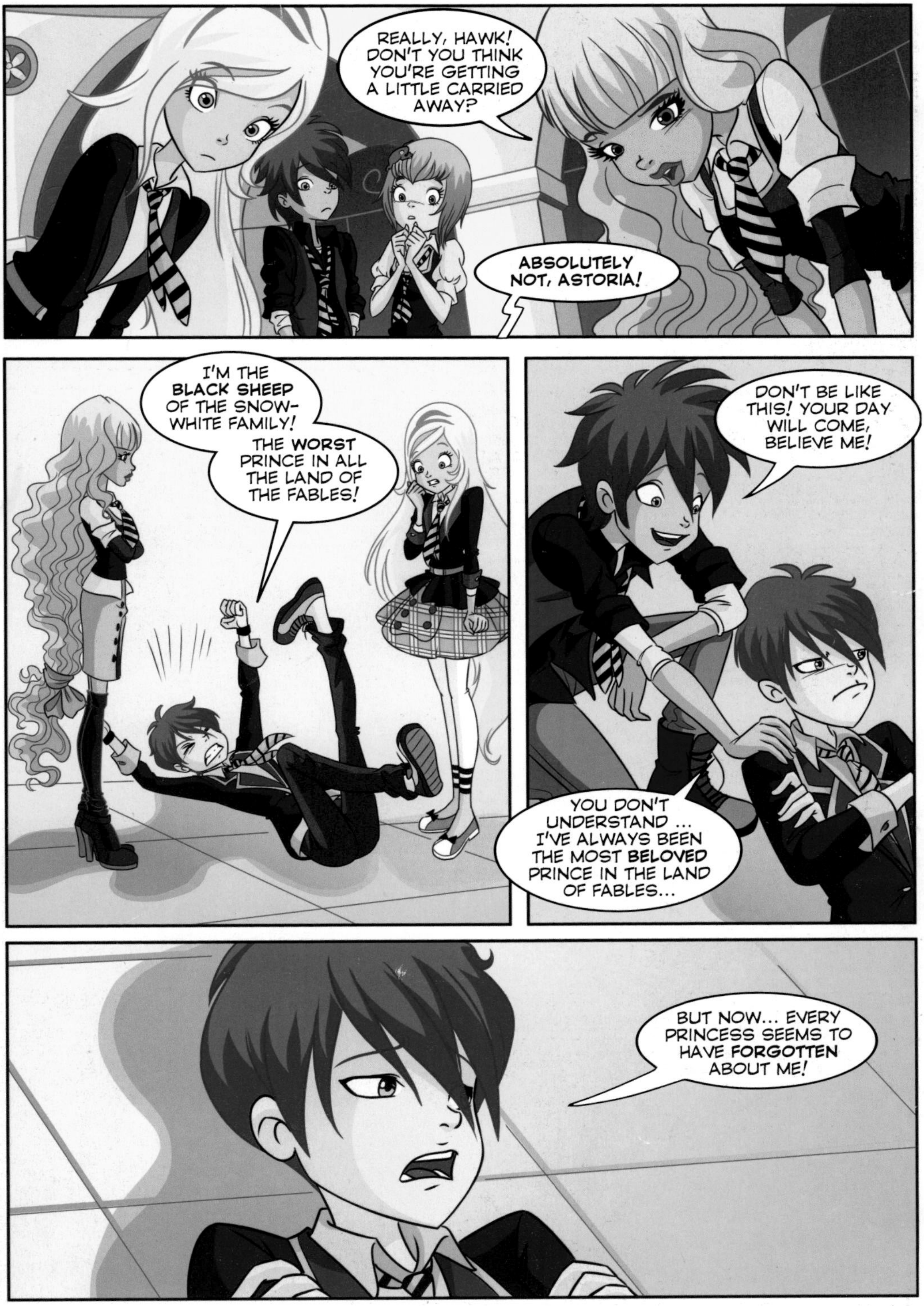
REALLY, HAWK! DON'T YOU THINK YOU'RE GETTING A LITTLE CARRIED AWAY?
ABSOLUTELY NOT, ASTORIA!
I'M THE BLACK SHEEP OF THE SNOW-WHITE FAMILY!
THE WORST PRINCE IN ALL THE LAND OF THE FABLES!
DON'T BE LIKE THIS! YOUR DAY WILL COME, BELIEVE ME!
YOU DON'T UNDERSTAND ... I'VE ALWAYS BEEN THE MOST BELOVED PRINCE IN THE LAND OF FABLES...
BUT NOW... EVERY PRINCESS SEEMS TO HAVE FORGOTTEN ABOUT ME!

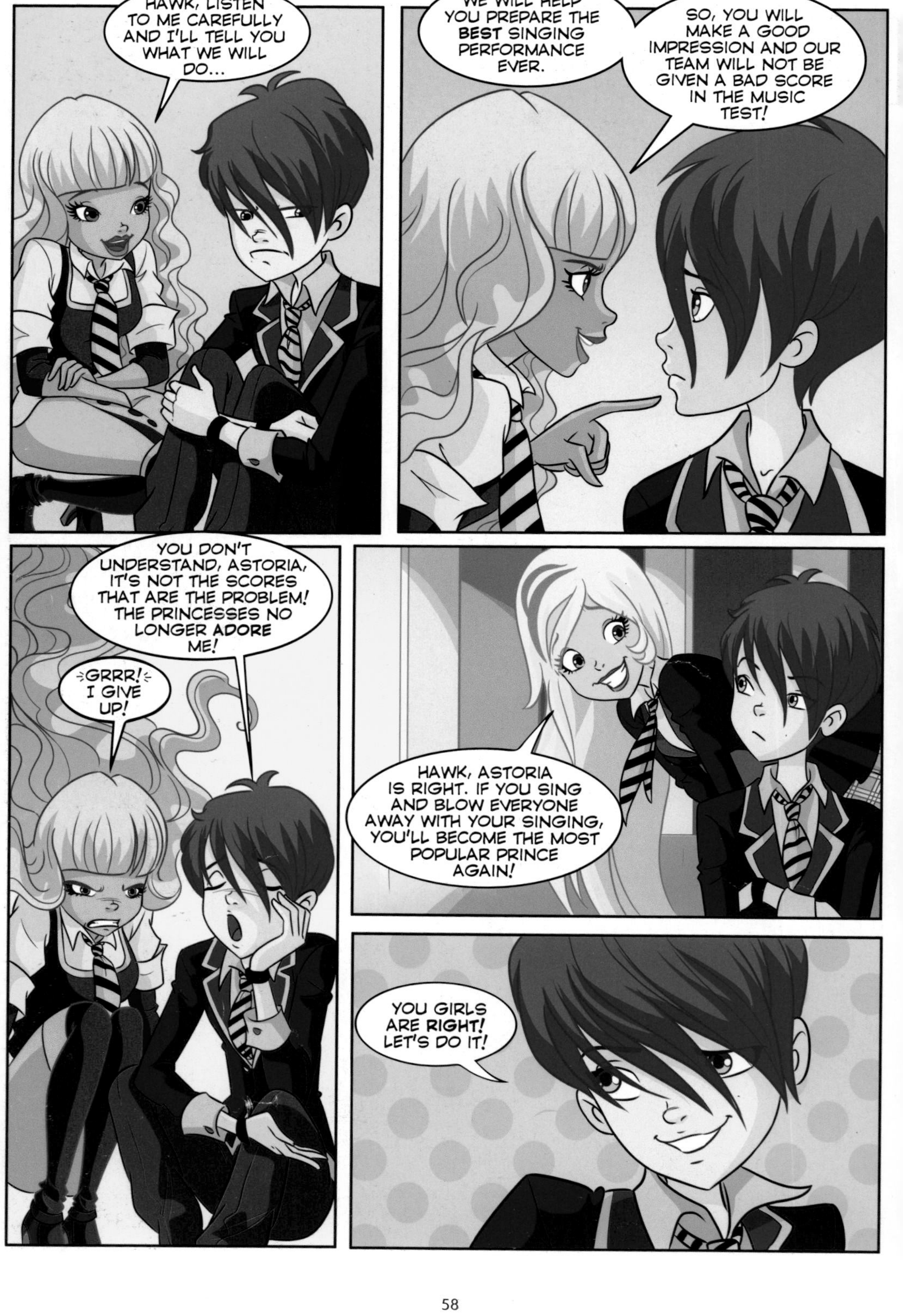
HAWK, LISTEN TO ME CAREFULLY AND I'LL TELL YOU WHAT WE WILL DO...
WE WILL HELP YOU PREPARE THE **BEST** SINGING PERFORMANCE EVER.
SO, YOU WILL MAKE A GOOD IMPRESSION AND OUR TEAM WILL NOT BE GIVEN A BAD SCORE IN THE MUSIC TEST!
YOU DON'T UNDERSTAND, ASTORIA, IT'S NOT THE SCORES THAT ARE THE PROBLEM! THE PRINCESSES NO LONGER **ADORE** ME!
GRRR! I GIVE UP!
HAWK, ASTORIA IS RIGHT. IF YOU SING AND BLOW EVERYONE AWAY WITH YOUR SINGING, YOU'LL BECOME THE MOST POPULAR PRINCE AGAIN!
YOU GIRLS ARE **RIGHT!** LET'S DO IT!

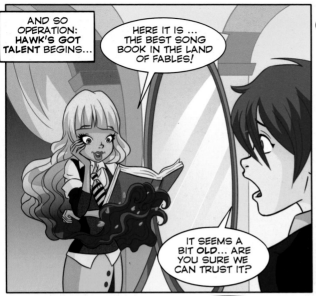

AND SO OPERATION: HAWK'S GOT TALENT BEGINS...

HERE IT IS ... THE BEST SONG BOOK IN THE LAND OF FABLES!

IT SEEMS A BIT OLD... ARE YOU SURE WE CAN TRUST IT?

LET'S SEE, IT SAYS...

"TO PITCH YOUR VOICE PROPERLY, IT IS IMPORTANT FOR ALL YOUR FACIAL MUSCLES TO BE TONED."

WHAT?!

WELL THEN? WHAT ARE YOU WAITING FOR? LET'S GET TO WORK!

I REALLY DON'T UNDERSTAND THIS THING ABOUT FACE MUSCLES...

BUT IT'S SIMPLE! LET ME DEMONSTRATE...

YOU HAVE TO STRETCH THE MUSCLES IN YOUR FACE... LIKE THIS!

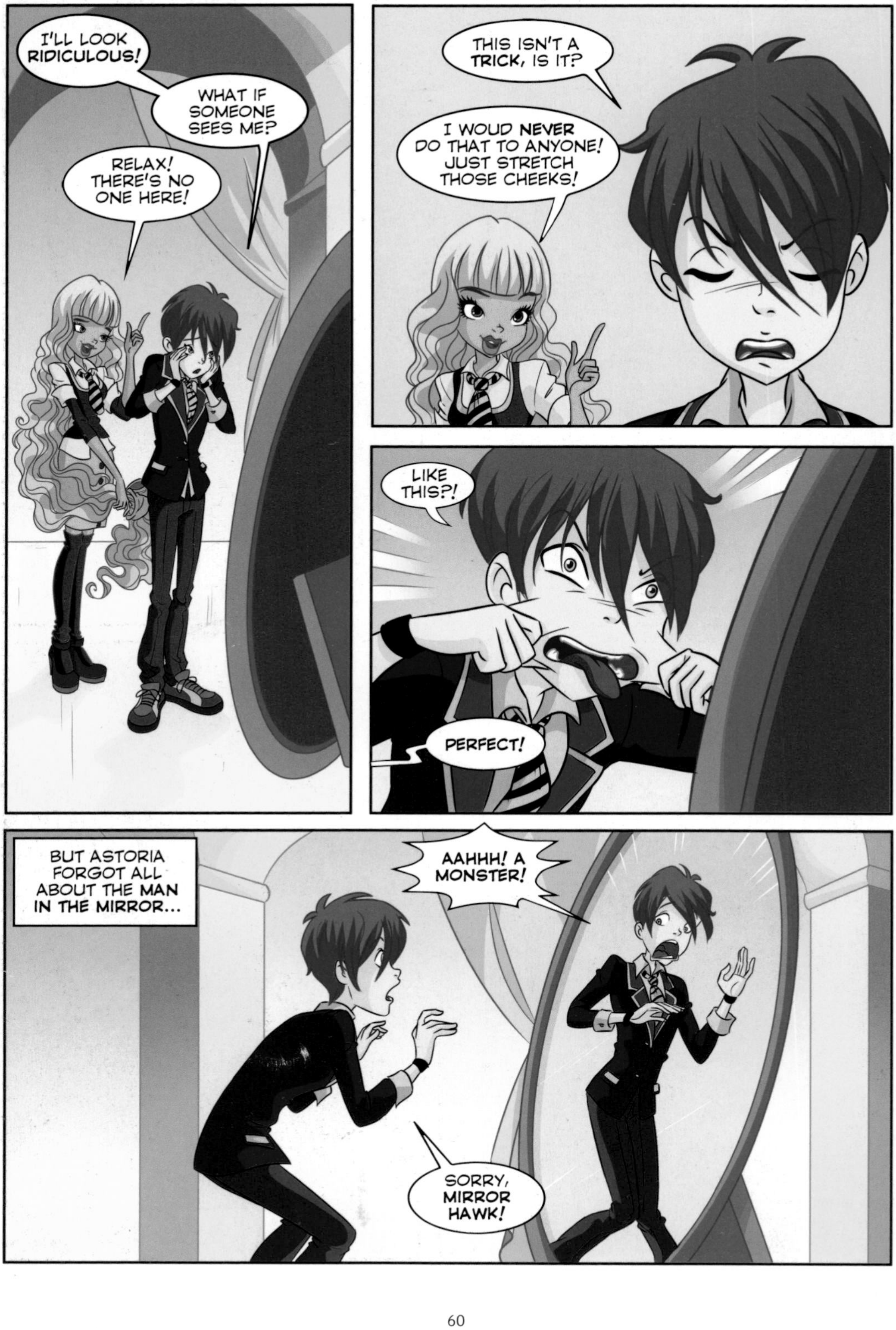
I'LL LOOK RIDICULOUS!
WHAT IF SOMEONE SEES ME?
RELAX! THERE'S NO ONE HERE!
THIS ISN'T A TRICK, IS IT?
I WOUD NEVER DO THAT TO ANYONE! JUST STRETCH THOSE CHEEKS!
LIKE THIS?!
PERFECT!
BUT ASTORIA FORGOT ALL ABOUT THE MAN IN THE MIRROR...
AAHHH! A MONSTER!
SORRY, MIRROR HAWK!

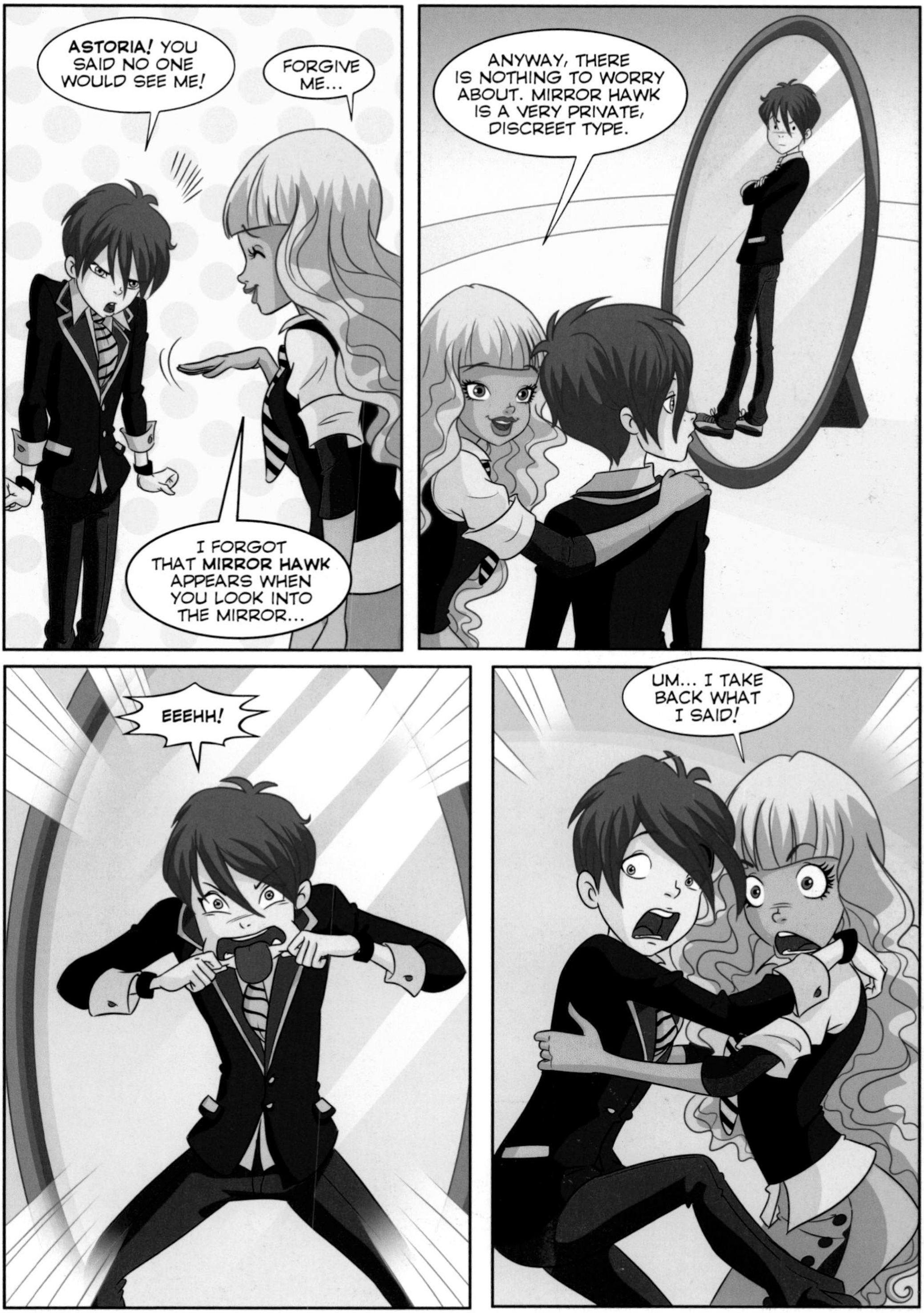

ASTORIA! YOU SAID NO ONE WOULD SEE ME!
FORGIVE ME...
I FORGOT THAT MIRROR HAWK APPEARS WHEN YOU LOOK INTO THE MIRROR...
ANYWAY, THERE IS NOTHING TO WORRY ABOUT. MIRROR HAWK IS A VERY PRIVATE, DISCREET TYPE.
EEEHH!
UM... I TAKE BACK WHAT I SAID!

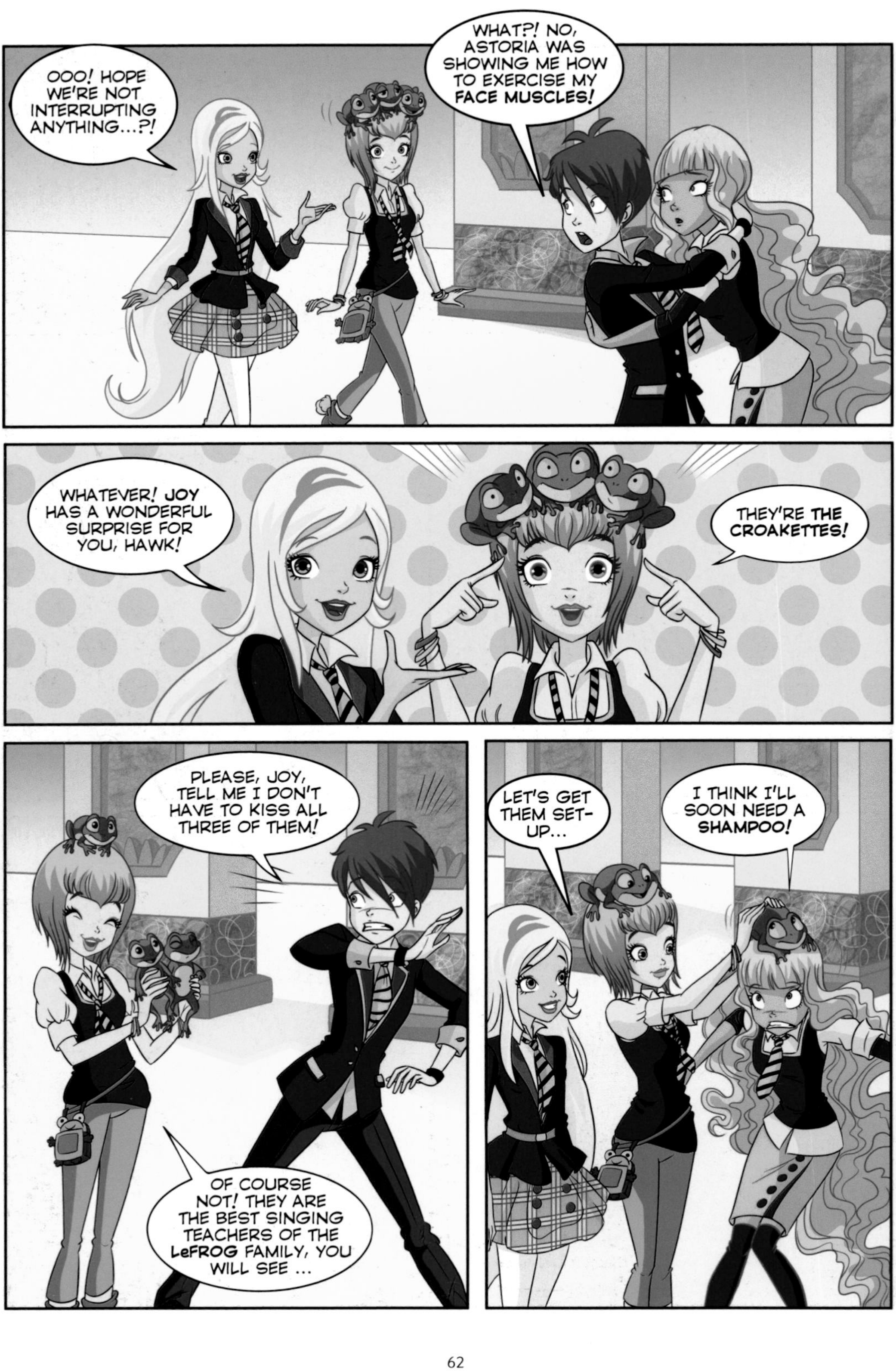
OOO! HOPE WE'RE NOT INTERRUPTING ANYTHING...?!
WHAT?! NO, ASTORIA WAS SHOWING ME HOW TO EXERCISE MY FACE MUSCLES!
WHATEVER! JOY HAS A WONDERFUL SURPRISE FOR YOU, HAWK!
THEY'RE THE CROAKETTES!
PLEASE, JOY, TELL ME I DON'T HAVE TO KISS ALL THREE OF THEM!
OF COURSE NOT! THEY ARE THE BEST SINGING TEACHERS OF THE LeFROG FAMILY, YOU WILL SEE ...
LET'S GET THEM SET-UP...
I THINK I'LL SOON NEED A SHAMPOO!

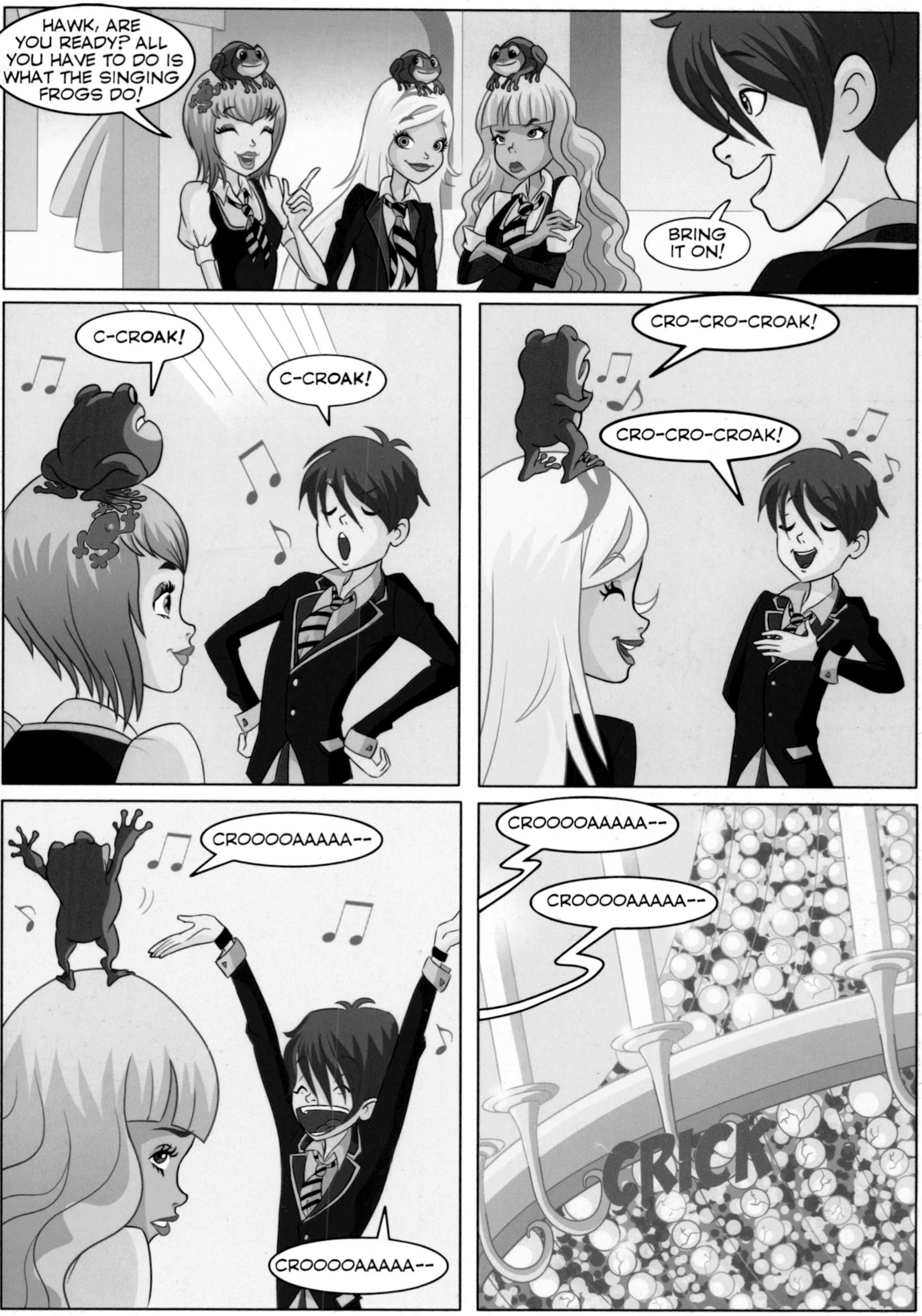
HAWK, ARE YOU READY? ALL YOU HAVE TO DO IS WHAT THE SINGING FROGS DO!
BRING IT ON!
C-CROAK!
C-CROAK!
CRO-CRO-CROAK!
CRO-CRO-CROAK!
CROOOOAAAAA--
CROOOOAAAAA--
CROOOOAAAAA--
CROOOOAAAAA--
CRICK

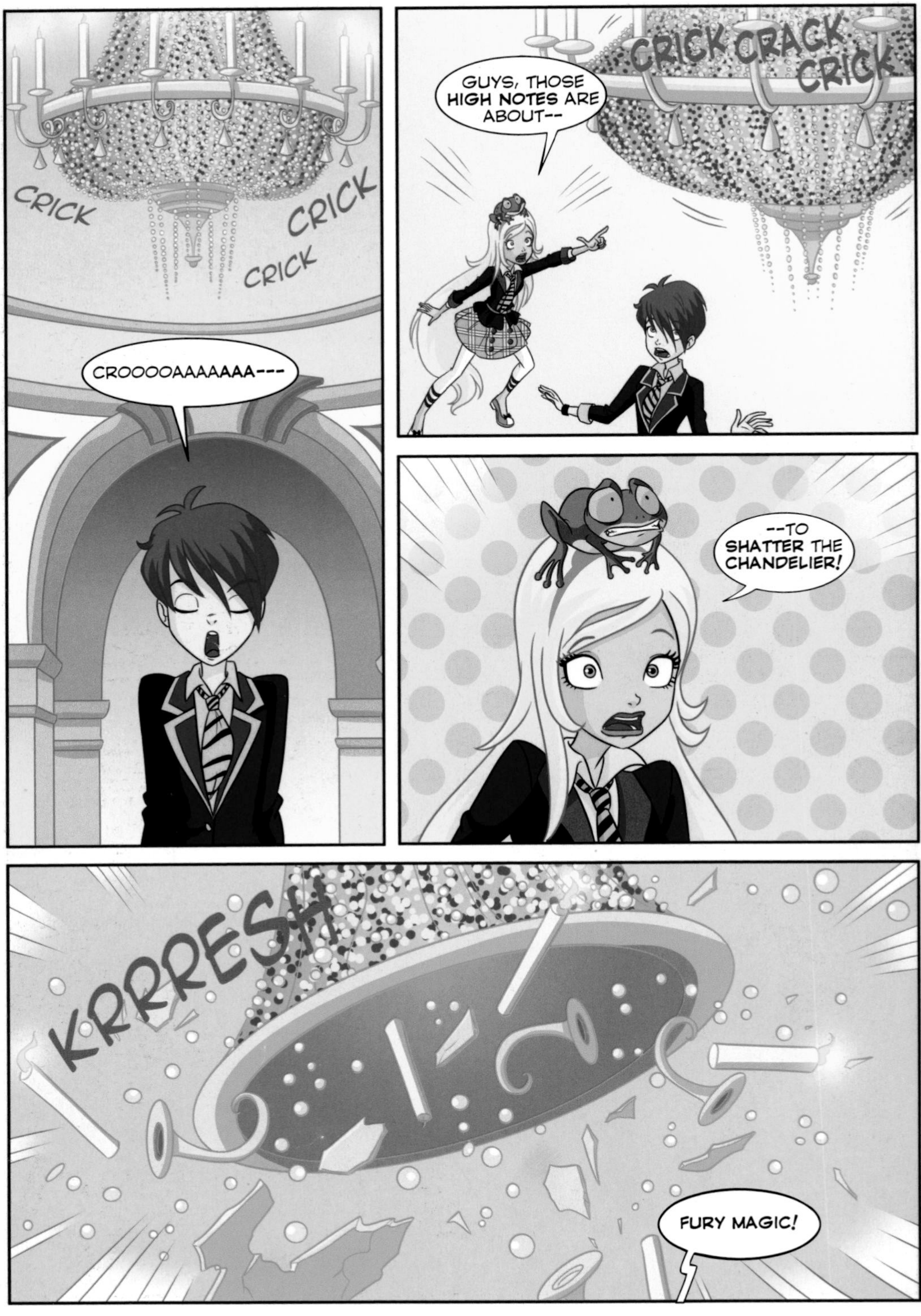
CRICK
CRICK
CRICK
CROOOOAAAAAAA---
GUYS, THOSE HIGH NOTES ARE ABOUT--
CRICK CRACK CRICK
--TO SHATTER THE CHANDELIER!
KRRRESH
FURY MAGIC!

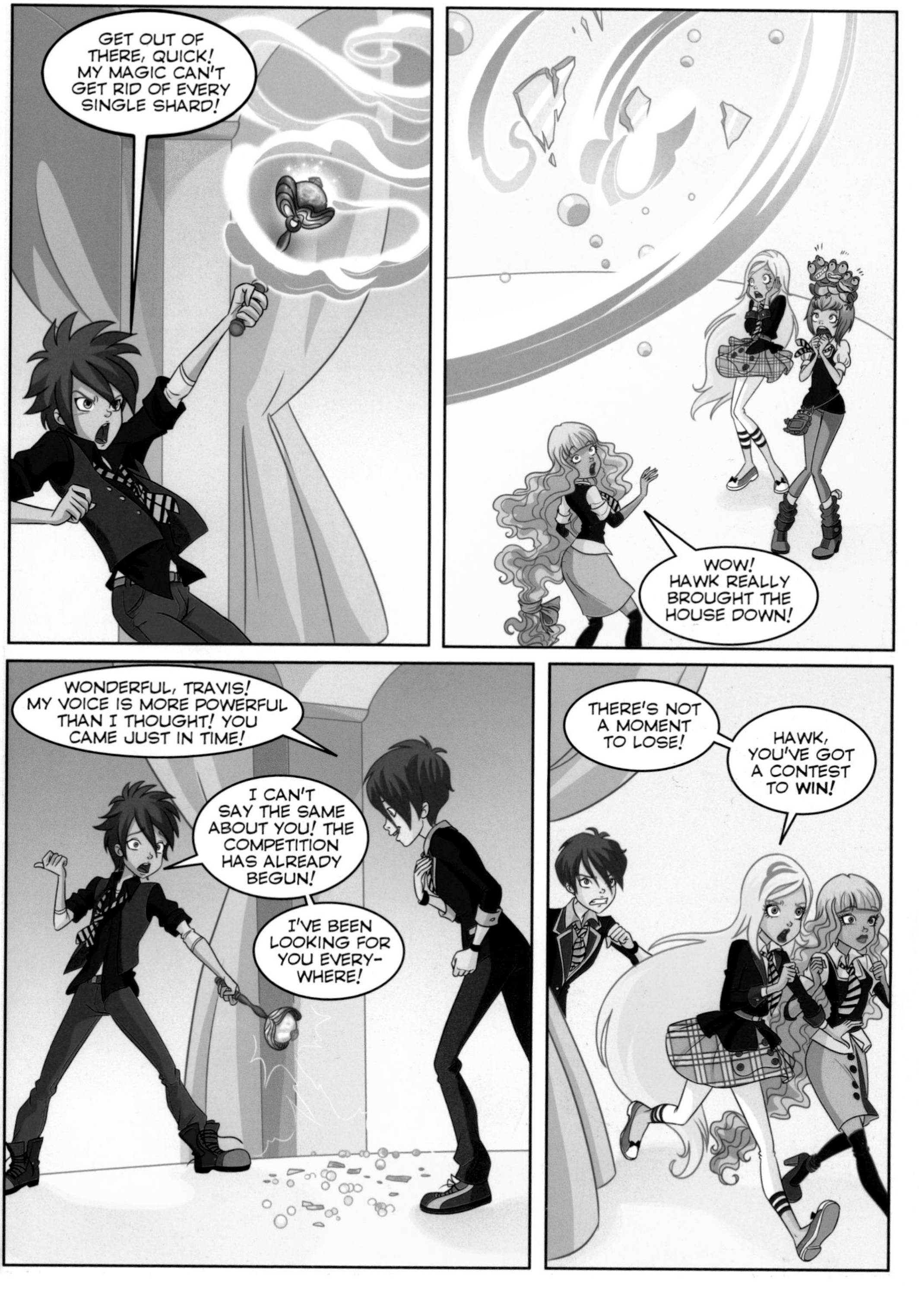
GET OUT OF THERE, QUICK! MY MAGIC CAN'T GET RID OF EVERY SINGLE SHARD!
WOW! HAWK REALLY BROUGHT THE HOUSE DOWN!
WONDERFUL, TRAVIS! MY VOICE IS MORE POWERFUL THAN I THOUGHT! YOU CAME JUST IN TIME!
I CAN'T SAY THE SAME ABOUT YOU! THE COMPETITION HAS ALREADY BEGUN!
I'VE BEEN LOOKING FOR YOU EVERY-WHERE!
THERE'S NOT A MOMENT TO LOSE!
HAWK, YOU'VE GOT A CONTEST TO **WIN**!

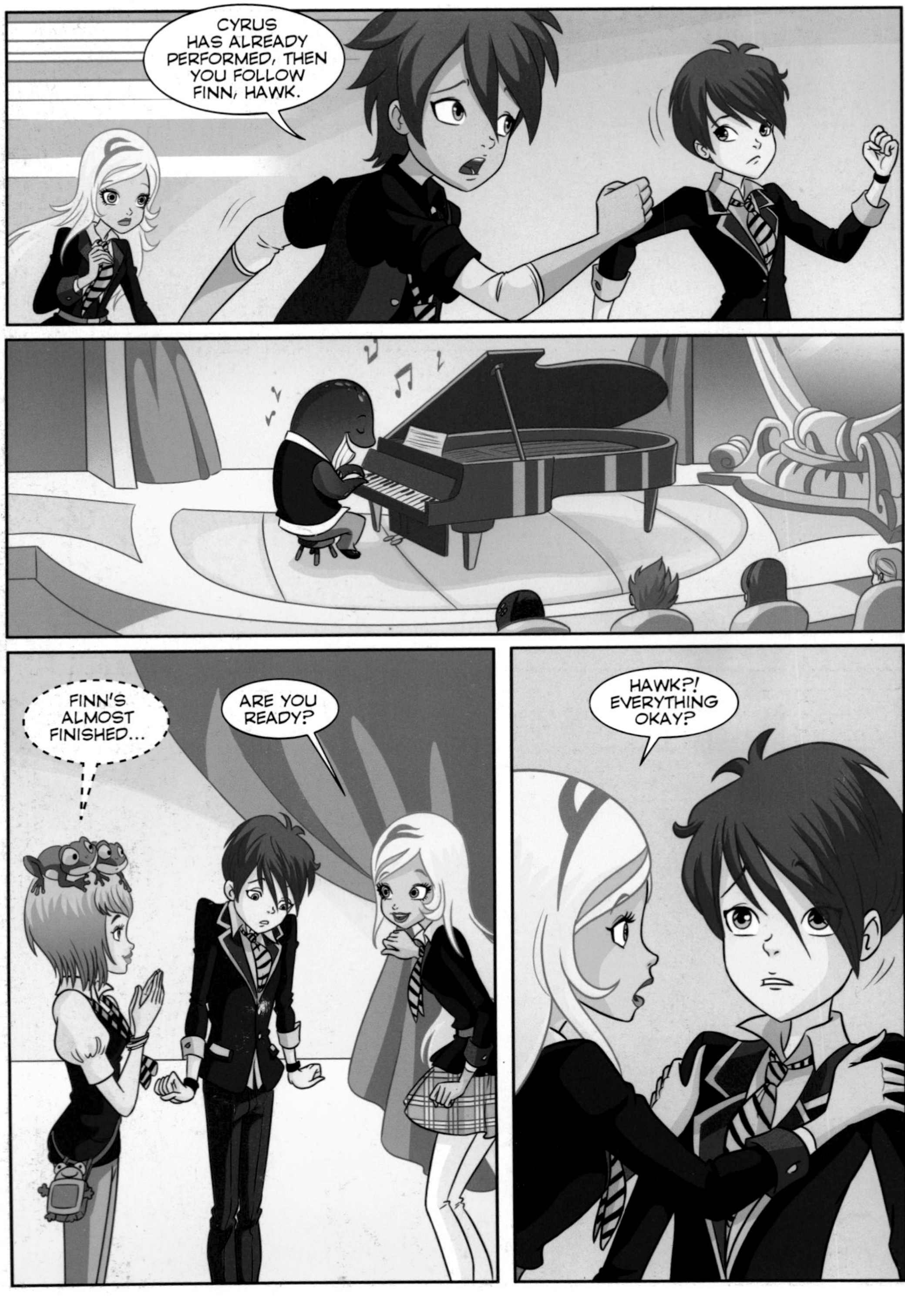
CYRUS HAS ALREADY PERFORMED, THEN YOU FOLLOW FINN, HAWK.
FINN'S ALMOST FINISHED...
ARE YOU READY?
HAWK?! EVERYTHING OKAY?

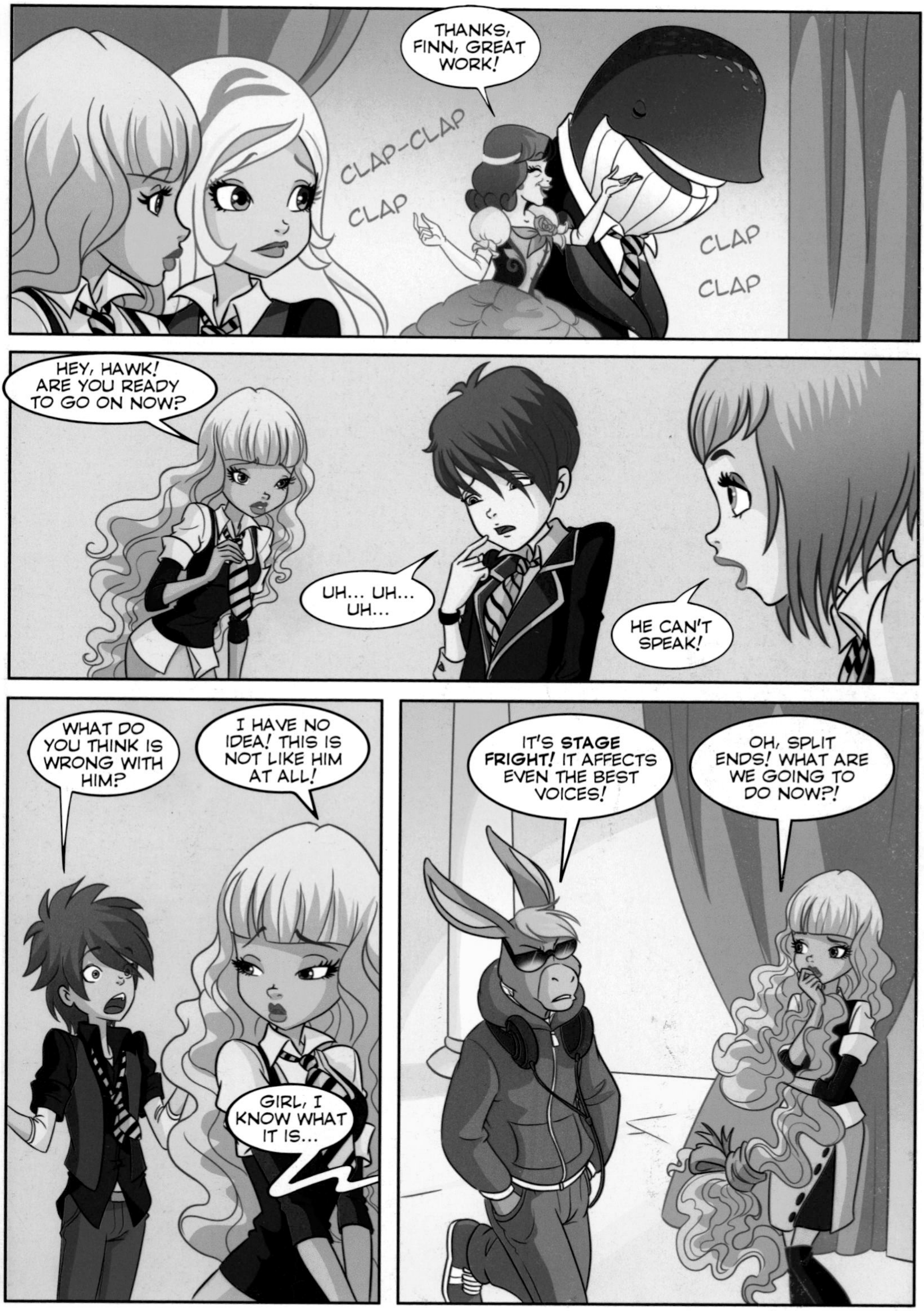
THANKS, FINN, GREAT WORK!
CLAP-CLAP
CLAP
CLAP
CLAP
HEY, HAWK! ARE YOU READY TO GO ON NOW?
UH... UH... UH...
HE CAN'T SPEAK!
WHAT DO YOU THINK IS WRONG WITH HIM?
I HAVE NO IDEA! THIS IS NOT LIKE HIM AT ALL!
GIRL, I KNOW WHAT IT IS...
IT'S **STAGE FRIGHT!** IT AFFECTS EVEN THE BEST VOICES!
OH, SPLIT ENDS! WHAT ARE WE GOING TO DO NOW?!

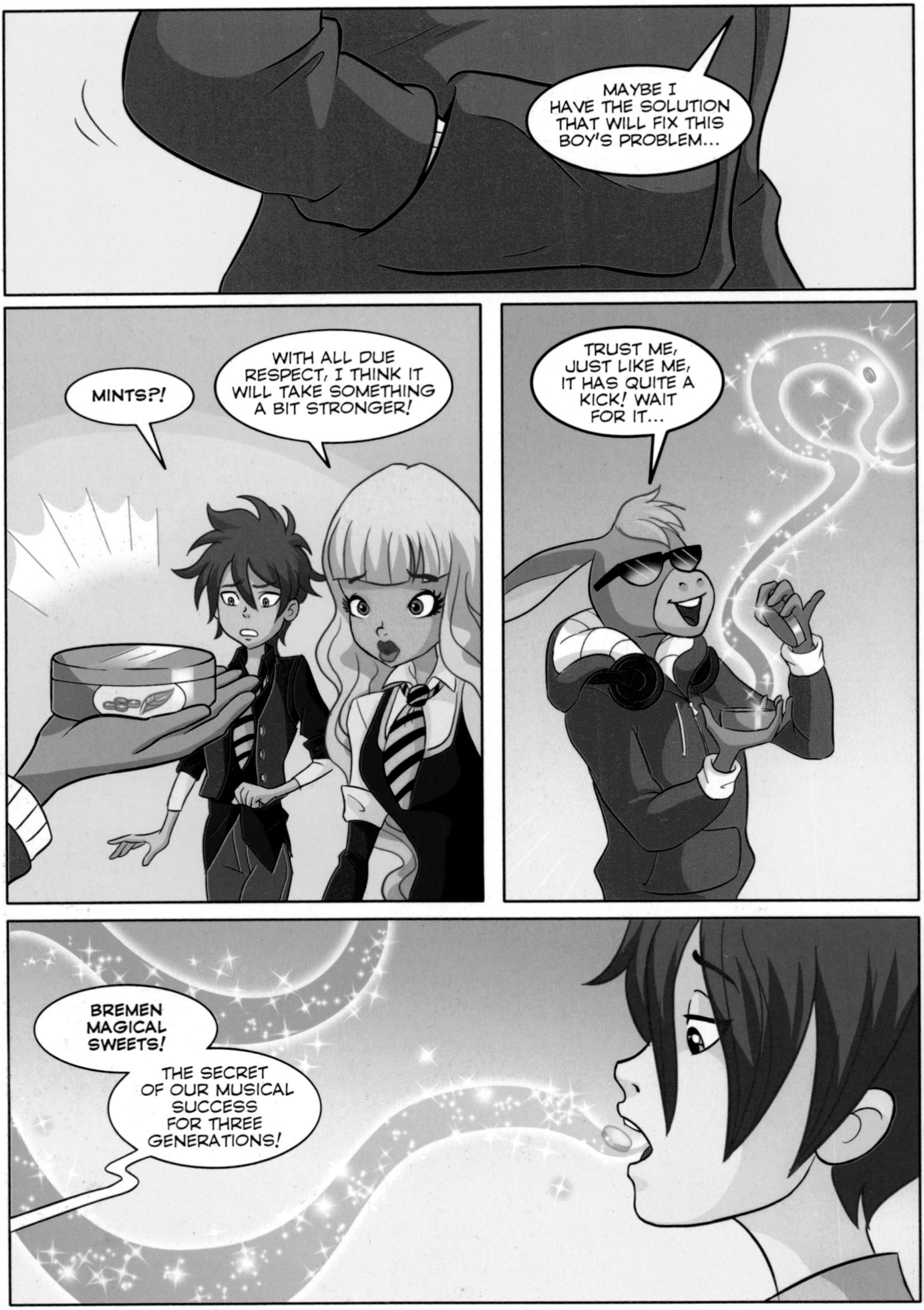
MAYBE I HAVE THE SOLUTION THAT WILL FIX THIS BOY'S PROBLEM...
MINTS?!
WITH ALL DUE RESPECT, I THINK IT WILL TAKE SOMETHING A BIT STRONGER!
TRUST ME, JUST LIKE ME, IT HAS QUITE A KICK! WAIT FOR IT...
BREMEN MAGICAL SWEETS!
THE SECRET OF OUR MUSICAL SUCCESS FOR THREE GENERATIONS!

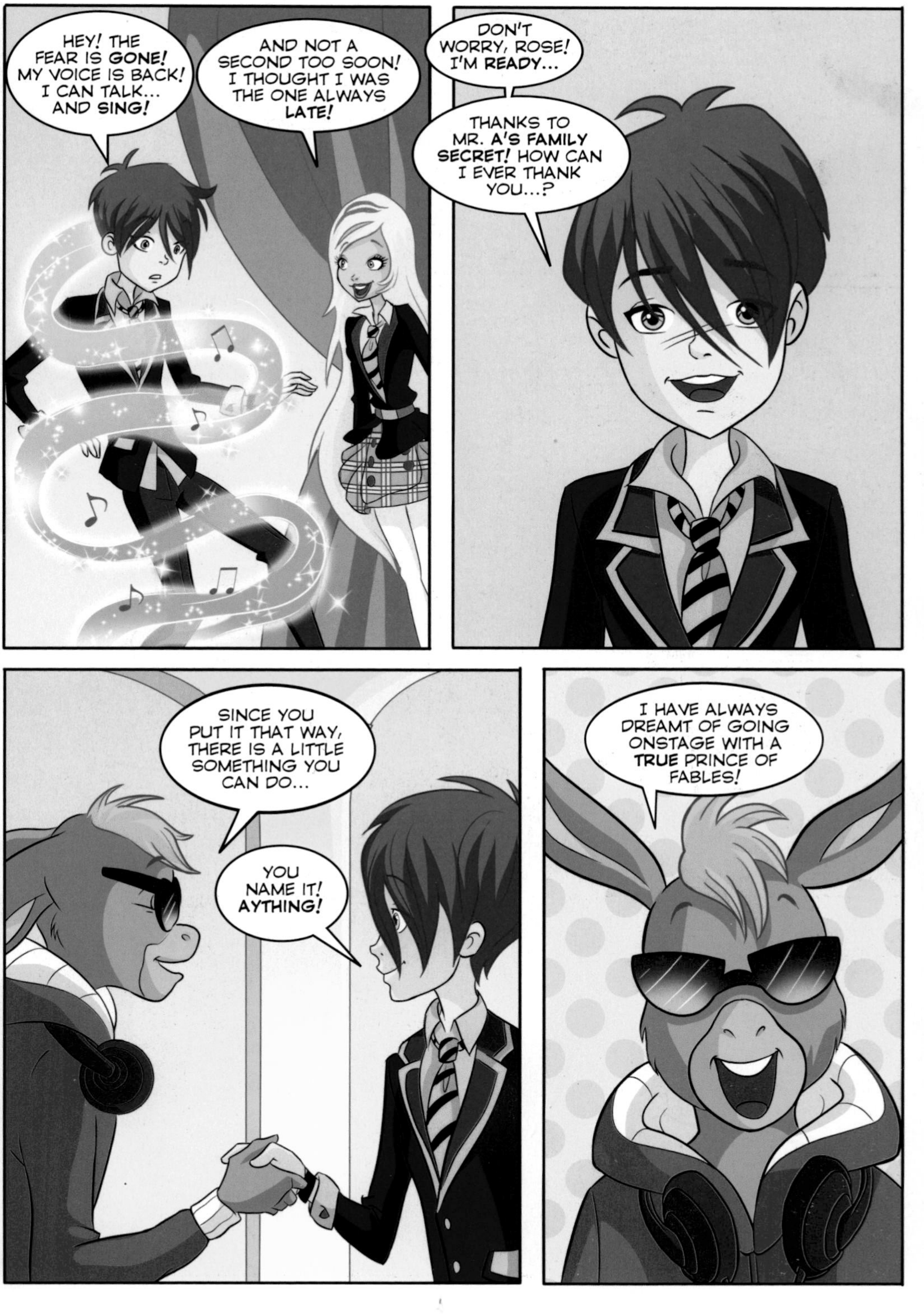
HEY! THE FEAR IS GONE! MY VOICE IS BACK! I CAN TALK... AND SING!
AND NOT A SECOND TOO SOON! I THOUGHT I WAS THE ONE ALWAYS LATE!
DON'T WORRY, ROSE! I'M READY...
THANKS TO MR. A'S FAMILY SECRET! HOW CAN I EVER THANK YOU...?
SINCE YOU PUT IT THAT WAY, THERE IS A LITTLE SOMETHING YOU CAN DO...
YOU NAME IT! AYTHING!
I HAVE ALWAYS DREAMT OF GOING ONSTAGE WITH A TRUE PRINCE OF FABLES!

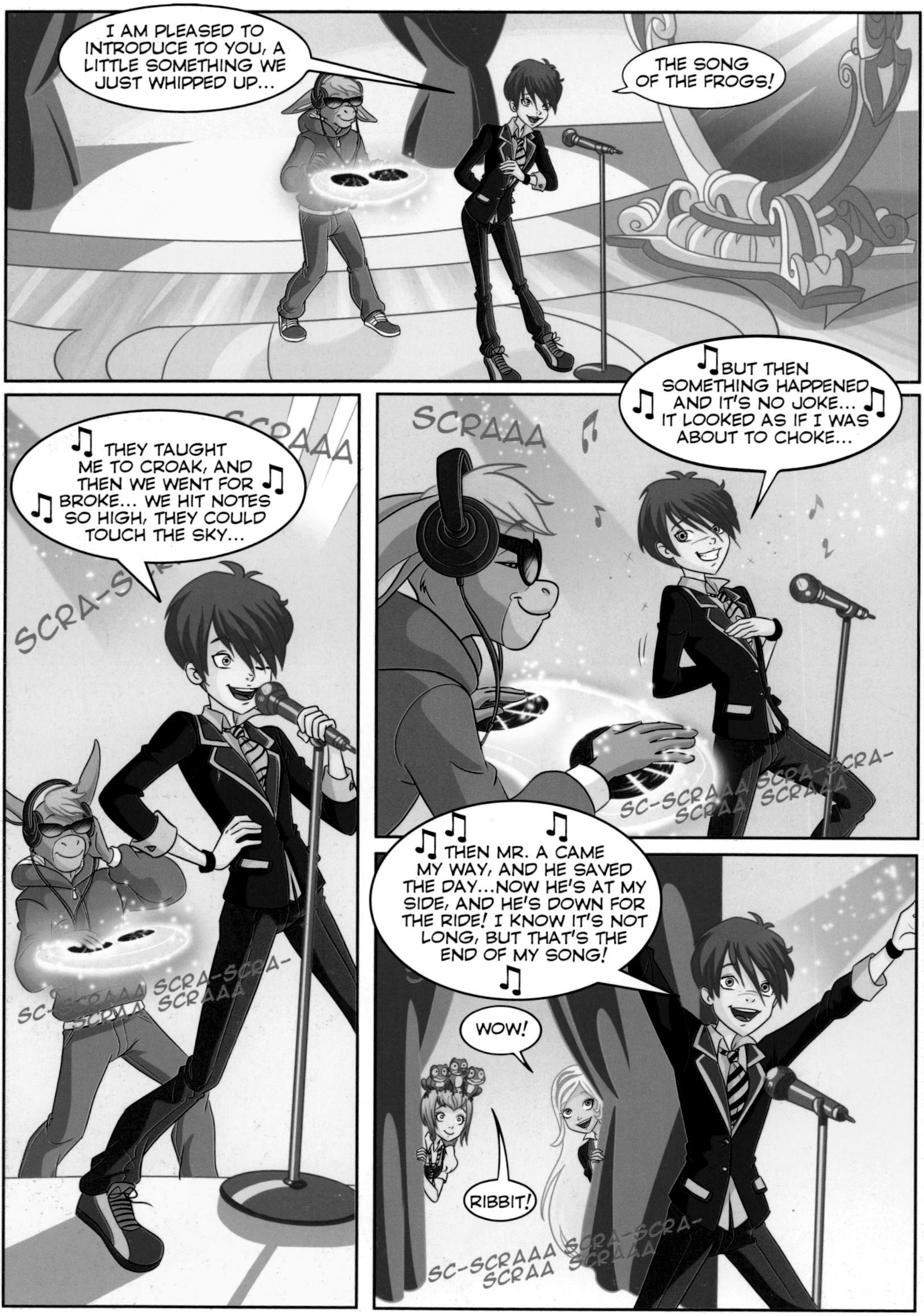
I AM PLEASED TO INTRODUCE TO YOU, A LITTLE SOMETHING WE JUST WHIPPED UP...
THE SONG OF THE FROGS!
♫ THEY TAUGHT ME TO CROAK, AND THEN WE WENT FOR ♫ ♫ BROKE... WE HIT NOTES SO HIGH, THEY COULD TOUCH THE SKY...
SC-SCRAAA SCRA-SCRA- SCRAA SCRAAA
SCRAAA
♫ BUT THEN SOMETHING HAPPENED ♫ AND IT'S NO JOKE... ♫ IT LOOKED AS IF I WAS ABOUT TO CHOKE...
SC-SCRAAA SCRA-SCRA- SCRAA SCRAAA
♫♫ ♫ THEN MR. A CAME MY WAY, AND HE SAVED THE DAY...NOW HE'S AT MY SIDE, AND HE'S DOWN FOR THE RIDE! I KNOW IT'S NOT LONG, BUT THAT'S THE END OF MY SONG! ♫
WOW!
RIBBIT!
SC-SCRAAA SCRA-SCRA- SCRAA SCRAAA

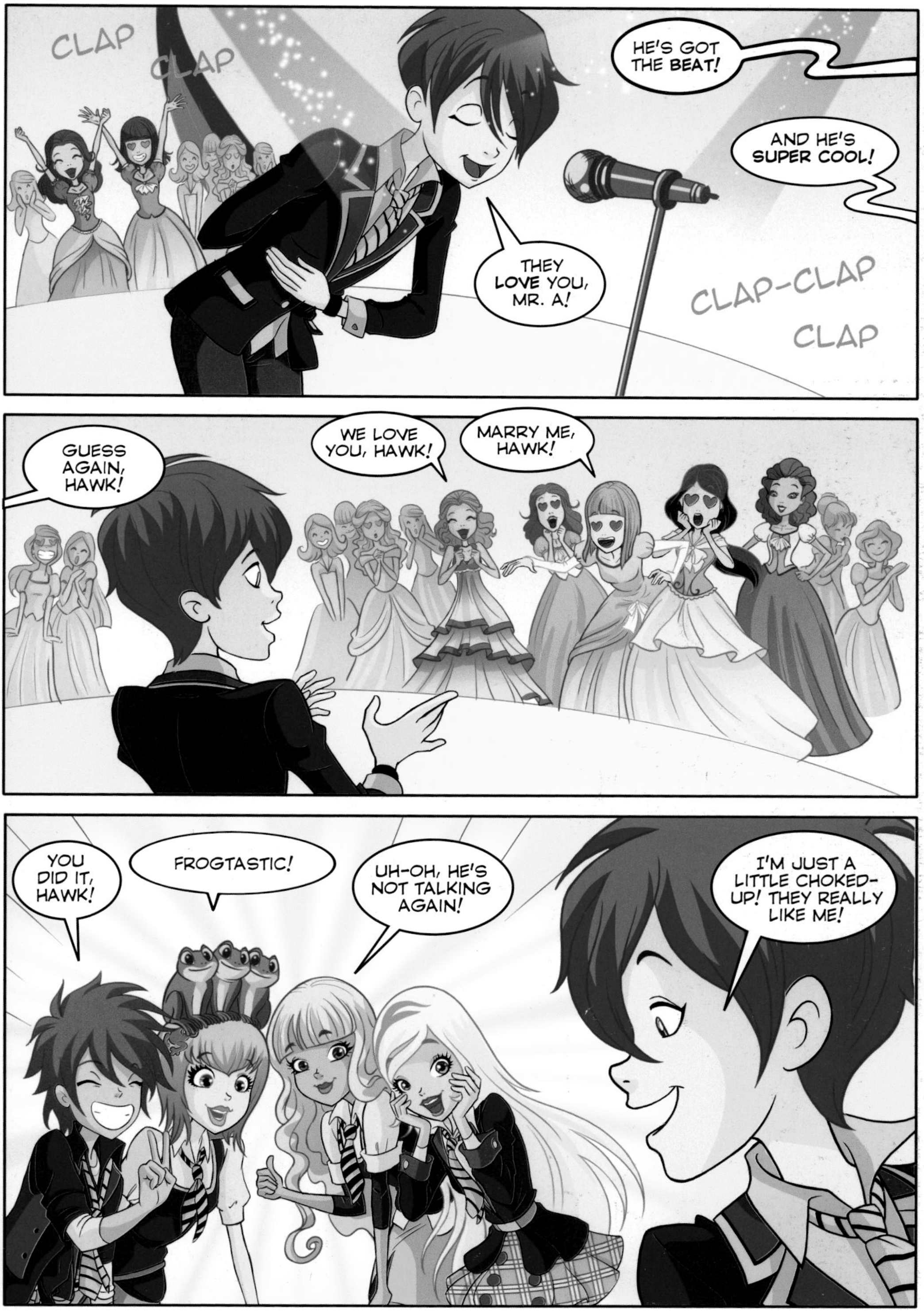
CLAP
CLAP
HE'S GOT THE BEAT!
AND HE'S SUPER COOL!
THEY LOVE YOU, MR. A!
CLAP-CLAP
CLAP
GUESS AGAIN, HAWK!
WE LOVE YOU, HAWK!
MARRY ME, HAWK!
YOU DID IT, HAWK!
FROGTASTIC!
UH-OH, HE'S NOT TALKING AGAIN!
I'M JUST A LITTLE CHOKED-UP! THEY REALLY LIKE ME!

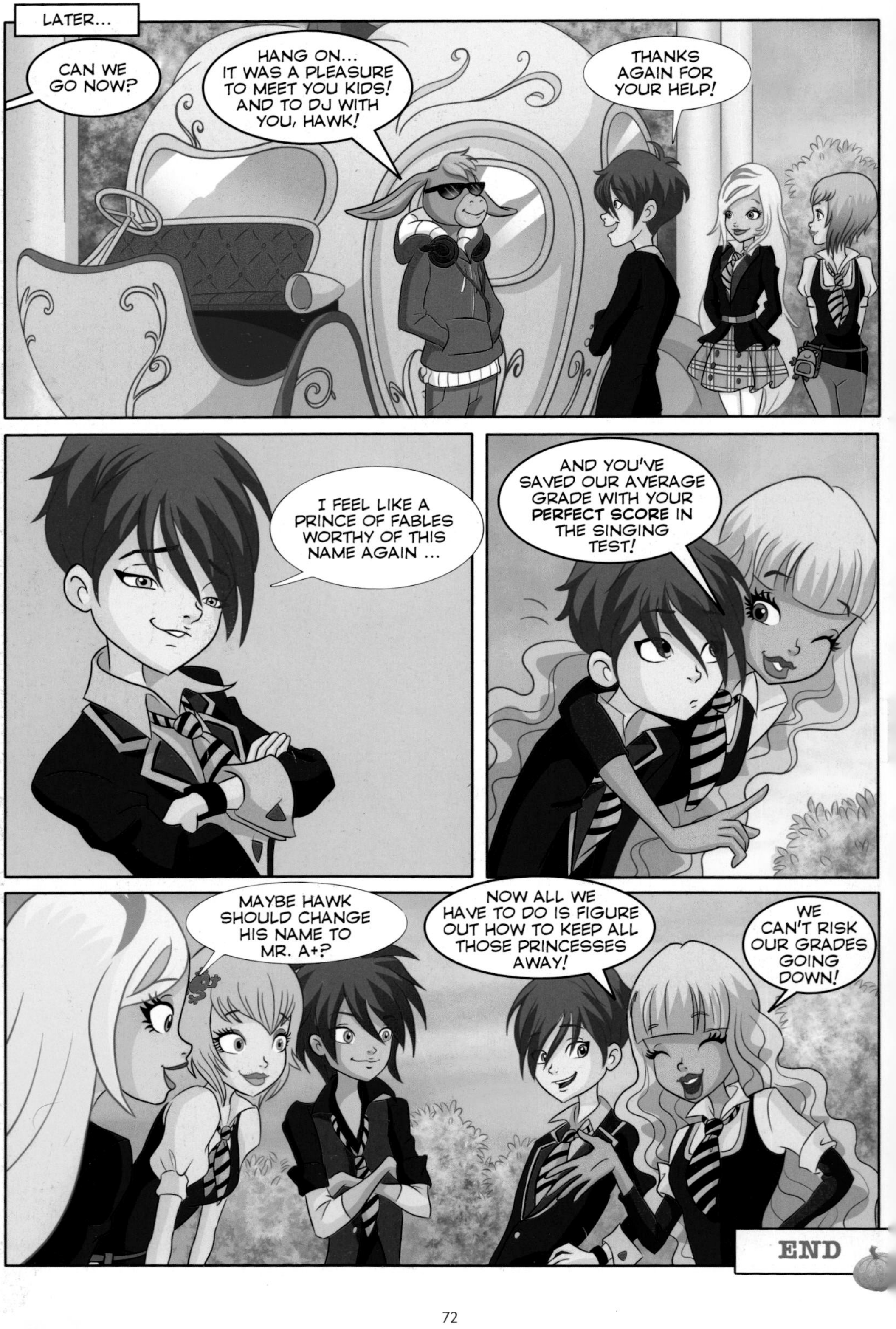
LATER...
CAN WE GO NOW?
HANG ON... IT WAS A PLEASURE TO MEET YOU KIDS! AND TO DJ WITH YOU, HAWK!
THANKS AGAIN FOR YOUR HELP!
I FEEL LIKE A PRINCE OF FABLES WORTHY OF THIS NAME AGAIN ...
AND YOU'VE SAVED OUR AVERAGE GRADE WITH YOUR **PERFECT SCORE** IN THE SINGING TEST!
MAYBE HAWK SHOULD CHANGE HIS NAME TO MR. A+?
NOW ALL WE HAVE TO DO IS FIGURE OUT HOW TO KEEP ALL THOSE PRINCESSES AWAY!
WE CAN'T RISK OUR GRADES GOING DOWN!
END

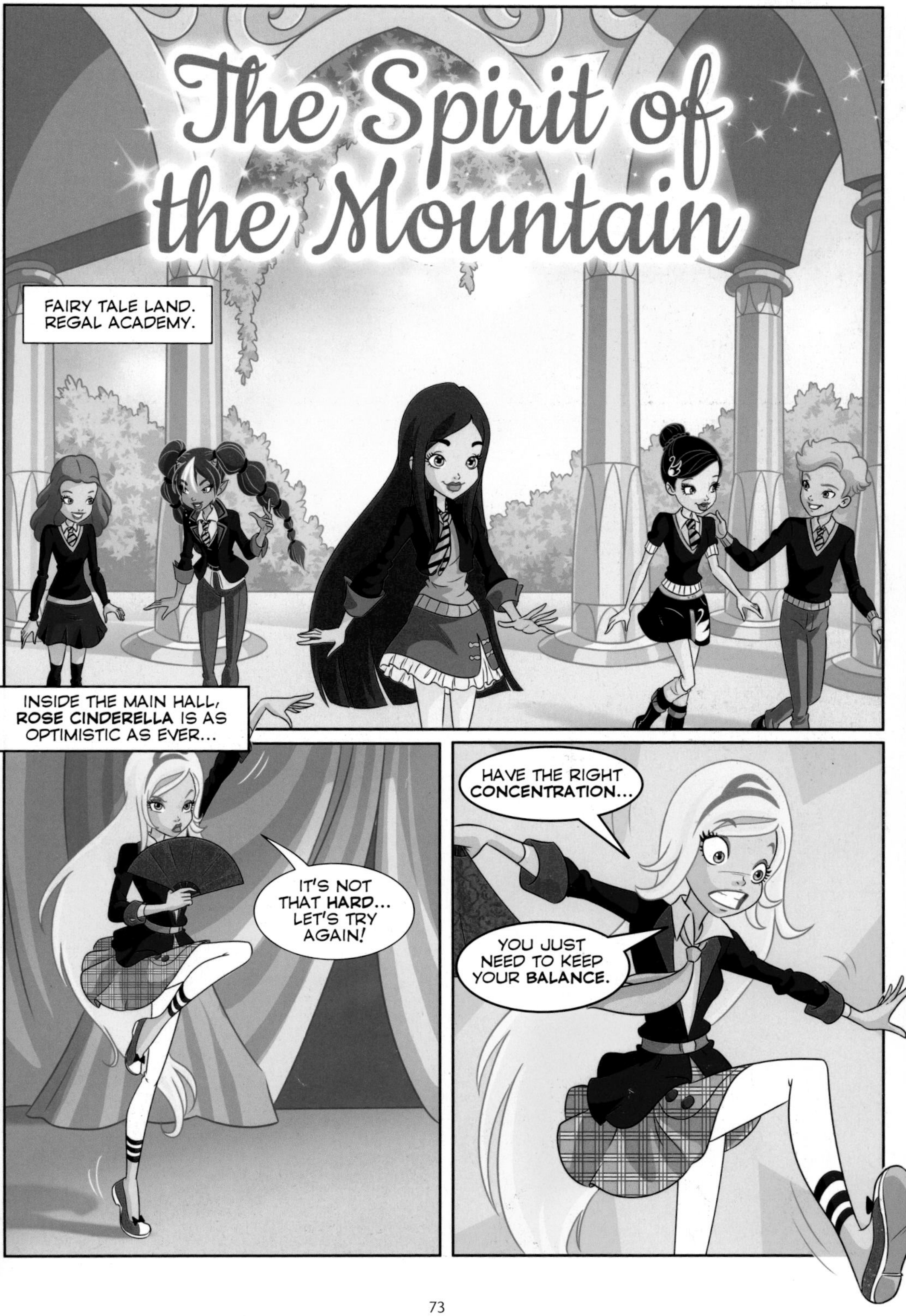
The Spirit of the Mountain
FAIRY TALE LAND. REGAL ACADEMY.
INSIDE THE MAIN HALL, **ROSE CINDERELLA** IS AS OPTIMISTIC AS EVER...
IT'S NOT THAT **HARD**... LET'S TRY AGAIN!
HAVE THE RIGHT **CONCENTRATION**...
YOU JUST NEED TO KEEP YOUR **BALANCE**.

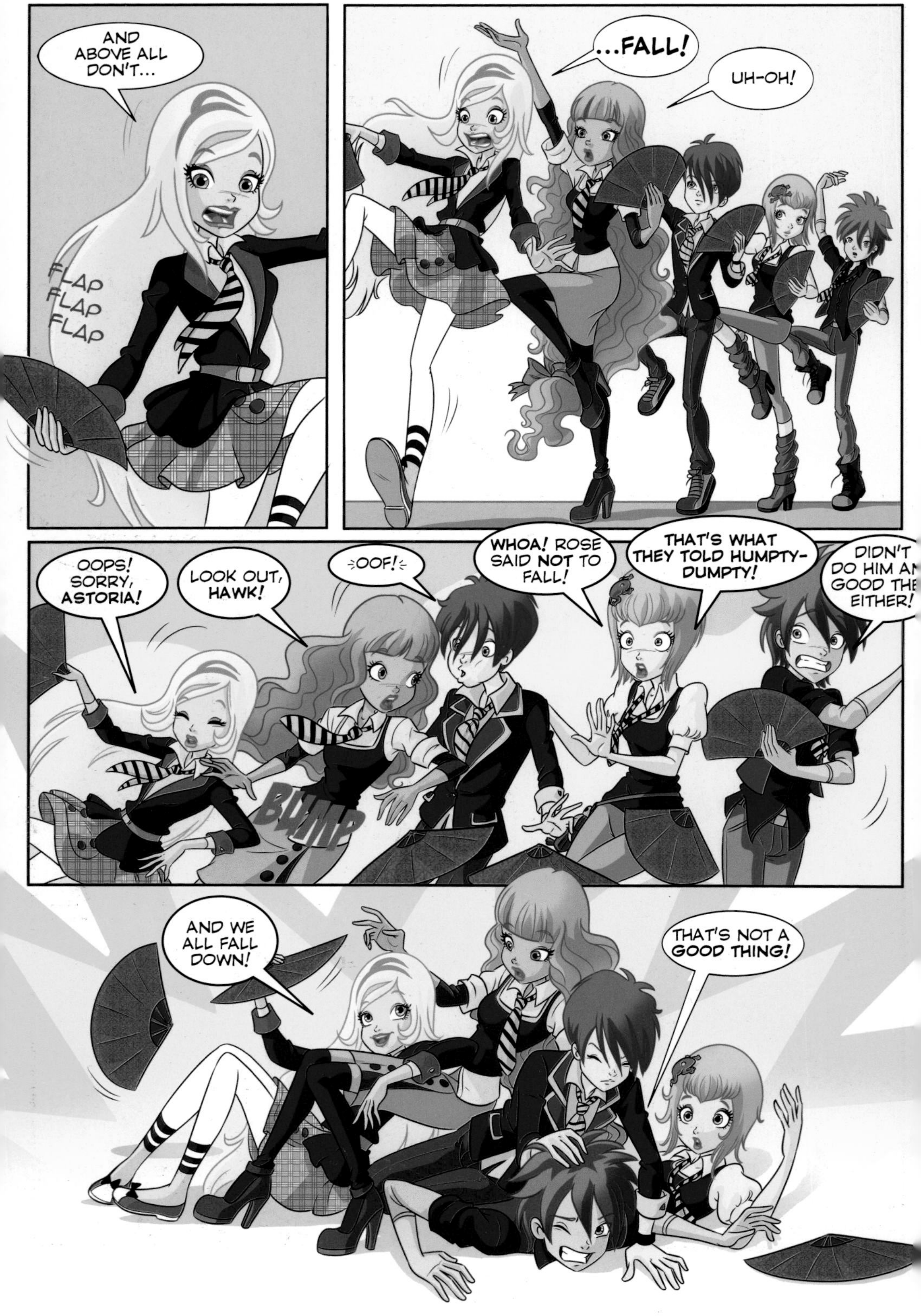
AND ABOVE ALL DON'T...
FLAP FLAP FLAP
...FALL!
UH-OH!
OOPS! SORRY, ASTORIA!
LOOK OUT, HAWK!
OOF!
WHOA! ROSE SAID NOT TO FALL!
THAT'S WHAT THEY TOLD HUMPTY-DUMPTY!
DIDN'T DO HIM A GOOD TH EITHER!
BUMP
AND WE ALL FALL DOWN!
THAT'S NOT A GOOD THING!

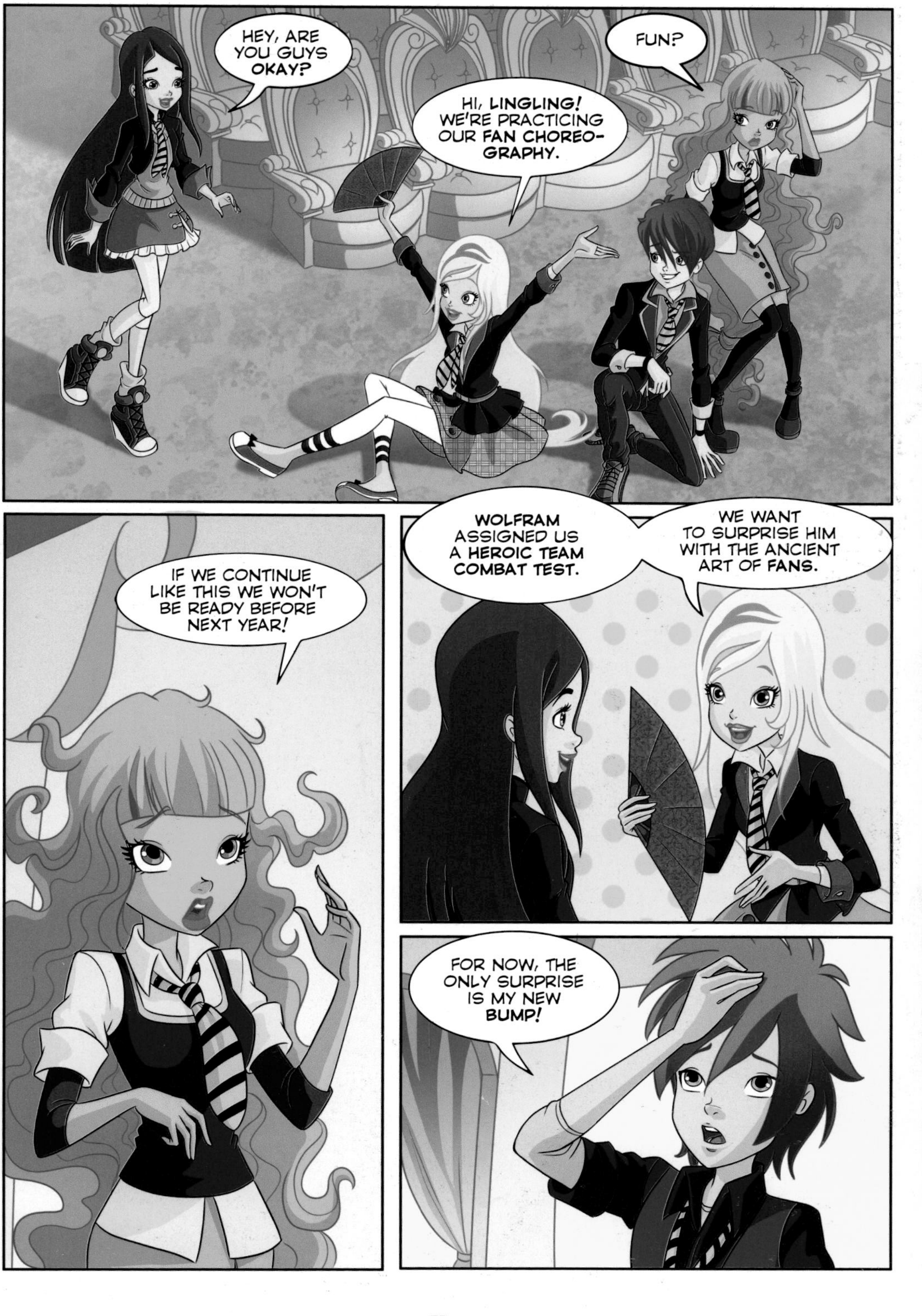
HEY, ARE YOU GUYS OKAY?
HI, LINGLING! WE'RE PRACTICING OUR FAN CHOREO-GRAPHY.
FUN?
IF WE CONTINUE LIKE THIS WE WON'T BE READY BEFORE NEXT YEAR!
WOLFRAM ASSIGNED US A HEROIC TEAM COMBAT TEST.
WE WANT TO SURPRISE HIM WITH THE ANCIENT ART OF FANS.
FOR NOW, THE ONLY SURPRISE IS MY NEW BUMP!

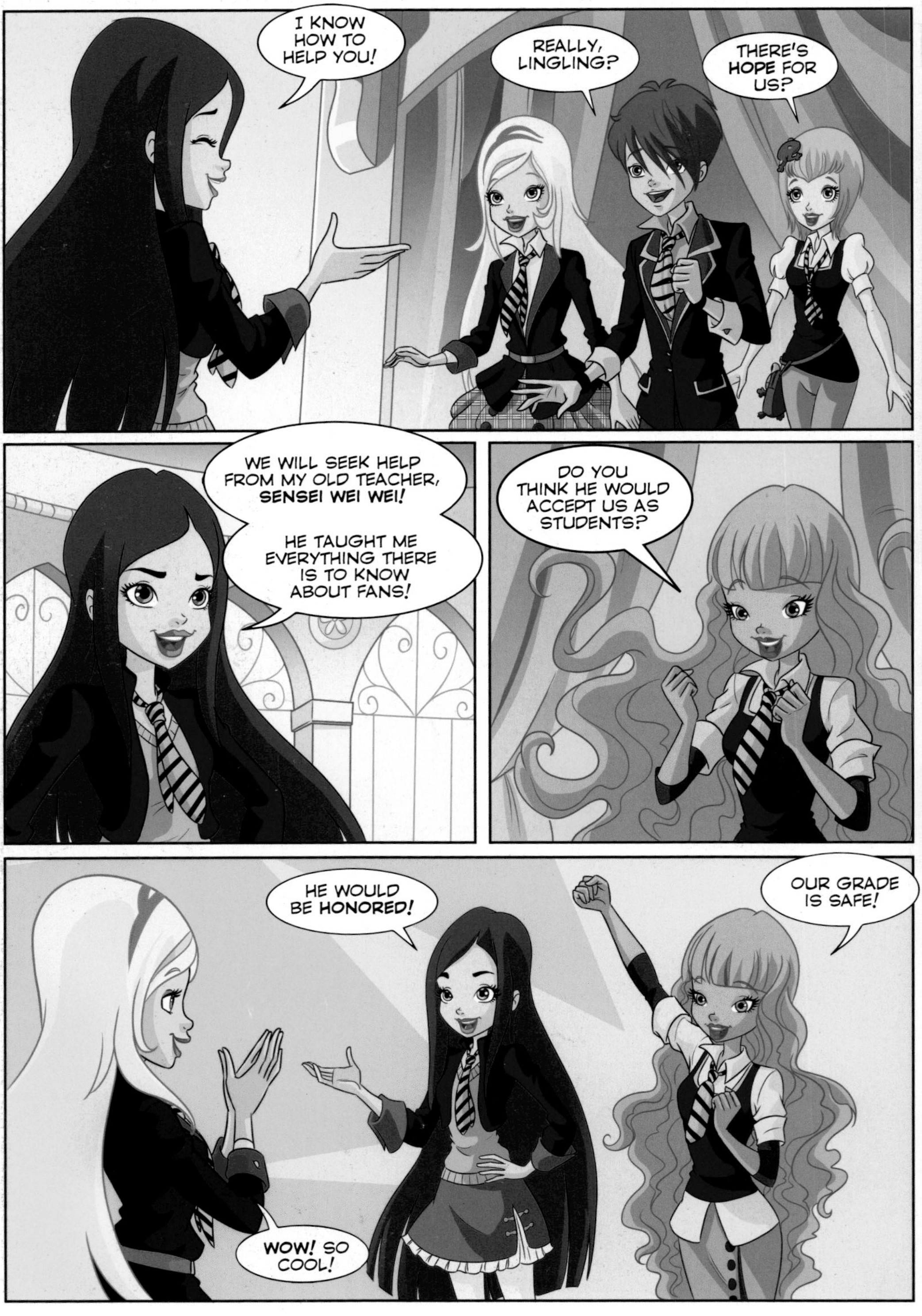
I KNOW HOW TO HELP YOU!
REALLY, LINGLING?
THERE'S **HOPE** FOR US?
WE WILL SEEK HELP FROM MY OLD TEACHER, **SENSEI WEI WEI!**
HE TAUGHT ME EVERYTHING THERE IS TO KNOW ABOUT FANS!
DO YOU THINK HE WOULD ACCEPT US AS STUDENTS?
HE WOULD BE **HONORED!**
OUR GRADE IS SAFE!
WOW! SO COOL!

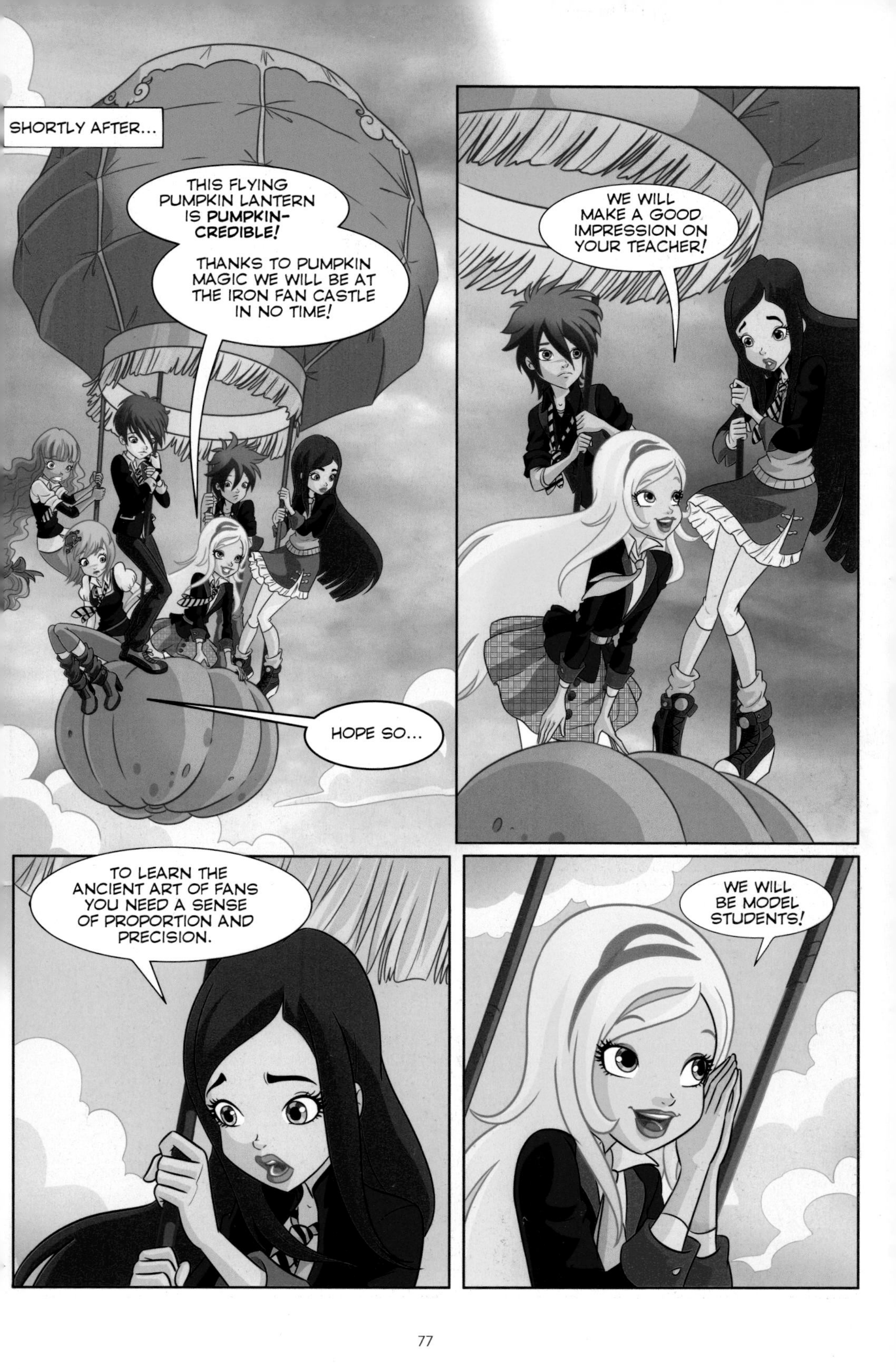
SHORTLY AFTER...
THIS FLYING PUMPKIN LANTERN IS **PUMPKIN-CREDIBLE!**
THANKS TO PUMPKIN MAGIC WE WILL BE AT THE IRON FAN CASTLE IN NO TIME!
HOPE SO...
WE WILL MAKE A GOOD IMPRESSION ON YOUR TEACHER!
TO LEARN THE ANCIENT ART OF FANS YOU NEED A SENSE OF PROPORTION AND PRECISION.
WE WILL BE MODEL STUDENTS!

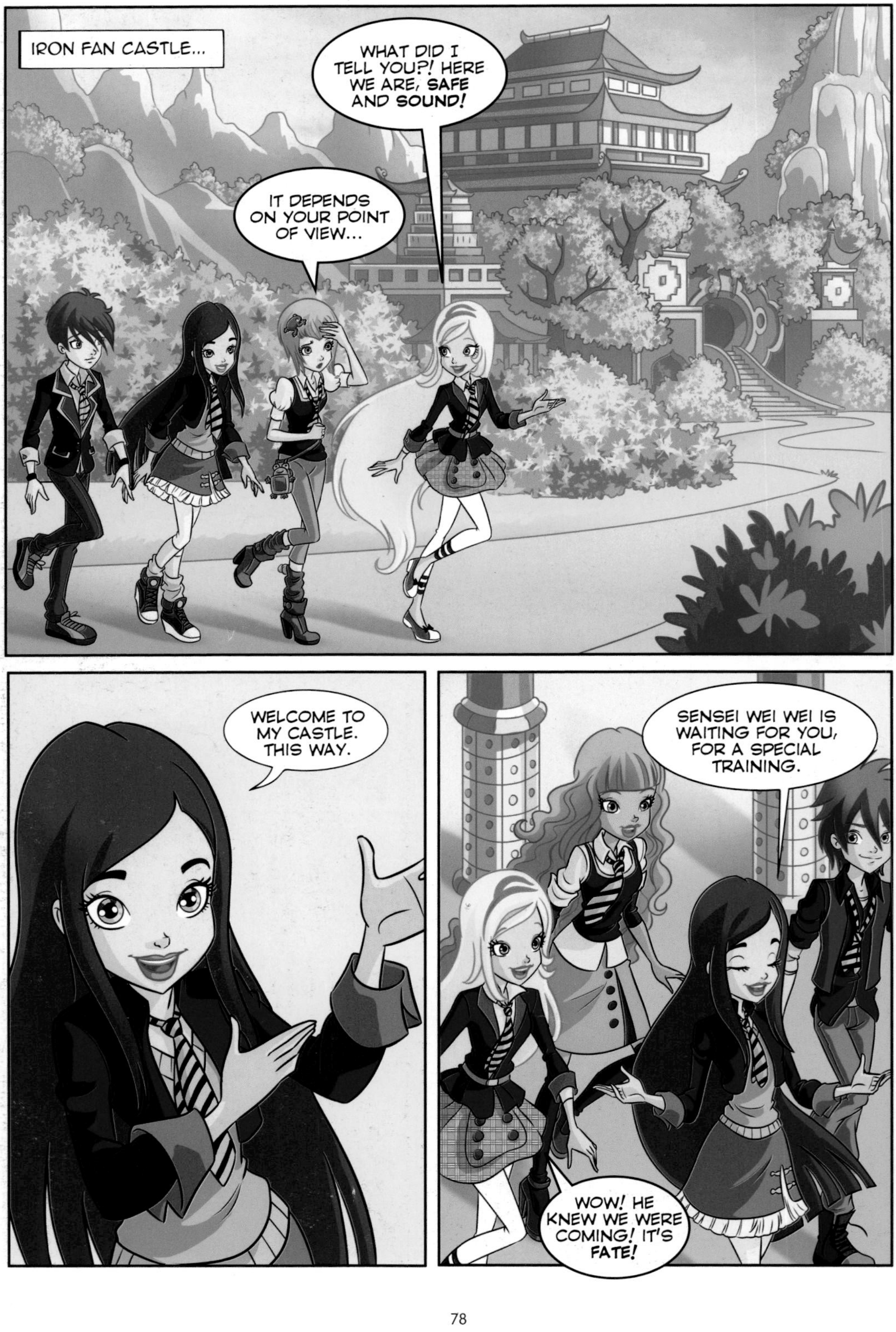
IRON FAN CASTLE...
WHAT DID I TELL YOU?! HERE WE ARE, SAFE AND SOUND!
IT DEPENDS ON YOUR POINT OF VIEW...
WELCOME TO MY CASTLE. THIS WAY.
SENSEI WEI WEI IS WAITING FOR YOU, FOR A SPECIAL TRAINING.
WOW! HE KNEW WE WERE COMING! IT'S FATE!

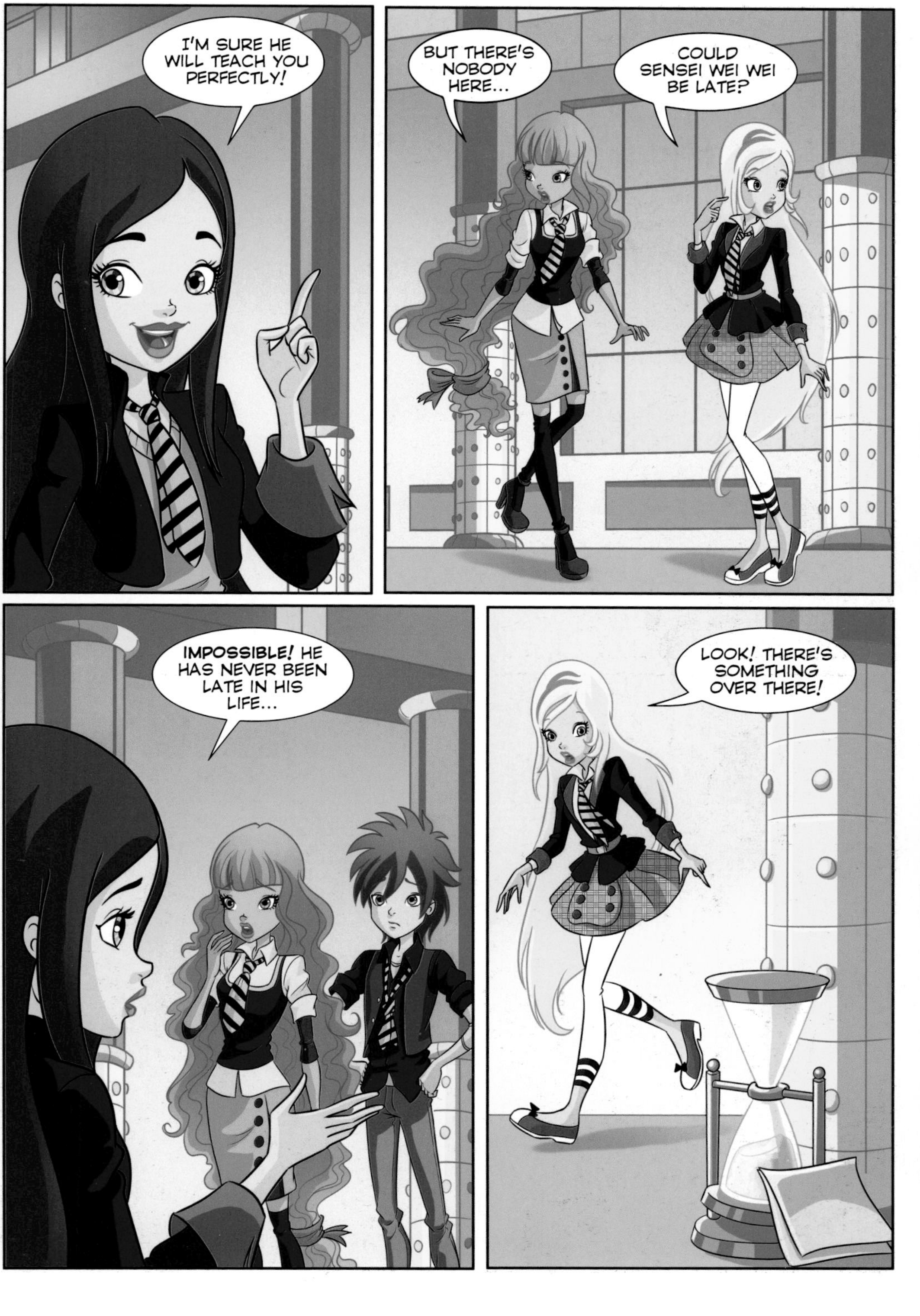
I'M SURE HE WILL TEACH YOU PERFECTLY!
BUT THERE'S NOBODY HERE...
COULD SENSEI WEI WEI BE LATE?
IMPOSSIBLE! HE HAS NEVER BEEN LATE IN HIS LIFE...
LOOK! THERE'S SOMETHING OVER THERE!

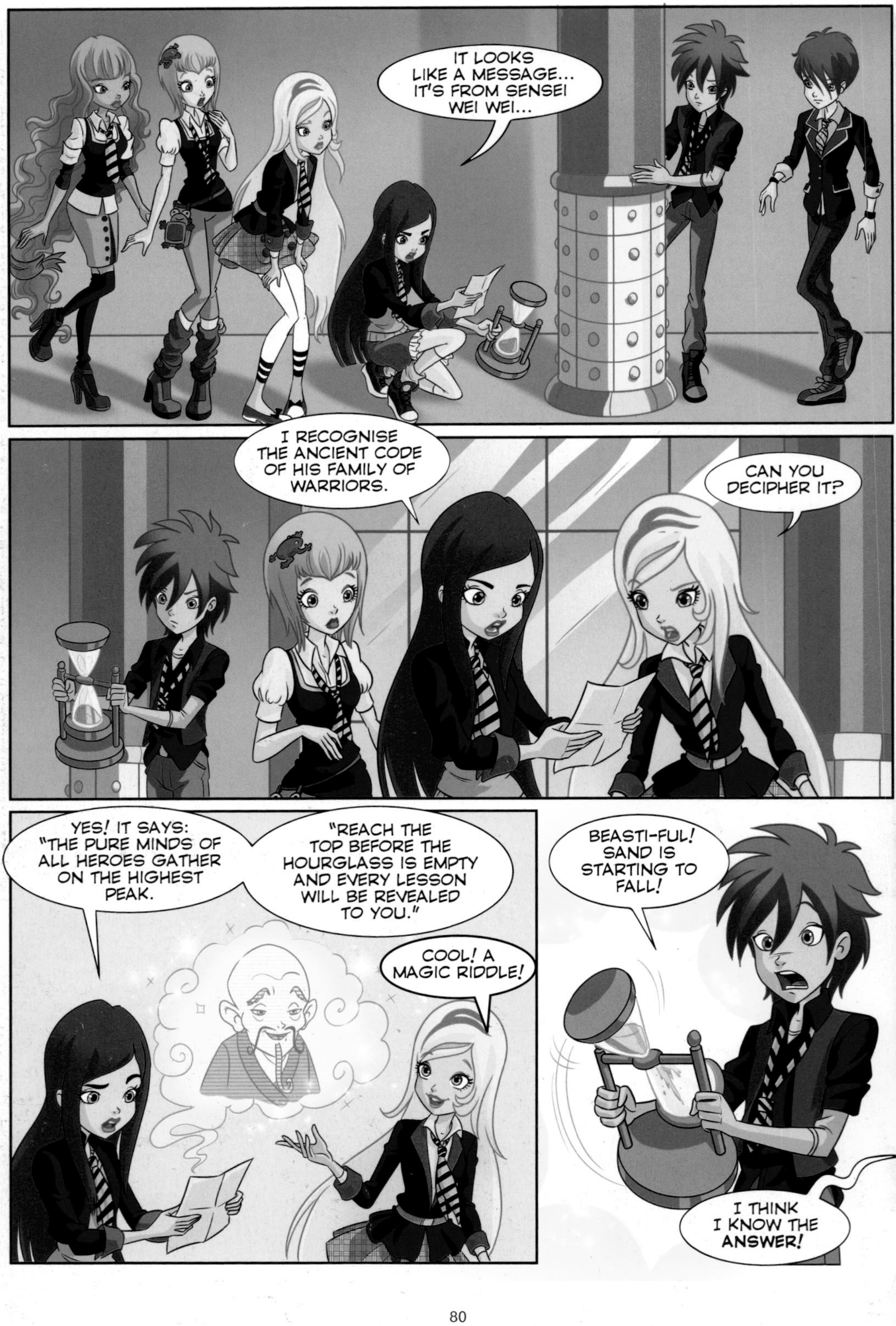

IT LOOKS LIKE A MESSAGE... IT'S FROM SENSEI WEI WEI...
I RECOGNISE THE ANCIENT CODE OF HIS FAMILY OF WARRIORS.
CAN YOU DECIPHER IT?
YES! IT SAYS: "THE PURE MINDS OF ALL HEROES GATHER ON THE HIGHEST PEAK.
"REACH THE TOP BEFORE THE HOURGLASS IS EMPTY AND EVERY LESSON WILL BE REVEALED TO YOU."
COOL! A MAGIC RIDDLE!
BEASTI-FUL! SAND IS STARTING TO FALL!
I THINK I KNOW THE ANSWER!

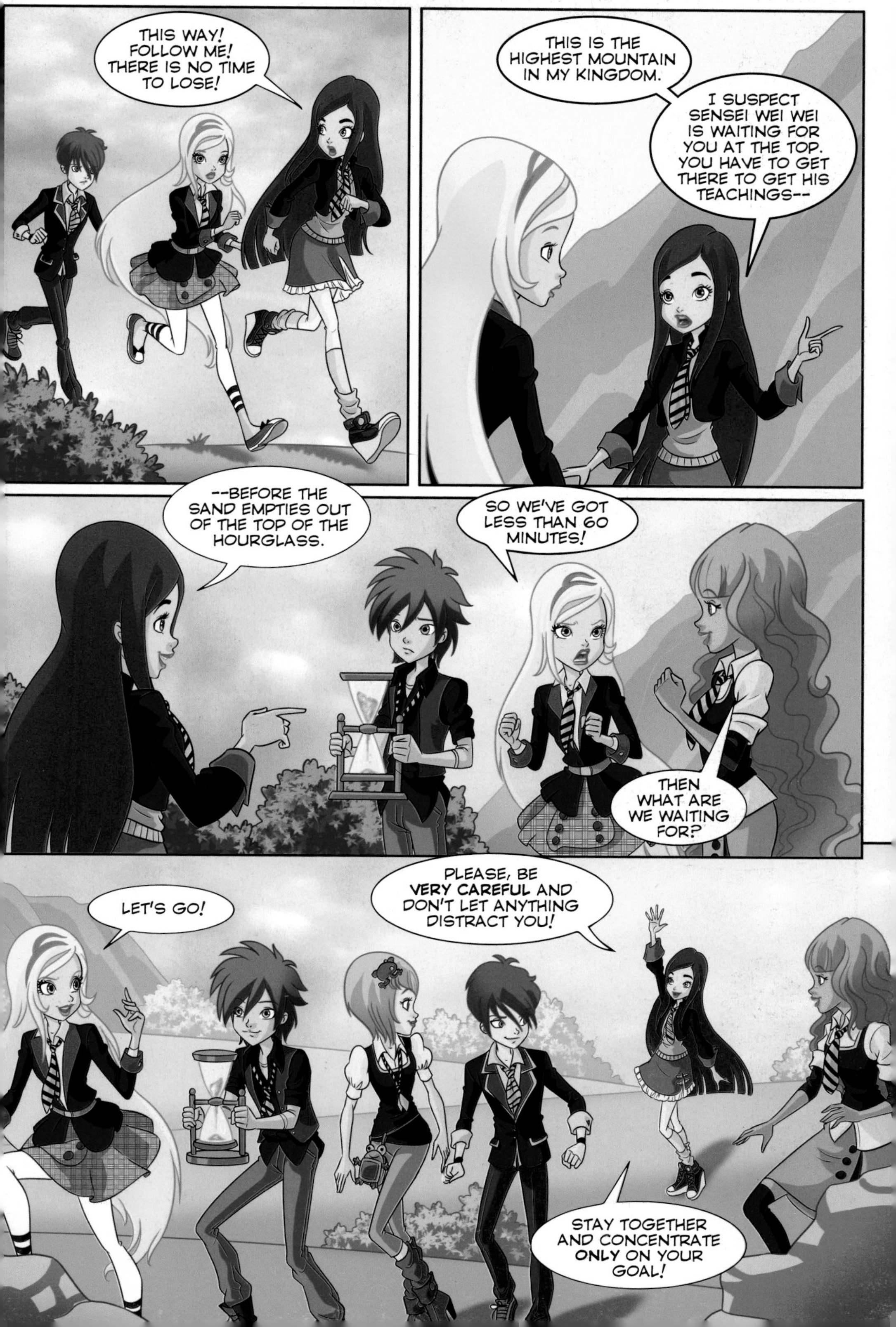
THIS WAY! FOLLOW ME! THERE IS NO TIME TO LOSE!
THIS IS THE HIGHEST MOUNTAIN IN MY KINGDOM.
I SUSPECT SENSEI WEI WEI IS WAITING FOR YOU AT THE TOP. YOU HAVE TO GET THERE TO GET HIS TEACHINGS--
--BEFORE THE SAND EMPTIES OUT OF THE TOP OF THE HOURGLASS.
SO WE'VE GOT LESS THAN 60 MINUTES!
THEN WHAT ARE WE WAITING FOR?
LET'S GO!
PLEASE, BE **VERY CAREFUL** AND DON'T LET ANYTHING DISTRACT YOU!
STAY TOGETHER AND CONCENTRATE **ONLY** ON YOUR GOAL!

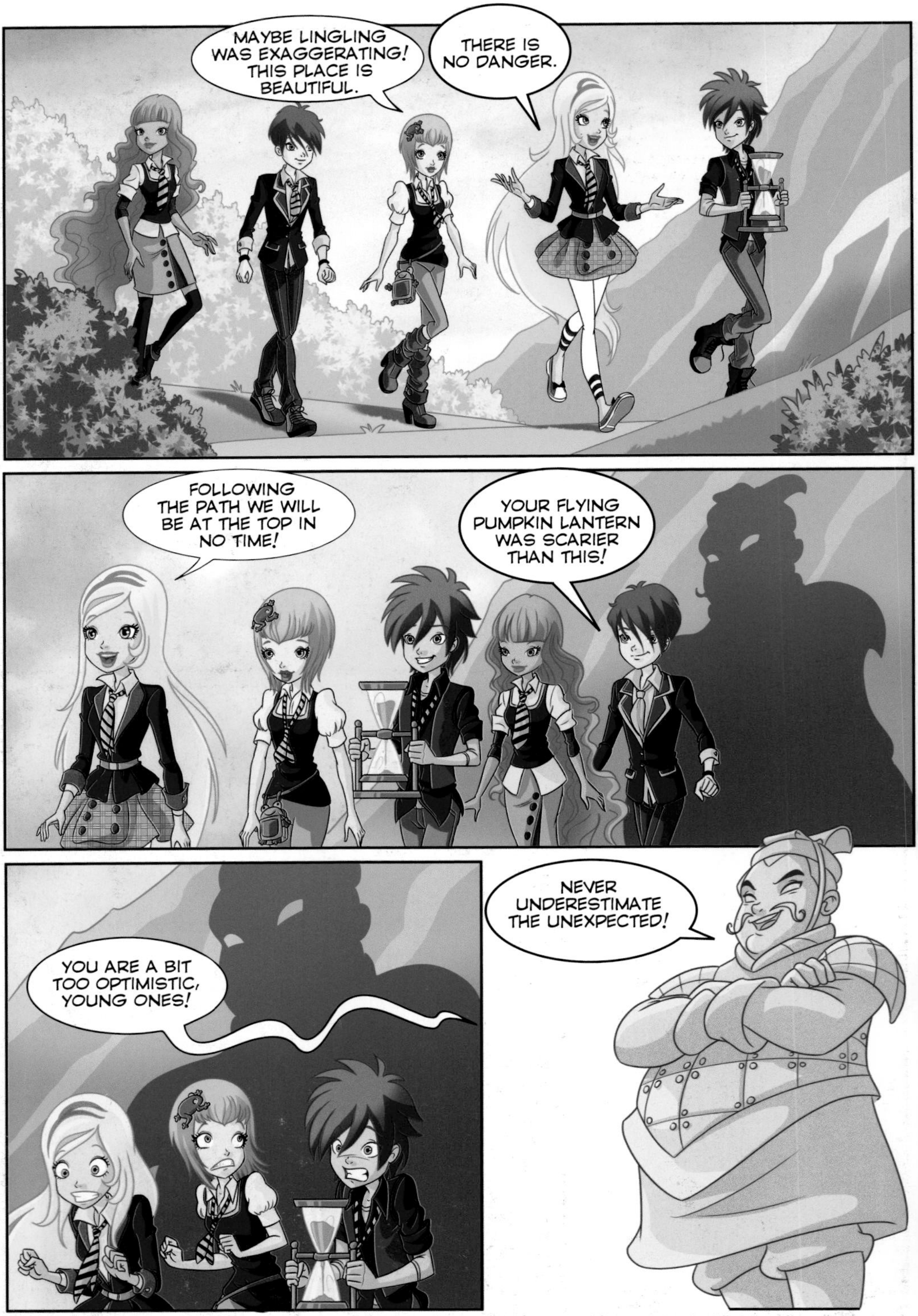
MAYBE LINGLING WAS EXAGGERATING! THIS PLACE IS BEAUTIFUL.
THERE IS NO DANGER.
FOLLOWING THE PATH WE WILL BE AT THE TOP IN NO TIME!
YOUR FLYING PUMPKIN LANTERN WAS SCARIER THAN THIS!
YOU ARE A BIT TOO OPTIMISTIC, YOUNG ONES!
NEVER UNDERESTIMATE THE UNEXPECTED!

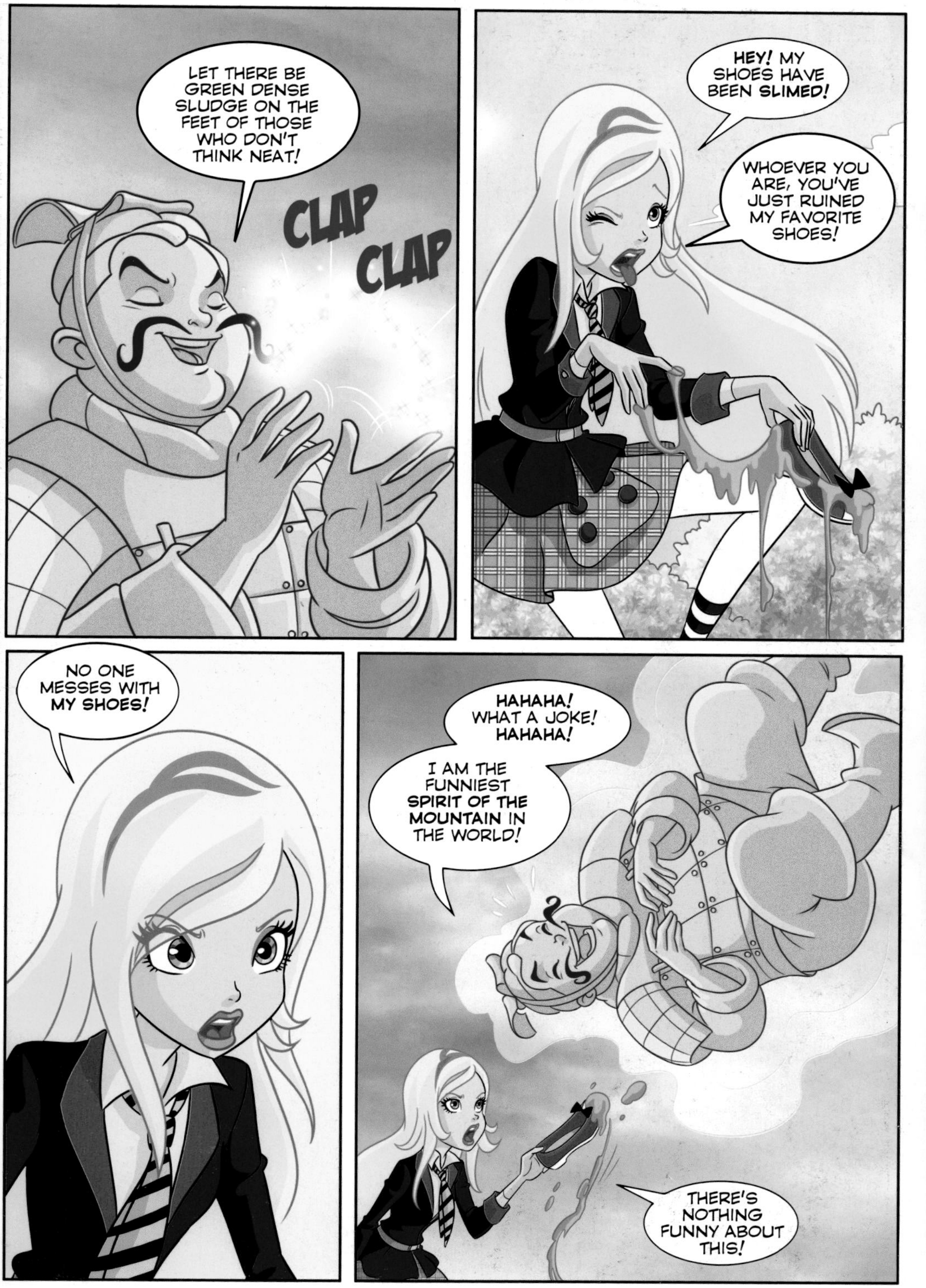
LET THERE BE GREEN DENSE SLUDGE ON THE FEET OF THOSE WHO DON'T THINK NEAT!
CLAP CLAP
HEY! MY SHOES HAVE BEEN SLIMED!
WHOEVER YOU ARE, YOU'VE JUST RUINED MY FAVORITE SHOES!
NO ONE MESSES WITH MY SHOES!
HAHAHA! WHAT A JOKE! HAHAHA!
I AM THE FUNNIEST SPIRIT OF THE MOUNTAIN IN THE WORLD!
THERE'S NOTHING FUNNY ABOUT THIS!

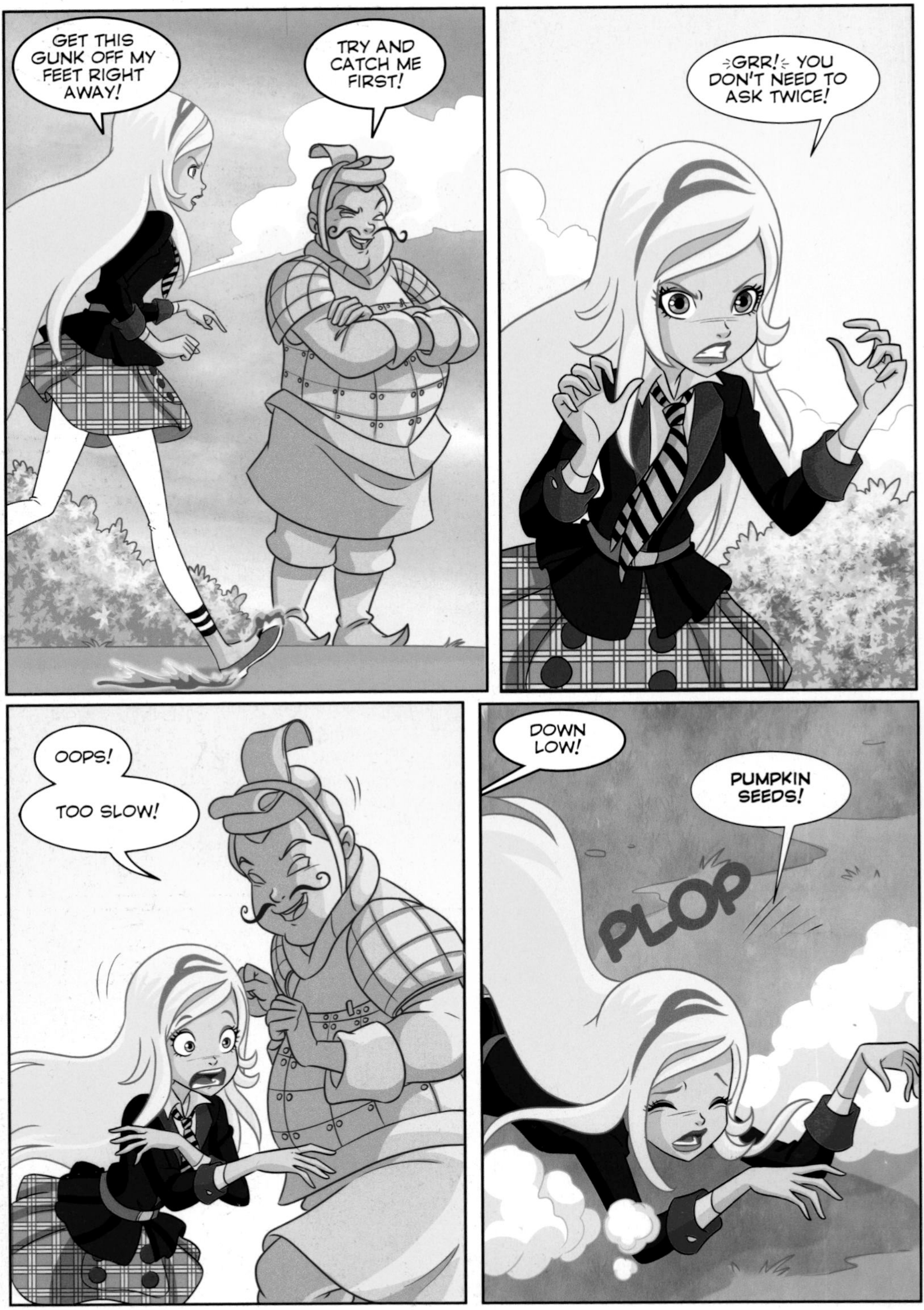
GET THIS GUNK OFF MY FEET RIGHT AWAY!
TRY AND CATCH ME FIRST!
GRR! YOU DON'T NEED TO ASK TWICE!
OOPS!
TOO SLOW!
DOWN LOW!
PUMPKIN SEEDS!
PLOP

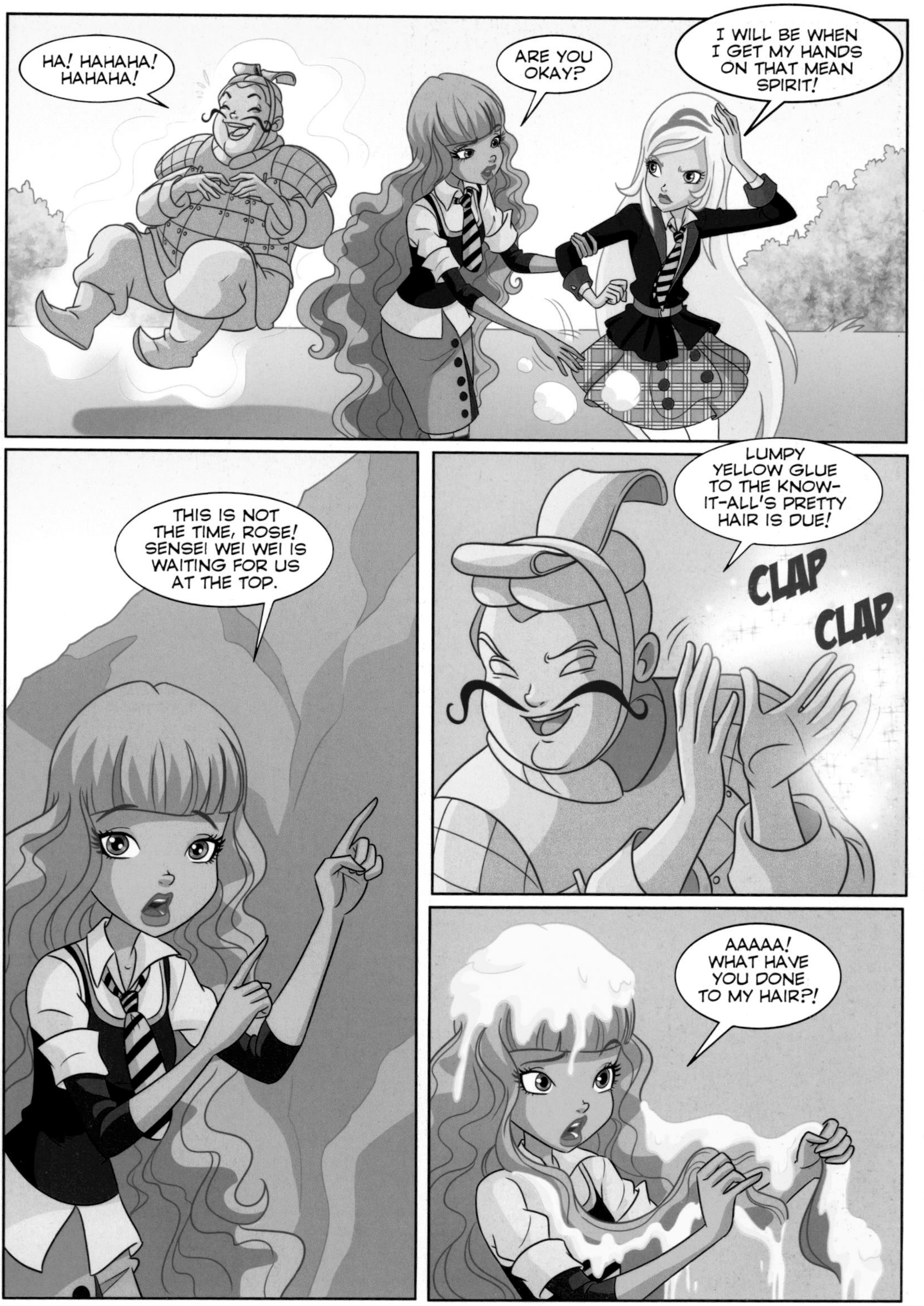
HA! HAHAHA! HAHAHA!
ARE YOU OKAY?
I WILL BE WHEN I GET MY HANDS ON THAT MEAN SPIRIT!
THIS IS NOT THE TIME, ROSE! SENSEI WEI WEI IS WAITING FOR US AT THE TOP.
LUMPY YELLOW GLUE TO THE KNOW-IT-ALL'S PRETTY HAIR IS DUE!
CLAP
CLAP
AAAAA! WHAT HAVE YOU DONE TO MY HAIR?!

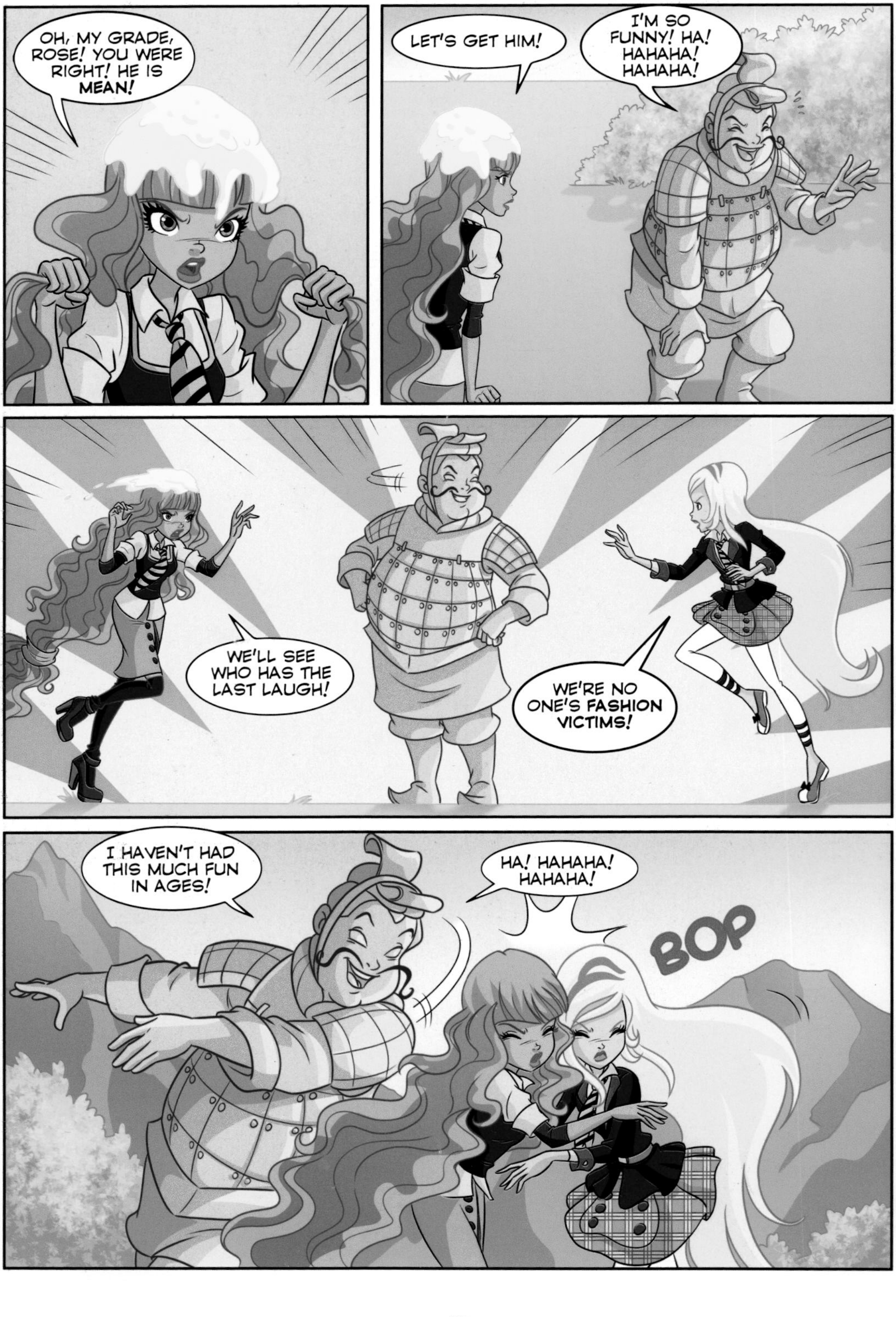
OH, MY GRADE, ROSE! YOU WERE RIGHT! HE IS MEAN!
LET'S GET HIM!
I'M SO FUNNY! HA! HAHAHA! HAHAHA!
WE'LL SEE WHO HAS THE LAST LAUGH!
WE'RE NO ONE'S FASHION VICTIMS!
I HAVEN'T HAD THIS MUCH FUN IN AGES!
HA! HAHAHA! HAHAHA!
BOP

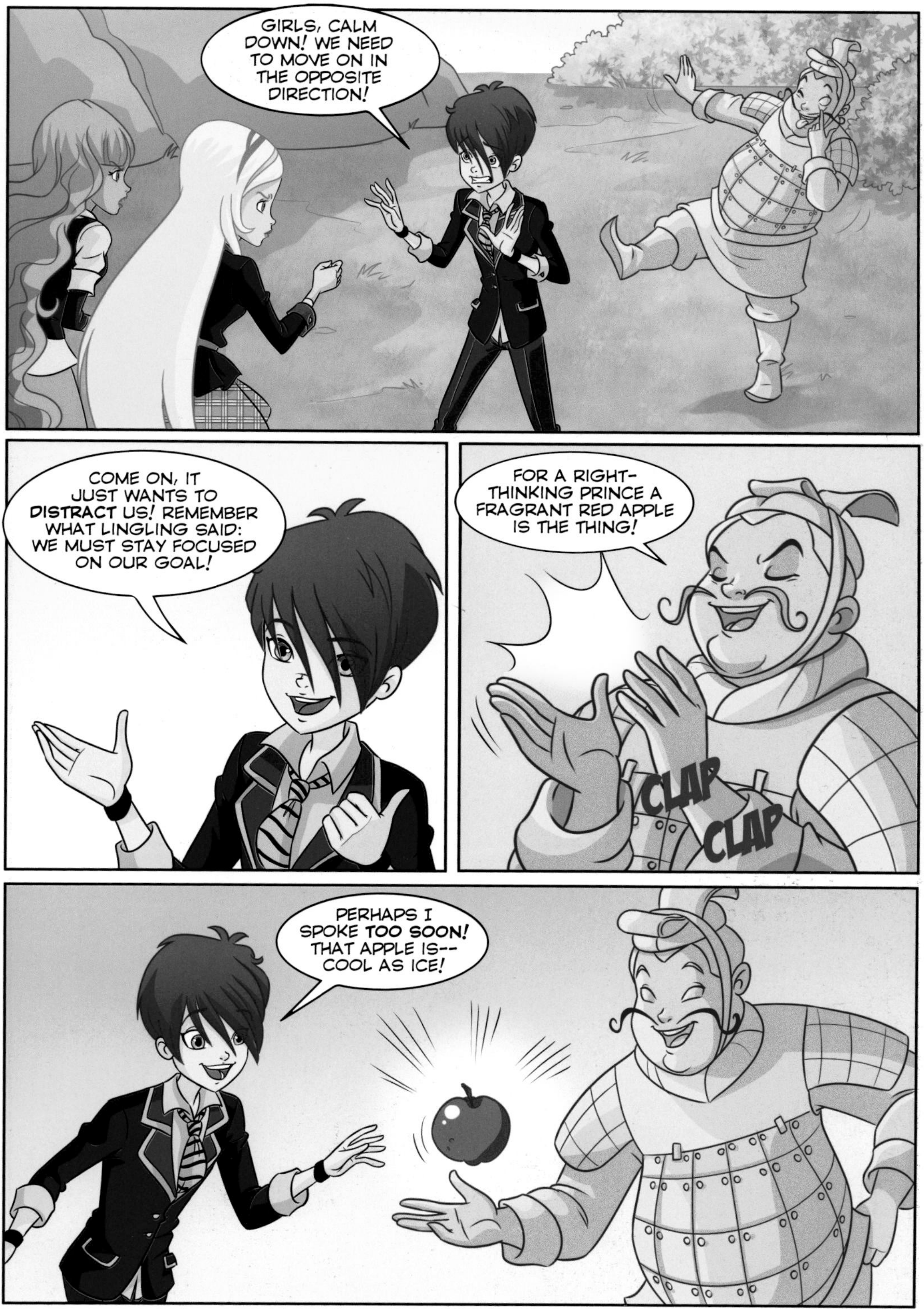
GIRLS, CALM DOWN! WE NEED TO MOVE ON IN THE OPPOSITE DIRECTION!
COME ON, IT JUST WANTS TO **DISTRACT** US! REMEMBER WHAT LINGLING SAID: WE MUST STAY FOCUSED ON OUR GOAL!
FOR A RIGHT-THINKING PRINCE A FRAGRANT RED APPLE IS THE THING!
CLAP
CLAP
PERHAPS I SPOKE **TOO SOON!** THAT APPLE IS-- COOL AS ICE!

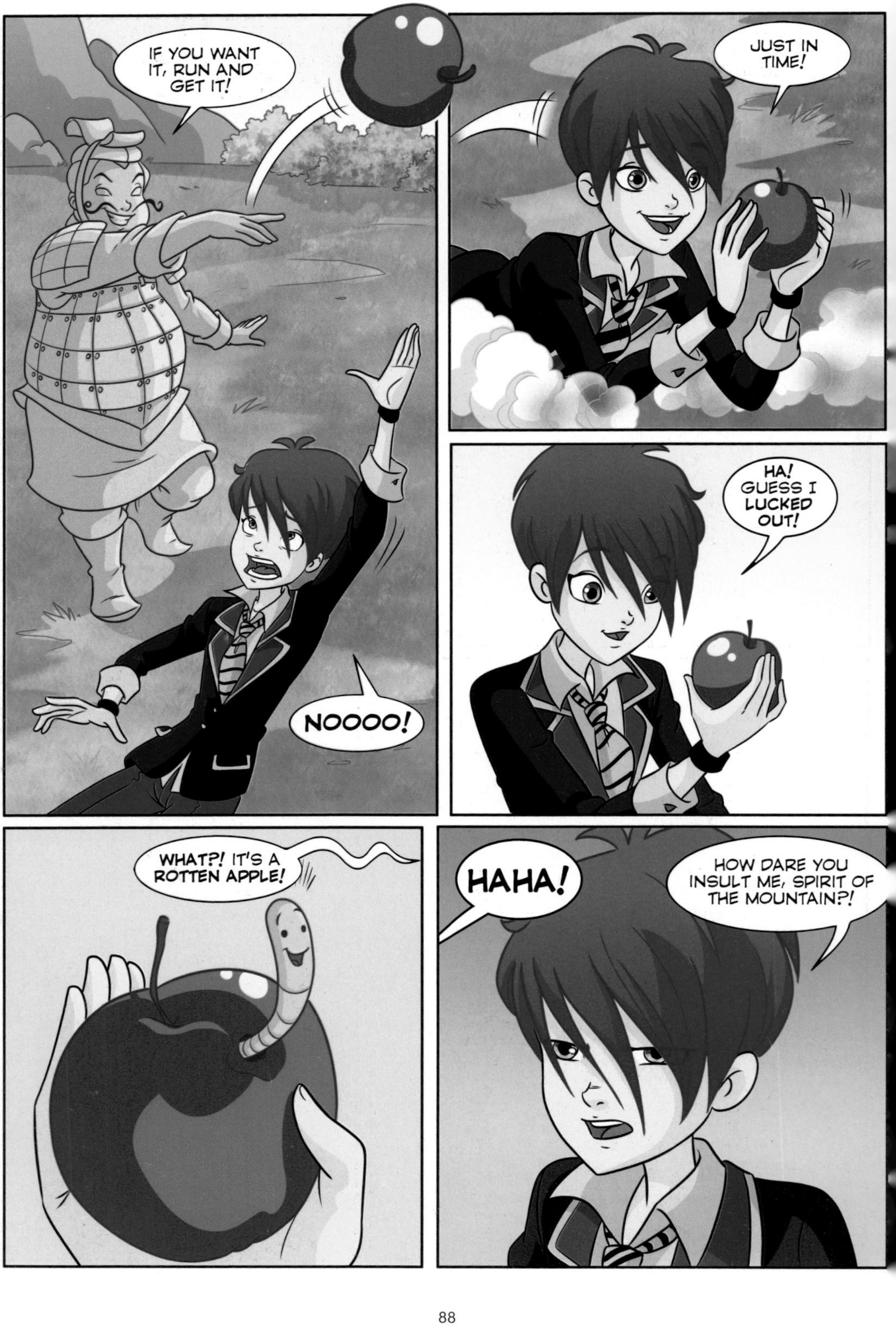
IF YOU WANT IT, RUN AND GET IT!
NOOOO!
JUST IN TIME!
HA! GUESS I LUCKED OUT!
WHAT?! IT'S A ROTTEN APPLE!
HAHA!
HOW DARE YOU INSULT ME, SPIRIT OF THE MOUNTAIN?!

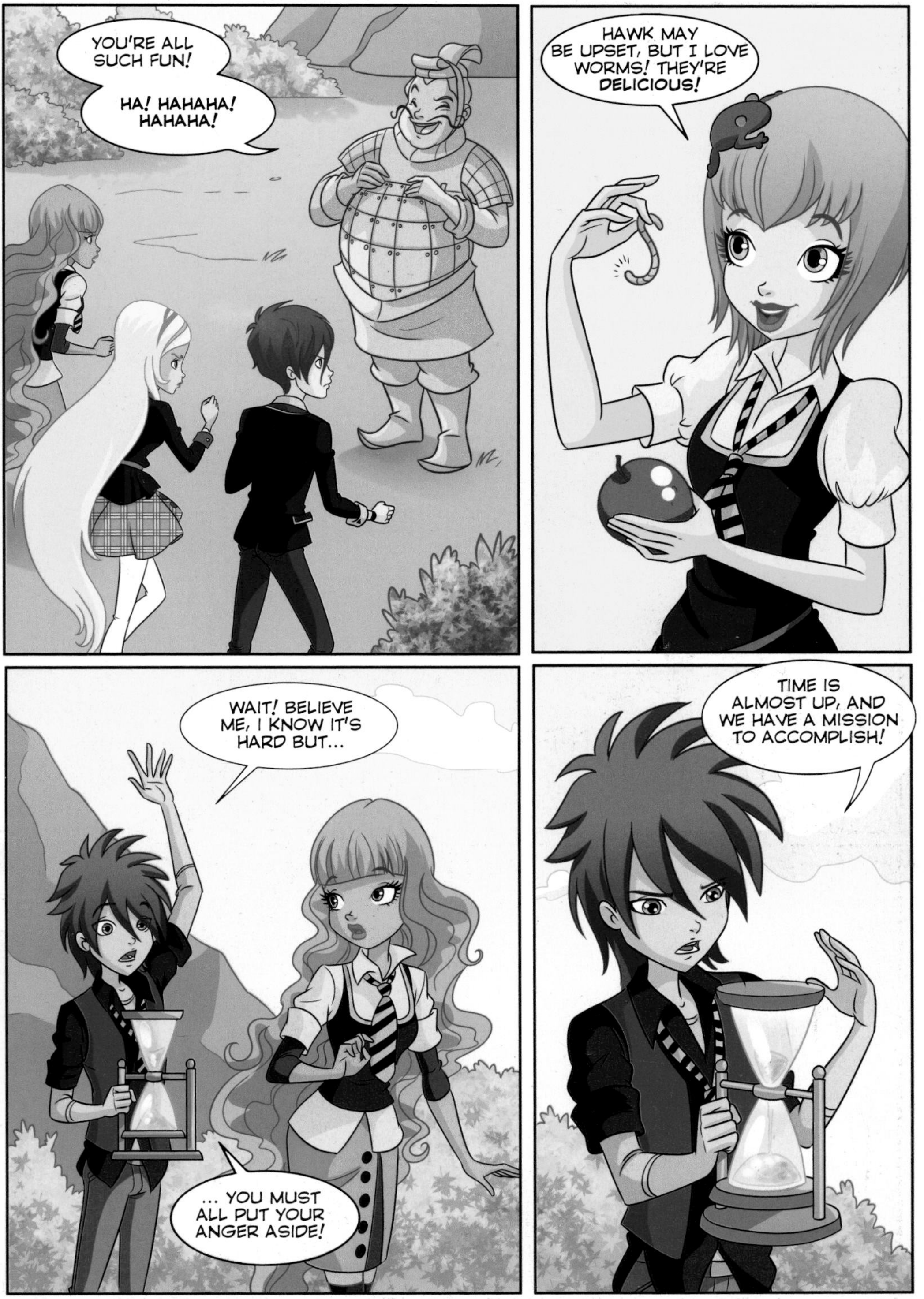
YOU'RE ALL SUCH FUN!
HA! HAHAHA! HAHAHA!
HAWK MAY BE UPSET, BUT I LOVE WORMS! THEY'RE DELICIOUS!
WAIT! BELIEVE ME, I KNOW IT'S HARD BUT...
... YOU MUST ALL PUT YOUR ANGER ASIDE!
TIME IS ALMOST UP, AND WE HAVE A MISSION TO ACCOMPLISH!

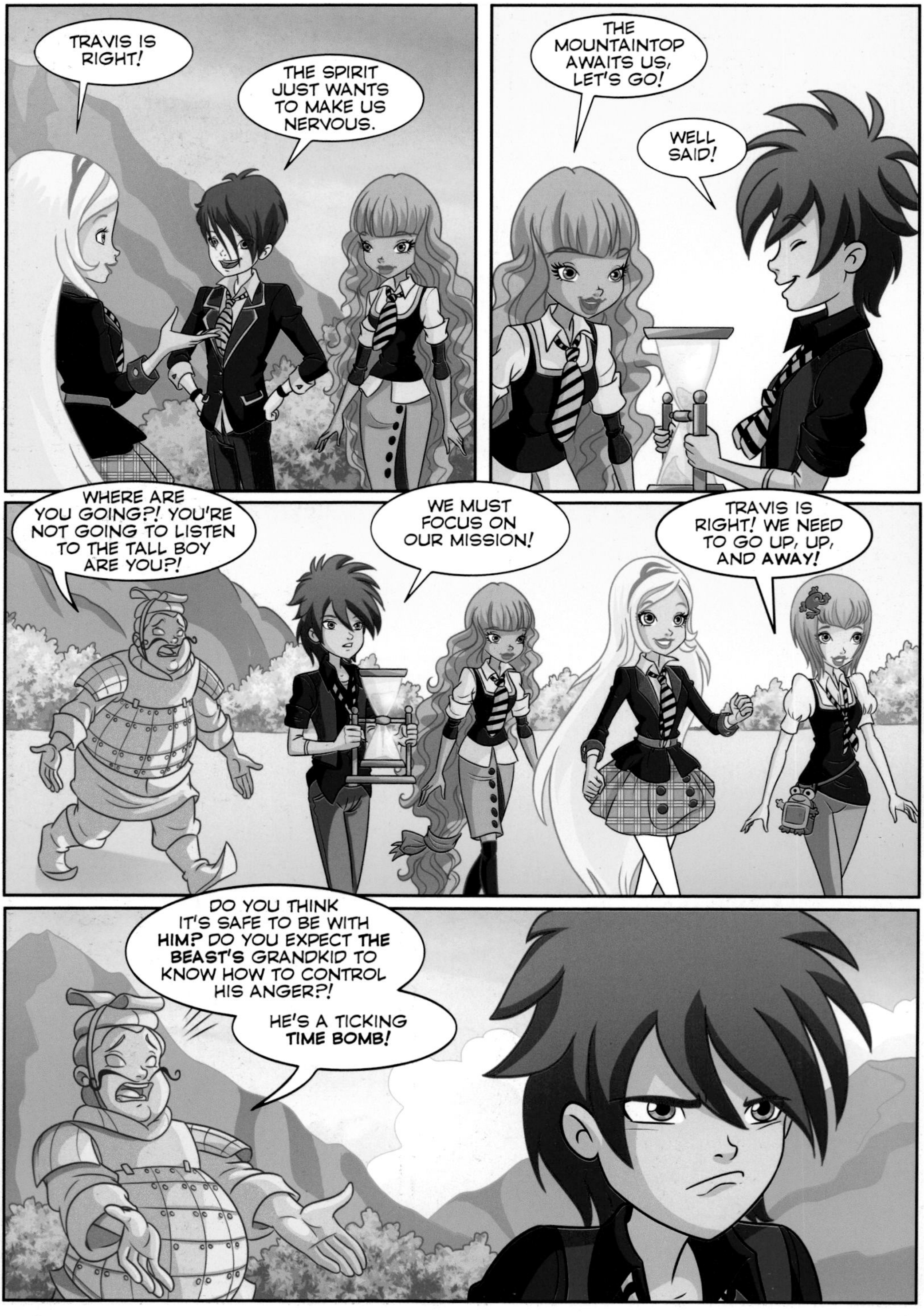
TRAVIS IS RIGHT!
THE SPIRIT JUST WANTS TO MAKE US NERVOUS.
THE MOUNTAINTOP AWAITS US, LET'S GO!
WELL SAID!
WHERE ARE YOU GOING?! YOU'RE NOT GOING TO LISTEN TO THE TALL BOY ARE YOU?!
WE MUST FOCUS ON OUR MISSION!
TRAVIS IS RIGHT! WE NEED TO GO UP, UP, AND AWAY!
DO YOU THINK IT'S SAFE TO BE WITH HIM? DO YOU EXPECT THE BEAST'S GRANDKID TO KNOW HOW TO CONTROL HIS ANGER?!
HE'S A TICKING TIME BOMB!

HERE WE ARE! AT THE TIPPY-TOP!

JUST IN TIME!

WHAT THE--?!

WELL DONE! I'M PROUD OF YOU!

YOU HAVE LEARNED THE FIRST LESSON.

SENSEI WEI WEI!

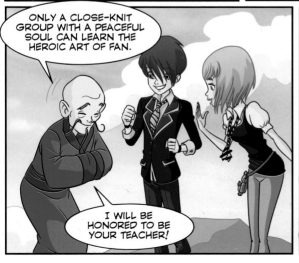

ONLY A CLOSE-KNIT GROUP WITH A PEACEFUL SOUL CAN LEARN THE HEROIC ART OF FAN.

I WILL BE HONORED TO BE YOUR TEACHER!

HOORAY!

YES!

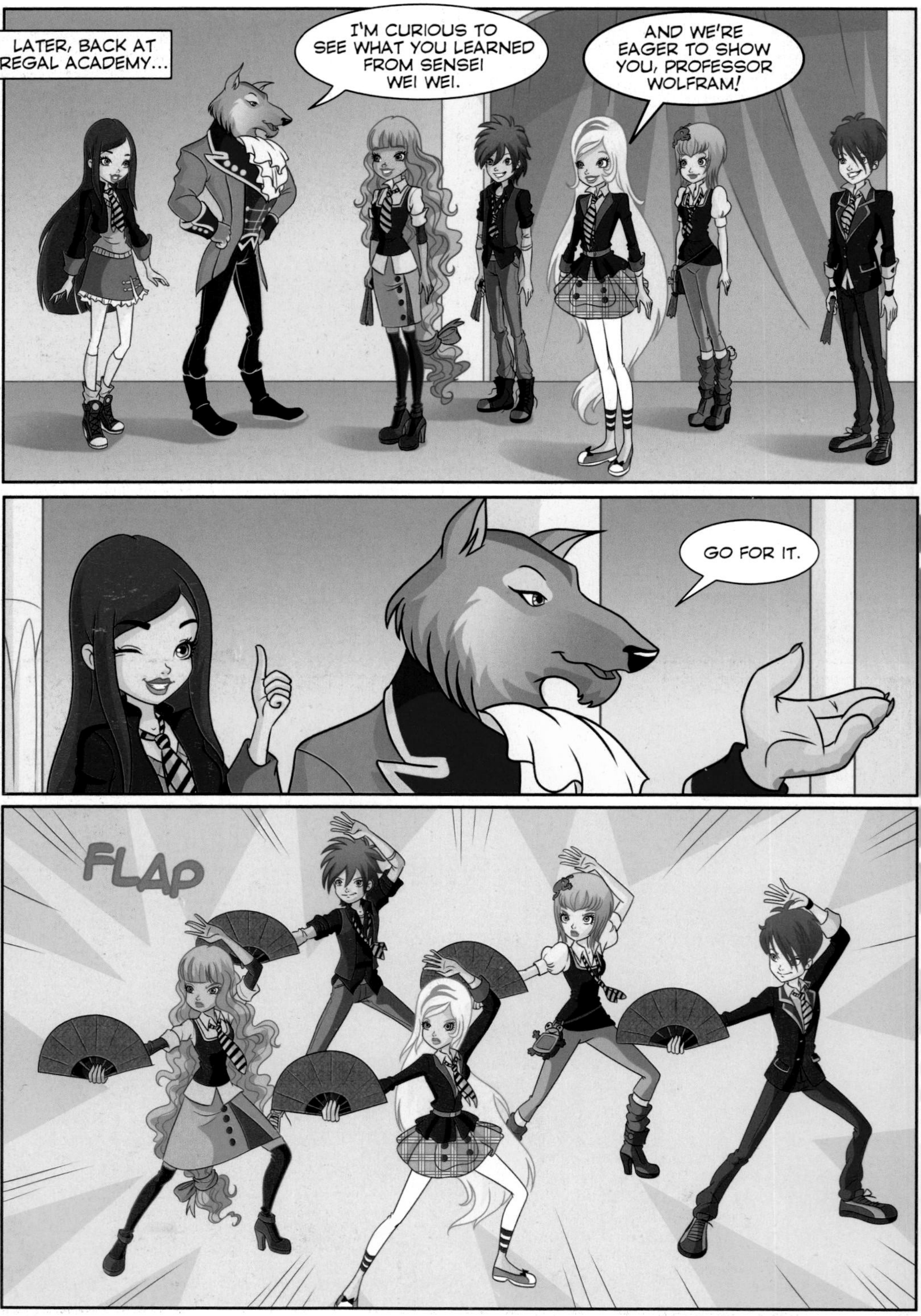
LATER, BACK AT REGAL ACADEMY...
I'M CURIOUS TO SEE WHAT YOU LEARNED FROM SENSEI WEI WEI.
AND WE'RE EAGER TO SHOW YOU, PROFESSOR WOLFRAM!
GO FOR IT.
FLAP

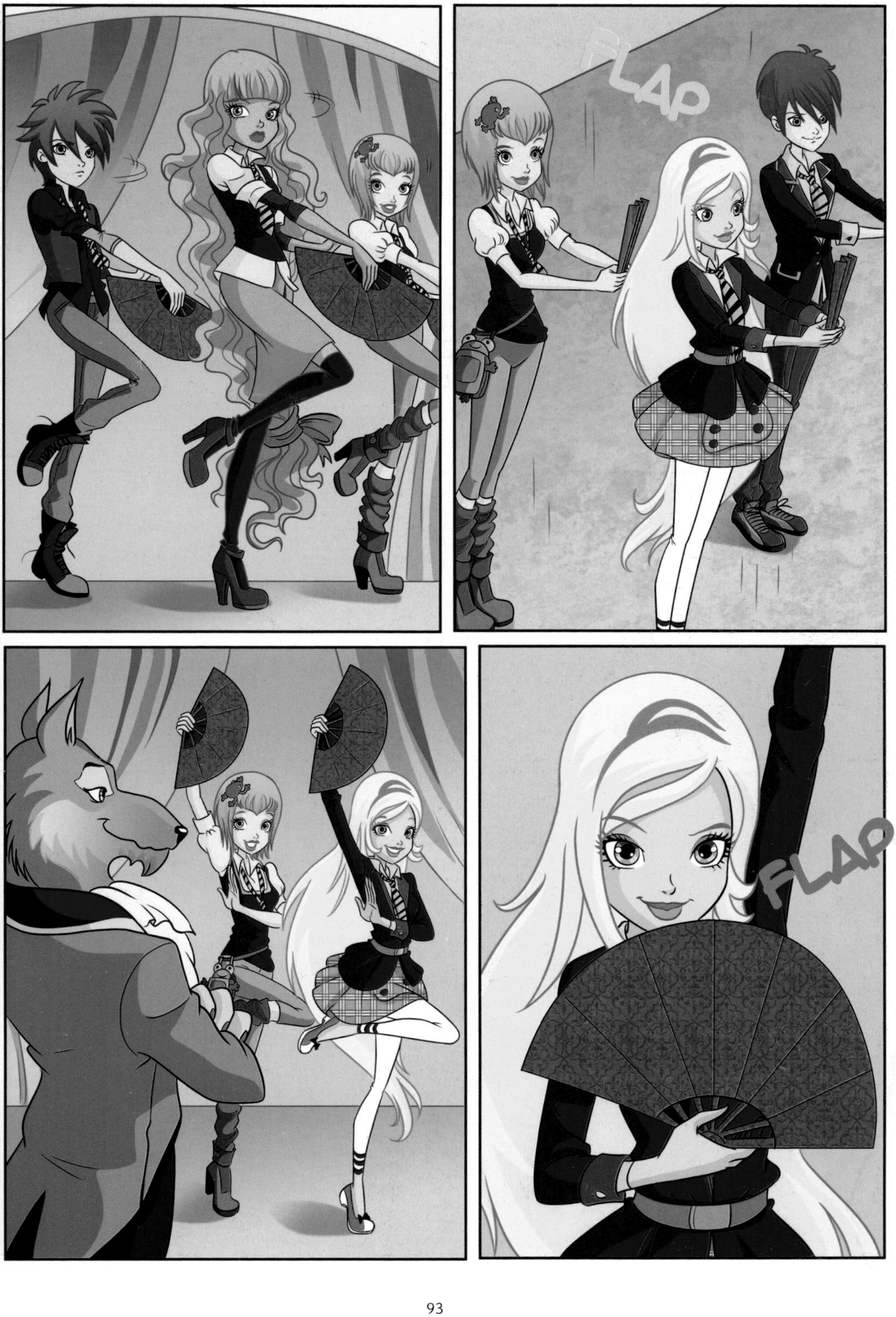
FLAP
FLAP

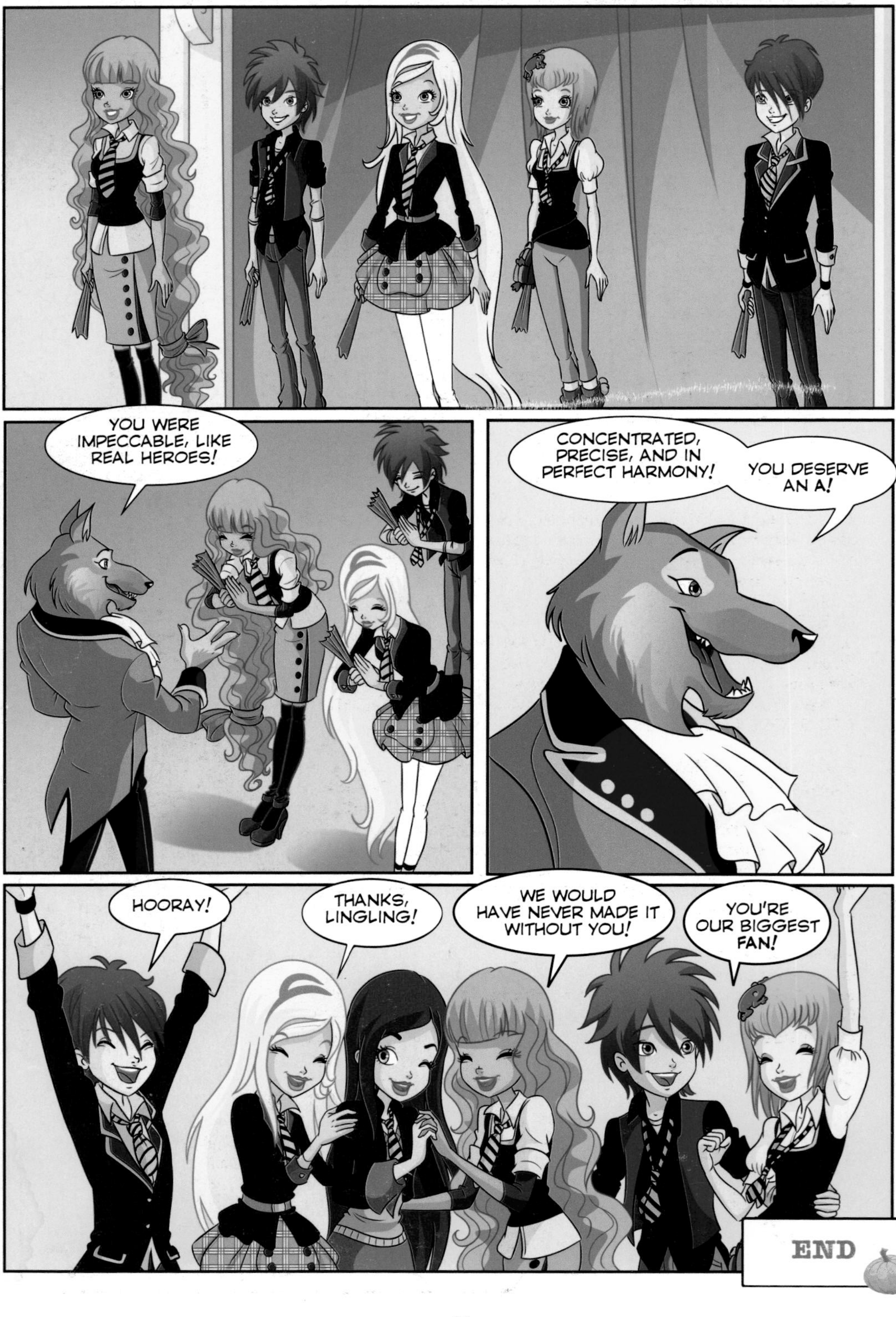
YOU WERE IMPECCABLE, LIKE REAL HEROES!
CONCENTRATED, PRECISE, AND IN PERFECT HARMONY!
YOU DESERVE AN A!
HOORAY!
THANKS, LINGLING!
WE WOULD HAVE NEVER MADE IT WITHOUT YOU!
YOU'RE OUR BIGGEST FAN!
END

WATCH OUT FOR PAPERCUTZ

Welcome to the third thaumaturgic REGAL ACADEMY graphic novel from Papercutz—those modern-day magicians dedicated to conjuring up enchanting graphic novels for all ages. I'm Professor Jim Salicrup, the Editor-in-Chief and your official marvelous guide to the wonders that await you, not only here at REGAL ACADEMY, but throughout the land of Papercutz.

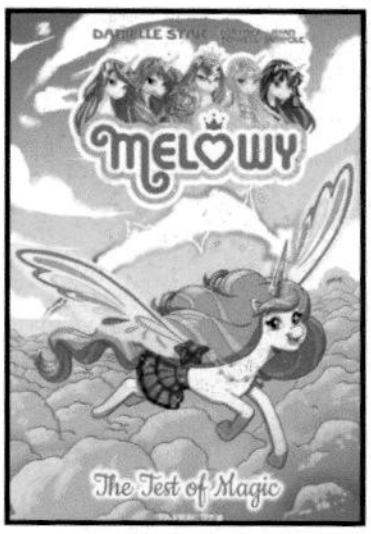
MELOWY
The Test of Magic

It seems that everything tends to be specialized these days. For example, REGAL ACADEMY tends to specialize in training the offspring of Fairy Tales. But, what if you were, let's say, a winged unicorn? Then where would you go to school? Well, would you believe that Papercutz has the answer? There's a world called Aura, where magical creatures live in harmony in four ancient island realms, separated by an enchanted ocean, and floating above it all on the clouds is a castle called Destiny, and that's where winged unicorns, called Melowies, go to school. Who knew? Well, you would if you picked up MELOWY #1 "The Test of Magic," the Papercutz graphic novel by Danielle Star (MELOWY creator), Cortney Powell (writer), and Ryan Jampole (artist)! Fear not—there's still time to attend! But you better hurry to your favorite bookseller or library now—you wouldn't want to get a Tardy!

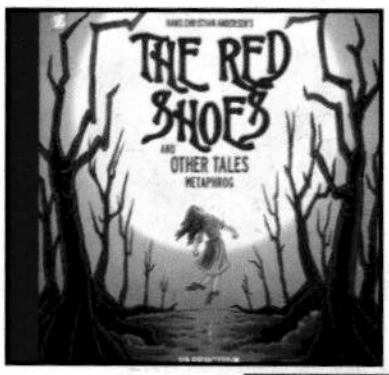
THE RED SHOES
AND OTHER TALES
METAPHROG

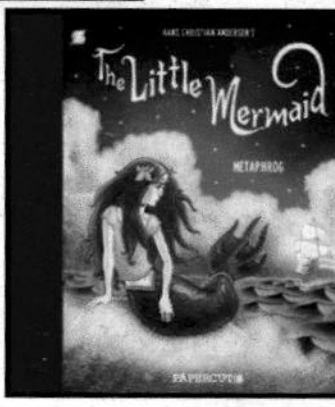
The Little Mermaid
METAPHROG

While REGAL ACADEMY features the children of fairy tales, Papercutz also offers beautiful graphic novel adaptations of the classic original fairy tales as well. Metaphrog, the award-winning husband and wife graphic novel creators, have adapted several tales by Hans Christian Andersen in THE LITTLE MERMAID and THE RED SHOES AND OTHER TALES. These beautiful books present comics a daptations of these stories that are a bit more faithful to the original stories than some of the big Hollywood animated versions, but are just as fun and exciting. They even created an all-new fairy tale, "The Glass Case," which is included in THE RED SHOES AND OTHER TALES.

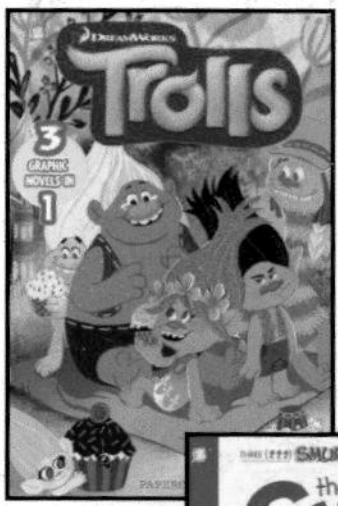
DreamWorks
Trolls
3 GRAPHIC NOVELS IN 1

And speaking of Hollywood movies, for those of you who've enjoyed The Trolls and The Smurfs movies, Papercutz has lots of graphic novels featuring these magical creatures as well! In fact, we've recently put together a couple of graphic novels that present the first three graphic novels of each series in one specially-priced graphic novel! So be sure to keep an eye out for THE SMURFS 3 IN 1 #1 and THE TROLLS 3 IN 1#1for thrice as much Troll fun and Smurfy shenanigans!

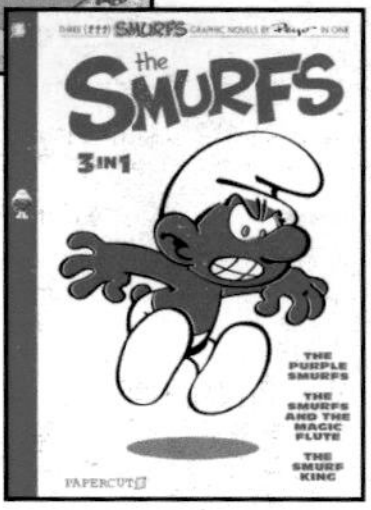
the SMURFS
3 IN 1
THE PURPLE SMURFS
THE SMURFS AND THE MAGIC FLUTE
THE SMURF KING
PAPERCUTZ

We've said it before, and we'll say it again—Papercutz is where the magic is! Be sure to visit papercutz.com for even more extraordinary enlightenment, and don't forget to pick up REGAL ACADEMY #4 "Best Furry Friends," featuring more fabulous tales of Rose Cinderella, Travis Beast, Astoria Rapunzel, Joy LeFrog, Hawk Snowwhite, and all the rest!

Class Dismissed!

Thanks,

Jim

STAY IN TOUCH!

EMAIL: salicrup@papercutz.com
WEB: papercutz.com
TWITTER: @papercutzgn
INSTAGRAM: @papercutzgn
FACEBOOK: PAPERCUTZGRAPHICNOVELS
FAN MAIL: Papercutz, 160 Broadway, Suite 700, East Wing, New York, NY 10038

Available on DVL!

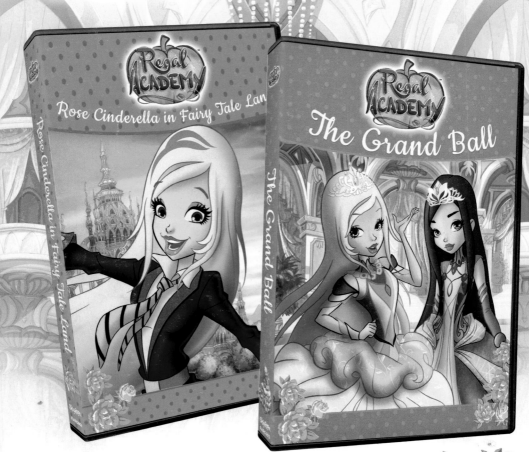

Join Rose Cinderella in Fairy Tale Land as she discovers that Cinderella is not only her grandmother, but also the headmistress of Regal Academy, a school where fairytale families teach the next generation how to become heroes! Then, come celebrate Regal Academy's first Grand Ball! Joy wants to go with Esquire Frog, but he's under a powerful curse! Can Joy and Rose come up with a plan to break the evil spell before the ball ends?